Extraordinary
Means

ROBYN SCHNEIDER

SIMON AND SCHUSTER

D0234506

FOR DANIEL,

who asked which book I recommend he read on an airplane.
I finally have an answer: this one.

First published in Great Britain by Simon & Schuster UK Ltd, 2015
A CBS COMPANY

Originally published in the USA in 2015 by Katherine Tegen Books,
an imprint of HarperCollins Publishers

Text copyright © Robyn Schneider 2015
Jacket illustration copyright © 2015 by Julie McLaughlin

1 3 5 7 9 10 8 6 4 2

Simon & Schuster UK Ltd
1st Floor
Gray's Inn Road
London WC1X 8HB

www.simonandschuster.co.uk

Simon & Schuster Australia, Sydney
Simon & Schuster India, New Delhi

A CIP catalogue record for this book
is available from the British Library

PB ISBN: 978-1-47111-548-6
eBook ISBN: 978-1-47111-549-3

Printed and bound by CPI Group (UK) Ltd, Croydon, CR0 4YY

MIX
Paper from
responsible sources
FSC® C020471

Simon & Schuster UK Ltd are committed to sourcing paper
that is made from wood grown in sustainable forests and supports the Forest
Stewardship Council, the leading international forest certification organisation.
Our books displaying the FSC logo are printed on FSC certified paper.

I didn't want to kiss you good-bye—that was the trouble—
I wanted to kiss you good night—
and there's a lot of difference.
—ERNEST HEMINGWAY

Draw your chair up close to the edge of the precipice
and I'll tell you a story.
—F. SCOTT FITZGERALD

CHAPTER ONE

LANE

MY FIRST NIGHT at Latham House, I lay awake in my narrow, gabled room in Cottage 6 wondering how many people had died in it. And I didn't just wonder this casually, either. I did the math. I figured the probability. And I came up with a number: eight. But then, I've always been terrible at math.

In fourth grade, we had to do timed tests for our multiplication tables. Five minutes a page, fifty questions each, and if you wanted to move on, you couldn't make a single mistake. The teacher charted our progress on a piece of hot-pink poster board taped up for everyone to see, a smiley-face sticker next to our name for each table we completed. I watched as the number of stickers next to everyone else's names grew, while I got stuck on the sevens. I did the flash cards every night, but it was no use, because it wasn't the multiplication table that was giving me trouble. It was the pressure of being told two things: 1. That I only had a short amount of time, and 2. That I had to get everything right.

When I finally drifted off to sleep, I dreamed of houses falling into the ocean and drowning. The water swallowed them, but they rose up again from the black depths, rotting and covered in seaweed as they rode the waves back to shore, looking for their owners.

I'M AN ONLY child, so the prospect of using the communal bathroom was pretty horrifying. Which is why I set my alarm that first morning for six o'clock, tiptoeing down the hall with my Dopp kit and towel while everyone else was still asleep.

It was strange wearing shoes in the shower, being completely naked except for a pair of flip-flops. Washing my hair with shoes on, and doing it in a Tupperware container of a shower stall, felt so different from my normal Monday-morning routine that I wondered if I'd ever get used to it.

I used to sleep in at home, waiting until the last possible moment to roll out of bed, grope for a clean shirt, and eat a cereal bar on the drive to school. I'd listen to whatever songs were on the radio, not because I liked them, but because they were my tarot cards. If the songs were good, it would be a good day. If they were bad, I'd probably get a B on a quiz.

But that morning, standing at the window of my dorm room as I buttoned my shirt, I felt like an entirely different person. It was as though someone had taken an eraser to my life and, instead of getting rid of the mess, had rubbed away all the parts that I'd wanted to keep.

Now, instead of my girlfriend, and my dog, and my car, I had a pale-green vinyl mattress, a view of the woods, and an ache in my chest.

I'd gotten in late the night before. My parents drove me up, Dad clutching the steering wheel and Mom staring straight ahead as we listened to NPR for six hours with the windows down, not saying anything. Dinner was long over and it was almost lights-out by the time I'd opened my suitcase.

Latham still didn't feel real. Not yet. I'd encountered it, tiptoeing around the corridors out of sync with the rest of its residents, but I hadn't yet become one of them.

It was the end of September, and I was seventeen, and my senior year was taking place four hundred miles away, without me. I tried not to think about that as I waited for my tour guide outside the dormitory, in the early-morning chill of the mountains. I tried not to think about any of it, because I was pretty sure the full weight of my situation would crush me. Instead, I thought about wet flip-flops and math problems and my cell phone, which I'd had for a few brief hours in the car, and which had been taken from me upon arrival.

According to my information packet, *Your First-Day Ambassador, Grant Harden, will meet you outside your dorm at 7:55 a.m. to take you to breakfast and help you find your first class.*

So I waited for Grant to show up while everyone else

streamed past me, shuffling toward the dining hall in a motley assortment of sweatpants and pajamas, like we were at summer camp.

Of course Grant was running late, so I stood there forever, getting more and more annoyed. It seemed ridiculous that I couldn't just find my own way to breakfast, or to Latham's one academic building, that I needed to be publicly escorted.

I glanced at my wrist: 8:09. I didn't know how much longer I was reasonably expected to stand there, so I waited another few minutes, then gave up and walked to the dining hall.

It was easy enough to find the place, to pick up a tray and join the line of half-asleep teenagers. I was right; I hadn't needed some kid to show me around after all. It was just a cafeteria line. I took a bowl of cereal and a little milk carton, noting that my old high school had carried the same brand of milk, featuring this weird, grinning cow's head. How strange, for everything to shift so drastically, but for the milk cartons to stay the same.

I slid my tray along the counter, past the plates of eggs and muffins and toast. But it wasn't until I heard someone yell for a friend to save him a seat that I realized my mistake: I was totally alone. I'd been so impatient to get to the dining hall that I hadn't thought it through. Maybe, if I'd gone into the bathroom that morning along with everyone else, pitching myself into the chaos instead of avoiding it, I could have found someone to walk over with. Now, I didn't even know who lived on my floor. And I was fast approaching the front of the line, without even a cell phone to rescue me from the total disaster of having nowhere to sit in a crowded dining hall.

I was thinking that I couldn't have screwed this up worse when the nutritionist frowned down at my tray like I'd personally disappointed her with my choice of breakfast cereal.

"That's it?" she asked.

"I'm not really hungry." I never was in the mornings; my appetite usually slept in until noon.

"I can't sign off on this," she said, as though I should have known better. "If you're too unwell to eat a full meal, you talk to the hall nurse *before* breakfast."

Too unwell. God, how embarrassing.

"It's my first day," I said desperately. "I didn't know."

I glanced behind me, uncomfortably aware that I was holding up the line. Way to make an impression. I hadn't known it was possible to fail breakfast.

Actually, I *should* have known. Grant should have told me.

"You can go back through for some protein. Or you can take a strike."

She glared at me, all pursed lips and leathery-tanned skin, waiting.

The thought of slinking to the back of the line, with everyone watching, filled me with a sense of horror. She couldn't mean it. But apparently, she did.

"Well?" the nutritionist asked.

I wished I were the sort of guy who'd take a strike, whatever that meant, just to prove that I didn't have to play by the system. But I wasn't. At least, not yet. I was a head-down-and-grades-up sort of guy. When the warning bell rang, I hustled. When Scantron tests were given, I brought a spare No. 2 pencil. And so, with everyone watching, I took a deep breath and went to the back of the line.

"THAT WAS BRUTAL," the boy in front of me said. He was my age, a pudgy Indian kid with a pair of old-fashioned glasses and a mess of black hair. Even at eight a.m., he was all nervous energy. "Not many people can say they've flunked breakfast on their first day."

"I didn't do the homework," I said. "I had too much on my plate."

He grinned, picking up on the pun.

"Or apparently, not enough," he said. "I'm Nikhil. Everyone calls me Nick."

"I'm Lane."

"So, Lane," he said. "Here's a crash course on meals: You take a dish from each station. You don't have to eat it all. Hell, you could sculpt the *Colosseum* out of eggs and toast, but you take full plates and bring back empty ones."

"Doesn't that defeat the purpose of having a nutritionist?" I asked.

"Precisely. Which is where *the plan* comes in."

"We have a plan?"

"We do indeed. Because lovely old Linda up there told you to go back for more, but she didn't tell you *how much* more."

I saw where he was going with this immediately.

"Oh no," I said. "I'm not really—"

"You're looking pretty hungry there, Lane." Nick grinned hugely as he slung a plate of scrambled eggs onto my tray. Before I could protest, he'd topped the scrambled eggs with hard-boiled ones.

I looked down at my tray. The damage was done. I'd been egged. And so, with Nick egging me on, I added a stack of toast.

"Perfect," he said. "Now how about a muffin?"

He reached into the case and held up an entire platter, offering it to me with a flourish.

"How about two?" I said.

We were halfway to the front when the line stopped moving again.

"You can't be serious," the nutritionist said.

Everyone craned forward to see what was going on. It was a girl. She was small and blond, with a messy ponytail. On her tray was a single mug of tea.

"So give me a strike," the girl said. It sounded like a challenge.

"Go back through."

"You and I both know there isn't enough time for that," the girl said.

It was true. There were maybe twenty minutes before we had to head to class.

"My tea's getting cold, so if you don't mind?" said the girl.

She held out her wrist with the black silicone bracelet, daring the nutritionist to scan it. The dining hall was silent. We were all watching to see what Linda would do.

And then she scanned the girl through, typing furiously into the computer bank.

"Strike two this month, Sadie," she warned.

"Ooh. After my third strike, do I get out?" the girl asked, laughing.

She exited the line in triumph, the mug of tea in front of her like a trophy. As she walked toward the tables, I saw her full-on for the first time. She was a miraculous, early-morning kind of pretty, with a ponytail she'd probably slept in and a sweater slipping off one shoulder. Her lips were painted red, and her mouth quirked up at the corner, and she looked like the last girl you'd expect to start trouble in the cafeteria on a Monday morning.

But that wasn't why I was staring. There was something oddly familiar about her. I had the unshakable impression that I'd seen her somewhere before, that we'd already met. And then I realized we had. At Camp Griffith, four years ago. That awful place in Los Padres my parents had shipped me off to when I was younger, so they could go on vacation without me.

"Well, that's the other way to handle it," Nick said, interrupting my train of thought.

Belatedly, I realized he was talking about Sadie.

"Won't she get in trouble?" I asked.

"Of course." Nick snorted. "But Sadie only gets in trouble when she wants to."

I didn't know what he meant, and I was about to ask, but we'd reached the front of the line.

"Hey there, Linda. Made you a Picasso this morning." Nick smirked, presenting the nutritionist with his tray, upon which he'd arranged his tofu sausage, eggs, and English muffin into the unmistakable shape of a penis.

I was scanned through with equal disgust, and was about to follow Nick over to his group of friends, when he gave me a chin nod and said, "You probably want to catch up with your tour guide and kick his ass for not warning you about the food stations, huh?"

"Something like that," I mumbled.

"Well, I'll see you around."

Before I could answer, he was gone.

I stood there alone, trying not to despair as my unwanted breakfast slid around on my tray. It was too dark inside the dining hall, the paneled wood and brass chandeliers swallowing all sense of time. The tables were small, round things. Six seats each, like some disastrous King Arthur's court. I thought longingly of Harbor High, with its palm trees and plastic-wrapped sandwiches, where my group and I hung out in the little courtyard behind the science labs.

We were the marginally acceptable AP crowd. Liked enough to hold officer positions in the Model United Nations Club, but not on the radar for something like student council. Most days, my girlfriend and I would check homework answers, or study for next period, and we'd pass a can of Coke back and forth while we ate our sandwiches. It wasn't the kind of group where we hung out at each other's houses, but I'd never once doubted that I had a place to sit.

I watched as Nick joined Sadie's table, striking a pose with his breakfast art that made everyone laugh. I understood then that he hadn't made the plate of, uh, junk food to piss off the nutritionist. He'd made it to amuse his friends. There were still two seats left, but Nick hadn't invited me to join him, and anyway, they probably belonged to people who were still in line.

I hoped that my missing tour guide would see me standing there and wave me over to his table with a sheepish apology, but no such luck. The 2.5 breakfasts on my tray were starting to get heavy, and I had to put the thing down somewhere. So I took a deep breath and walked to the back of the dining hall like I knew where I was going.

I SAT DOWN randomly, at a table with four empty seats and two boys intensely playing a game of travel chess, who seemed to be off in their own world. I sighed and poured my milk into my cereal, dumping in the whole carton instead of trying to get the proportions right. The Cheerios floated to the top, bobbing like empty life rafts.

"Hi, I'm Genevieve. Are you new?" a girl asked, taking the seat next to mine. Her smile was friendly, but there was something about the combination of freckles and ponytail and teeth that made me certain she had a dozen horse-riding ribbons pinned over her desk.

"First day," I said.

"You'll love it here," she promised. "What's your dorm?"

"Um, six?" I said.

"John's in six!" she said, as though this was the biggest coincidence in the world. "He's my boyfriend. He'll be here in a minute; the line's taking forever today."

I was at the wrong table. I knew it then, as the girl introduced me to John, her acne-ravaged boyfriend, and to Tim and Chris, the two chess players I'd mistakenly assumed were sitting by themselves, not waiting for the rest of their group.

"Are you really going to eat all that?" John asked, staring at my tray.

"It's a joke," I explained, halfheartedly. "The nutrition-ist said—"

"Oh, you don't want to make her mad," Genevieve warned. "She'll give you a strike against privileges, and if you get three in a month, you're banned from *the social*."

"The social?" I asked.

"Didn't your tour guide tell you anything?" Genevieve asked.

"Not really," I said, not wanting to get into it.

"Oh. Well, we get some big activity every month," Genevieve explained.

"I think this time it's line dancing," John put in, sounding scarily excited.

I snorted. No wonder Sadie had baited the nutritionist. I'd assumed it was detention, or chores, or whatever else bad kids are punished with, not a free pass from making a fool of yourself to "Cotton-Eye Joe." But then, Nick *had* said she only got in trouble when she wanted to.

Genevieve launched enthusiastically into a description of line dancing, just in case I wasn't already aware how much I would rather go to the dentist. I smiled and nodded, wishing I could have breakfast in peace. But I was the one who'd sat at their table, and they were just being nice.

And as awful as they were, it looked like I could have picked tables far worse. The group to my left was totally checked out, and I couldn't tell if they were just early-morning zombies, or if the glazed expression was permanent. And on my right was a table of girls who were actively Not Talking to Each Other as they glared at their scrambled eggs.

I glanced across the dining hall, toward Nick and Sadie's table. There was something magnetic about it, about them, even from all the way where I sat, in the outer rings. I couldn't figure out what they were—not that your typical social groups applied at a place like Latham. There were four of them, and they were laughing. Nick had picked up his breakfast sausage and was holding it aloft like an orchestra conductor, waving it slowly and deliberately.

Next to me, Genevieve started coughing. She scrambled for a napkin, pressing it over her mouth.

"Sorry," she said. "The orange juice had pulp."

"You okay, bunny-wunny?" John asked, rubbing her back.

God, I really had picked a winner of a table. But something about Genevieve's choking made me realize that, beyond the talking and the eating and the scraping of chairs, the dining hall echoed with coughing. It was like a symphony of sickness.

I glanced over at Sadie's table again, and sure enough, that's what they were laughing at. Nick, with his tofu sausage, was conducting the coughing.

THANKFULLY, ALL THE classrooms were in the same building, so I found my way to English without too much trouble. It was in a large, wood-paneled room with huge open windows, like an atrium. There was an old-fashioned chalkboard and twenty desks.

Twenty. I was used to SMART Boards. Lockers. Public school. And something told me that Mr. Holder, a balding crane of a man in a shapeless tweed blazer, had never been near a public school in his life.

"Yes?" he asked as I hesitated in the doorway, wondering if seating was assigned.

"I'm Lane Rosen," I said. "I'm new?"

"Welcome to the rotation," he said grimly. "Take the seat next to Mr. Carrow."

He pointed toward a sullen-looking boy in the first row. I sat, taking out my notebook and pencil. Holder slapped a copy of *Great Expectations* and a photocopied packet on my desk.

"Read a chapter, answer the questions. Rinse and repeat. When you're done, I'll give you an essay topic," he said, leaving me to it.

I stared down at the paperback on my desk. All around me, students were working. Some of them had different books. I spotted *Lord of the Flies*, *Moby Dick*, and *The Sun Also Rises*. I sighed and opened my packet, skimming the questions so I knew what answers to look for when I started reading, a trick I'd picked up in SAT prep.

When class was over, Holder said, "See you on Wednesday," and everyone started to pack up. I was about halfway through the questions for chapter two.

"Wait," I said to the boy next to me. "What's the homework?"

"Good one." He snorted, as though I'd said something funny.

In history, we watched a documentary on the black plague and filled in a worksheet during the movie. The teacher didn't even stay in the room. When she left, I expected the class to erupt into chaos, but everyone continued watching, except for a couple of kids who put their heads down on their desks and went to sleep.

I sat at the same table for lunch, which I hadn't meant to do, except Genevieve was two places behind me in line, so there really wasn't an exit tactic. I'd hoped my missing tour guide would have found me by now, but no such luck. I could feel the monotony setting in, and I wished it wouldn't.

I didn't want to be at Latham. I didn't want this routine of having my meals checked and my teachers write me off at first glance. I wanted to be in third-period AP Euro, in Mr. Verma's classroom with all the old newspapers framed on the walls, where we got pizza the Friday before an exam.

Back at Harbor, being in AP was like belonging to the club that teachers liked best. We were going somewhere in life, the teachers said, handing us extra-credit assignments instead of detention, study guides instead of busywork. I'd just never thought that where I was going was Latham House.

WE TOOK A long break after lunch. As I trudged across the quad, toward the cottages, I saw four students cut out toward the woods. Nick and Sadie's crowd. They walked quickly, heads down, as though hurrying toward something far more interesting than rest period. And even though they did it in plain sight, no one seemed to care.

The eight cottages were arranged in a half-moon, around a gazebo in desperate need of a paint job. They were more like ski lodges than actual cottages, with dark wood and deep porches and neat rows of windows.

Each cottage had around twenty residents, if I had to guess. The first floor was a lounge area with dilapidated plaid sofas, a long study table, and stacks of board games. There was a separate television room, and a microkitchen, even though we weren't supposed to cook anything.

The best places in the lounge had already been staked out by early arrivers. I watched as a group of four Asian kids played a loud game of Settlers of Catan on the rug, and two boys with a deck of Magic cards hunched over the coffee table.

My new and hopefully temporary acquaintances from earlier were setting up a game of Chinese checkers, and they cheerfully waved me over.

"We can play teams," John suggested.

"I should finish unpacking," I said, edging toward the door.

"Well, later then," Tim called. Or maybe it was Chris. I didn't want to stick around long enough to figure it out.

As I made my way back to my room, muffled music and the unmistakable sound effects of video games leaked from behind closed doors. It was reassuring to hear the Smiths and someone's Pokémon battle, for some small part of my day to be normal.

I reached into my pocket, forgetting for a moment that it was empty. I felt so lost without my cell phone, like I might get the most important email of my life and it would just sit there for hours, unread. Not that I was expecting an email like that, but still.

My room was at the very end of the hall, a corner room. I assumed that was why it was so narrow. Best coffin in the place, I thought, and then instantly hated myself for going there. It wasn't terrible. I mean, sure, all the furniture was miniaturized. There was a twin extra-long bed, which still didn't make it any roomier. I had a massive bed at home, and I loved her dearly. She was my queen, and I was her loyal subject. Well, her loyal subject in exile.

At the foot of my minibed was a wardrobe that looked suspiciously like a locker, a vestige of when this place had been an all-boys' boarding school. I'd tried and failed to squish my still-packed suitcase inside the night before, and had kicked it under the bed in defeat. It stuck out, and I'd already tripped over it. Twice.

I also had a wooden desk and chair, and two huge windows that were stuck open permanently, for fresh air. The best part about my room, though, was the view: an endless stretch of woods and sky, with a distant haze of mountains. If I hadn't known why we were in the middle of nowhere, it might have been peaceful.

I rummaged through my desk drawers until I found the thick, glossy handbook I'd been given the night before, and climbed into bed to read it. I figured studying the rules was the best thing to do, since I didn't want to accidentally fail breakfast again.

God, the handbook was tedious. I could feel myself falling asleep as I read about *suggested Wellness dress options*. I tried to stay awake, but I'd been up for most of the night, and there hadn't been any coffee at breakfast. . . .

I woke up groggy and disoriented. The handbook was on the floor, pages down, like it was trying to scuttle away. I didn't blame it. When I checked my wrist, I realized I'd been out for a while.

I stretched and walked over to the window that faced the woods, watching for the four students to return. It was getting late, and I wondered if I'd missed them entirely. We were all supposed to dress out for PE, which was ironically called Wellness, by two thirty. Except I wasn't cleared for Wellness yet. I was supposed to go to the medical building instead.

I was just about to head over when I saw them emerge from a grove of trees. Sadie was out front, an expensive camera swinging over her shoulder. Nick was there, too, his horn-rimmed glasses glinting in the sun. Bringing up the rear was this punk kid in black skinny jeans and Docs who looked like he was in a band, and a tall black girl who was shaking leaves from the hem of a billowing lace dress like she'd just stepped off the stage in a school play. They strolled back toward the dorms as though they owned the place, and in that moment, they did.

I watched as Sadie stopped to take a picture of the group, solemnly raising her camera and fiddling with the lens. Instead of posing, they stopped where they were, as though frozen, letting her capture the moment forever.

I remembered at least this much about her: she'd taken photos all the time at summer camp, sneaking out to the woods and disappearing for hours. She was all elbows and skinned knees back then, and I was one of the shortest boys in my cabin.

My memories of that summer were hazy and mostly had to do with being terrified of this one asshole cabinmate of mine who threatened to piss on everyone's beds if we didn't give him our commissary snacks. We were starting eighth grade in the fall, and almost overnight everyone had gone from pointing out girls with visible bra straps to girls who were definitely gonna blow them after the lower-seniors dance, at this rock in the woods. For their sake, I'd hoped the rock had a sign-up sheet.

I hadn't exchanged more than a couple of sentences with Sadie. I didn't say much of anything during that terrible summer, where two guys got kicked out of my cabin for stealing and a disgusting game of soggy cookie had ended so badly that my only real friend went home two weeks early, his parents threatening a lawsuit. But I still remembered

Sadie, with purple rubber bands in her braces and these tie-dyed shorts, always alone, and always stooping to photograph a leaf, or a flower.

It had seemed impossible that I'd recognize anyone at Latham, that there could be a familiar face up in the Santa Cruz Mountains, hundreds of miles from home. But the more I considered it, the more it made a terrible kind of sense.

At Latham House, we were asked to believe in unlikely miracles. In second chances. We woke up each morning hoping that the odds had somehow swung in our favor.

But that's the thing about odds. Roll a die twice, and you expect two different results. Except it doesn't work that way. You could roll the same side over and over again, the laws of the universe intact and unchanging with each turn. It's only when you consider the past that the odds change. That things become less and less likely.

Here's something I know because I'm a nerd: up until the middle of the twentieth century, dice were made out of cellulose nitrate. It's a material that remains stable for decades but, in a flash, can decompose. The chemical compound breaks down, releasing nitric acid. So every time you roll a die, there's a small chance that it won't give you a result at all, that instead it will cleave, crumble, and explode.

CHAPTER TWO
SADIE

WE WERE OUT in the woods behind the cottages when Nick mentioned what had happened in the breakfast line. It was one of those beautifully crisp fall days that was starting to give way to a warmer afternoon, and we'd all taken off our sweaters and tossed them into a pile with our book bags.

Charlie was sitting under a tree, sketching sword ferns. Marina was modeling for me in this great old dress she had. And Nick was sorting the leaves that we'd collected, stacking them by color family.

"Is this one more jaundice yellow or liver-failure yellow?" he asked, holding up a leaf.

"I can't look," I said, because I was using a fixed-length lens and had finally managed to get Marina perfectly in frame. "But please tell me you're not sorting them by pathology."

"Two pathologies diverged in a yellow wood," Nick said, using his Mock Trial voice. "And I, I took the one less traveled."

"Ugh, that was awful," Marina complained. "Besides, that's not even the quote."

"Of course it's the quote," Nick said, but he sounded unsure.

"It's two *roads* diverged," Marina insisted.

"We'll Google it," said Nick. "You'll see."

I laughed, because Nick was always doing that. Messing up and stubbornly defending himself, like he could argue his way out of being wrong.

"The poem is literally called 'The *Road* Not Taken,'" I informed him. "Now, can you put three more leaves on Marina's skirt, the gold-yellow ones?"

"Path, road, lane, whatever," he said, adding the leaves. "Actually, that was the new kid's name. Lane. The one I helped piss off the nutritionist."

My camera almost slid off the rock.

"Lane Rosen?" I asked.

"I have no clue." Nick placed the last leaf with a flourish. "Who introduces themselves with their full name?"

He had a point, but I wasn't going to admit it.

"Maybe *I* will from now on, just to annoy you," I said.

I took a test photo, to check that it wasn't still blurry, but my lens wasn't the only thing out of focus. I had to force myself to concentrate, because my head was spinning over the possibility.

Lane wasn't a common name. I vaguely remembered some hiccup at the front of the line, but I'd figured it was just the nutritionist being a raging bitch, per usual. Not the casual arrival of someone I hadn't thought of in a long time, and was perfectly happy never to see again.

"Hello, Sadie?" Marina sounded like she'd been trying to get my attention for a while. "I asked how it looks."

"Sorry," I said, scrolling through the memory card. "Um. Hold your right arm a little higher."

I took a couple of shots, then made Nick add in some more leaves, even though Marina complained that they'd never come out of her skirt and that her arm ached from holding it up.

"Art is pain," I said, mock-seriously.

"And so is life," Charlie put in. "Which makes life the art from which we are all afflicted. Aahhh, that would make such an awesome lyric. . . ."

I could never tell when Charlie was paying attention. He had the suffering-in-silence thing down to an art, which actually made sense, because he was our group's resident artist. He'd sit there covering his notebook with song lyrics and sketches, all of them dark and painfully brilliant. And then he'd look up and ask something ridiculous, like whether we thought it was possible that dinosaurs had glowed in the dark.

"Almost done?" Marina asked.

"Almost," I promised. "You look great."

She really did. The combination of her dark skin and curly hair and vintage dress covered with leaves was enchanting and almost eerie. Marina did theater back home, designing the costumes. I decided I liked her after I caught her reading a fantasy novel under her desk in Finnegan's class.

I'd never had a group of friends like this back in real school. We wouldn't have existed. Charlie would have been some misunderstood loner. Nick would have been off with his mock-trial cult, pretending they weren't just a glorified drama club. Marina would have hung around with those backstagey cosplay kids who watch *Doctor Who* and wear interesting hats. And I would, well . . . I would have hung out with the same three girls I'd met in eighth grade, who always seemed to get into relationships with non-statusy boys while I sat there being this mildly entertaining friend who they kept apologizing to when they went on group dates without me.

But Latham had reinvented us. Made us more offbeat, more interesting, more noticeable than we would have been anywhere else. I'd expected to hate Latham, but I hadn't expected to find friends who hated the exact same things about it, mocking the rules and the teachers and Dr. Barons until we were laughing so hard we could barely breathe.

We'd gone out to the woods because I was finishing up this thematic series, which involved photo manipulations of my friends escaping in fantastical ways. This one was eventually going to be an image of a miniaturized Marina flying away, held aloft by a bunch of balloons. Except the balloons would be leaves.

A couple of weeks ago, I'd done one of Charlie gliding above the cottages on a paper airplane made of sheet music. And before that it had been Nick boating across the lake on an antique pocket watch, with a twig as a paddle. It had taken forever to put them together in Photoshop.

We walked back to the cottages after I got some pictures I thought I could use. I'd wanted to take more, but we still had to change for Wellness, and if we waited too long and hurried, it would show on our med sensors.

Because Big Brother was always watching. Except we could trick him sometimes, if we were clever enough, and if we timed the distractions perfectly.

"So what's the new kid like?" I asked.

"Curious much?" Nick teased, not very nicely.

"I'm just trying to find your replacement," I said, smiling sweetly.

"You couldn't replace me if you tried," Nick boasted. "I'm impossible to replace. Like a girl's virginity."

"But not a boy's virginity?" I asked.

"Oh, shut up," Nick muttered, embarrassed, as everyone laughed. "Go talk to the new kid yourself, if you care so much."

"I don't," I said, because being interested wasn't the same thing as caring. Caring meant eagerness, and how I felt about running into Lane was the opposite of eagerness. It was a combination of embarrassment and dread. Dreadbarrassment.

- 25 -

"Something feels off today," Marina announced.

I could feel it, too, but I hadn't wanted to say anything.

And it wasn't just the appearance of a new kid, folded into the rotation with minimum fanfare only weeks after the last dorm lockout. There was a definite ripple. A weirdness, which usually meant one thing at Latham.

"Oh God, who died?" Nick deadpanned.

He was joking, but he wasn't.

"One day that's not going to be funny," Charlie warned.

It wasn't funny now. But we all knew what he meant.

We were back by the cottages then. Back in time for Wellness, like we'd never been gone. Charlie and Marina were lagging behind, Charlie because he was always stopping to catch his breath, and Marina because she'd been right, it was going to be hell getting those leaves out of her skirt.

"Hey, wait," I said, holding up my camera and documenting the moment.

The light was perfect there, slanting through the trees and toward the cottages, and the day was turning unseasonably warm. I could almost imagine that we were at camp. That we'd pull a prank on the counselors and toast s'mores at the campfire. That we'd go home tanned, our clothes smelling of bug spray. That we'd go home.

But it was possible not all of us would. Four out of five residents returned home from Latham House. That fact was in the brochure, and it was the part of all this that had struck me the most deeply. Deeper than the day I'd fainted in phys ed from the cardio conditioning sprints and wound up in the ER in my embarrassingly unwashed gray jersey gym set. Deeper than how Dr. Crane had gotten my test results and, staring straight through me, had said, "There is an active case of tuberculosis," a sentence hauntingly absent of a pronoun. Like, I had once been there, but my person-hood was now irrelevant, because when anyone looked at me from that moment on, all they would see was a grim and incurable disease.

In the old days, they used to lay us out on the porch in rows. We'd sleep under the stars in our patient beds, instructed to breathe deeply and to think only of getting better. But that was before first- and second-line drug treat-ments. Before scientists developed a cure and the whole thing began to sound ridiculous, as though bored ladies had imagined it in their drawing rooms, gasping in their fashion-able corsets. Before the disease rose from its ancient grave like some sort of zombie, immune to the drugs that doctors had once fought it with, as it shambled toward our unsuspecting towns, determined to catch its prey young.

Before it caught me.

I'd been at Latham House for more than a year, and time ran slower here. Boredom seeped in, and instead of seeming like there weren't enough hours in a day, it felt like there were far too many.

This was my life now: a dining hall that echoed with

coughing, and teachers who kept the windows open and made any excuse to leave the room. It was a life of X-rays and nurse checks, of feeling feverish before bed and having an ache in your chest after taking the stairs. Some days were worse, but really, all of them were the same, because every day at Latham was a sick day.

I barely remembered what it was like to have homeroom and Twitter and hours of freedom after school let out, while my sister was still at gymnastics, and before my mom got home from work. And Latham wasn't just a lack of freedom, but a lack of privacy. The med sensors we wore around our wrists at all times saw to that, monitoring our temperatures and heart rates and sleep cycles, and reporting everything back to a remote computer system, as much for our own benefit as for medical research.

Dr. Crane had been right. Where I once was, there was now an active case of TB. Everything of who I was and who I wanted to be had been evicted to make room for the disease.

CHAPTER THREE
LANE

ONE THING I'VE realized about new places is that they're like jeans. Sure, they might fit, but they're not comfortable. They need time to be broken in. I was thinking about this as I sat in the sterile waiting room of the medical building, trying not to cough from the air-conditioning. The whole place smelled like a hospital, a combination of antiseptic and misery. It was completely different from the boarding-school atmosphere of the cottages and classrooms, a reminder of what was lurking just around the corner. Literally.

The posters on the wall, marked with the Cross of Lorraine—the skull and crossbones of tuberculosis—urged us to "fight the war against contagion" or "crusade for a TB-free America." I almost would have preferred a cat telling me to hang in there. At least that would have been generically terrible. Instead, I was staring at posters claiming I was the enemy.

I sighed and slouched in my chair, waiting for the nurse

to summon me. Up until a few weeks ago, I was a novice at hospitals. Before all this happened, I'd been to the emergency room exactly twice. Once for an ear infection, and once when I'd wiped out on the quarter pipe in Josh Dow's driveway in seventh grade and broken a bone in my foot. But it's like they say: third time's the charm.

A nurse took me back to an exam room, which was even colder than the waiting room. When I sat down on the exam table, the thin paper crackled. I had a theory it was the same paper that covered toilet seats in public restrooms, except on a much larger, much more depressing roll.

Once again, my hands itched for my phone. My mom always complained I was addicted to the thing, but that wasn't true; I just didn't like sitting around with nothing to do, wasting time instead of spending it.

It took forever for the doctor to come in, and when he did, he was in a rush.

"Sorry for the wait," Dr. Barons said, taking a seat on the little metal stool by the computer. "So, Lane. How are we getting on?"

"Fine," I said automatically.

"Good, good." He stared at me in this probing, obvious way, and I could tell that despite the friendliness, I was being evaluated. "Tired at all? In any pain?"

"No, I'm okay."

I mean, I was a little tired, from not getting enough

sleep, but I wasn't, like, medically exhausted.

"On a scale of one to ten," he prompted, waiting for a number.

"Um, two?"

"That's what we like to hear," Dr. Barons said, taking out his phone and tapping the screen. "Let me get a read on your vitals here. . . ."

I stared down at the bracelet on my wrist, black and silicone and bulky. I wasn't used to the thing, or how it worked to give the doctors and nurses most of the data they needed, so they could spend as little time alone with me as possible. It felt strange, being recorded, having the way my body worked chronicled in some database that they could pull up on their phones and tablets, either across the room, while I was watching, or secretly, from rooms away.

"Excellent," Dr. Barons said, still looking at his screen. "Now let's see what's going on with those lungs of yours. . . ."

And then he pivoted toward the computer and pulled up two side-by-side X-rays of my chest. One from the day in the hospital when I'd been diagnosed, and one from the night I arrived at Latham.

Dr. Barons talked a little, gesturing toward the cavities with the tip of his pen, like some bizarre PowerPoint presentation where I was both subject and viewer.

"This area here is what we need to watch out for, to make sure these two lesions in the right lobe don't get any bigger," he said, speaking so slowly and loudly that it was almost insulting. "Can you see what I'm talking about? These black shadows?"

I nodded, waiting for him to continue. I didn't need Tuberculosis 101. None of this was new to me. Back at St. Luke's, when I'd spent two weeks going stir-crazy in the infectious disease ward, I'd at least had the internet to keep me company. And even though I knew Googling "total-drug-resistant TB" wasn't the best idea, I hadn't been able to help myself.

So I knew how to identify the small, tuberculous lesions on an X-ray. I knew all about how the infection in my lungs affected the red blood cells that passed through them, which was what made this new strain of tuberculosis so much worse than the ones that had come before it. TDR-TB, the news reports called it, since none of the old medications worked on it. But unlike so many other incurable diseases, it was contagious. Whenever I coughed, I put everyone near me at risk. Hence the whole reason for shipping me off to a sanatorium in the middle of the mountains, surrounded by woods and sealed with iron gates. Walling off the infection, literally.

But even though I'd read a lot about what was wrong with me, I'd read even more on how doctors couldn't do anything to fix it until scientists managed to develop a treatment that actually worked. Essentially, every doctor's appointment I'd had over the past few weeks had boiled down to this: the only thing to do was wait and see. Sanatoriums like Latham had statistically higher and faster rates of recovery than being quarantined in your bedroom, but they couldn't promise anything.

"So," Dr. Barons said, "how are we going to tackle your TB? While you're here at Latham, the best course of treatment is to follow your schedule."

"My schedule?"

He couldn't possibly mean the daily schedule I'd taped over my desk, which began with *Breakfast, eight a.m.* and ended with *Lights-out, nine p.m.*

"You'll find it in the front of your handbook," he continued. "And I think you'll discover that having a routine gives you something outward to focus on. Rest periods are for resting quietly in your room, or the common room if you're feeling up to it. Wellness periods are spent engaging in gentle physical activities, like nature walks, lawn games, and yoga."

"Yeah, sounds great," I said, without enthusiasm. Naptime and nature walks, the foolproof Latham Treatment Plan. I'd known that going in, but there hadn't been a choice. I couldn't stay at home: my parents were both teachers, and if either of them tested positive for exposure to what I had, the school board would be forced to fire them.

Dr. Barons smiled at me, like he thought I was actually raring to go on a nature walk that very second.

"Of course, you should still listen to your body. If you're

feeling tired, spend your Wellness time resting in bed. If you're feeling ill, check in at the nurse's station in your dorm. And of course once a week you'll check in with me, so we can see how much progress you've made."

"Once a week?" That seemed ridiculously drawn out, like I'd be at Latham forever.

"Your hall nurse is available twenty-four hours a day." He smiled, misunderstanding.

"No, I mean, how long am I going to be stuck here?"

I didn't realize what a dangerous question it was until I'd asked it, and Dr. Barons's smile widened.

"That's a good question, Lane. First, we have to get your X-rays looking better. Wall off that pesky infection in your right lung. Make sure your hemoglobin levels have stabilized. And how long that takes is really up to you, not me."

Yeah, no kidding.

"Two months?" I pressed. "Three?"

I couldn't imagine being away for longer than that. In three months, I'd have missed the entire fall semester. Even with the binders of makeup assignments my teachers had sent over, I still wouldn't be able to keep up. Not in the Advanced Placement classes. And then I wouldn't get the scores I needed on the AP exams in the spring, and I wouldn't get college credit, which meant I'd have to take intro courses instead of skipping ahead to the classes I actually wanted.

"What's so important that you need to get back for?" Dr. Barons asked.

He had this condescending smile, and in that moment, I knew he wouldn't understand.

I was ranked second in my graduating class. I'd almost killed myself to get there, too. I'd bussed over to the community college all of junior year for the AP Physics lab, volunteered at the health clinic on Wednesday afternoons, given up most of my weekends for Model UN practice and SAT prep courses, and started the Carbon Footprint Awareness Club after my adviser told me I needed to demonstrate "unusual hobbies and passions" to set my application apart.

I was good at being smart. At studying the textbooks until I had them memorized. At knowing the right answer so often that I'd stopped raising my hand in class, because I didn't need to prove anything. My parents had always pushed me to succeed, and after a while, I hadn't needed the push anymore.

Until a couple of weeks ago, it was a straight shot to the college of my choice. To Stanford. I could land a summer banking internship at twenty, graduate in three years, and recruit straight to Wall Street. I'd have my loans paid back by the time I turned twenty-three, just in time for business school, or law school, I wasn't quite sure yet. But that was the plan.

And I intended to stick to it. Anyway, I healed fast. I'd recovered in a weekend when I got my wisdom teeth out, so I didn't have to miss the exam review in English. All I needed were a couple of weeks for my body to get its shit together and then I could go home. I didn't even feel that sick. I was a little tired, and I coughed sometimes, but it felt like having a cold, not some serious illness.

"Well, it's my senior year—" I began.

"Lane," Dr. Barons interrupted. "What you need to do is to think of Latham as a vacation. A calm, welcoming place to relax and to escape from all the stresses and toxins of the real world."

"A vacation. Right," I said, my shoulders sagging.

I didn't do vacations. Vacations were for people who had time to relax, and I didn't. Stanford's acceptance rate was only 5 percent. I couldn't afford to be better than 94 percent of the other applicants. I had to be better than almost everyone.

But I could see that I wasn't getting through to Dr. Barons about how important it was for me to stay on track. I'd have to show him that Latham was working. That I was improving. And then he'd send me home. I just had to make sure I wasn't too far behind when I got there.

CHAPTER FOUR
SADIE

I LOOKED FOR Lane at dinner, wondering if I'd recognize him. And then I wondered if he'd recognize me. To be honest, I hoped he wouldn't. I'd been a total mess at thirteen, with frizzy hair and the wrong type of shorts and Deathly Hallows symbols inked onto my sneakers.

But the thing about being a disaster in middle school is that the shame of it never fully goes away. Even after your braces are off and your hair is exactly the way girls wear it on Tumblr, underneath it all, you're still just as unsure whether someone actually likes you, or is only talking to you so they can laugh about it afterward.

And even though stuff like that never happened anymore, even though it had been years since I'd experienced anything you could really call bullying, I was still terrified I'd wake up one day and someone would declare everything about me totally and irreparably wrong. I knew it was dumb, but I didn't want some boy around who could tell embarrassing stories about me. I didn't want anyone to look at me and see Sadie Bennett, the outcast girl who sat alone in the arts and crafts tent making friendship bracelets for her American Girl doll.

The cafeteria line inched forward, and I grabbed a turkey burger and two fruit cups. Nick snickered at me for taking two, and I was like, "Sorry for having an appetite."

And that was when I saw him. It *was* him, after all. He was taller than I'd imagined, with unruly brown hair that seemed to defy gravity. He was pale and thin, which we all were, with dark circles under his eyes, and his clothes were too formal for Latham, like something you'd wear to a country club. But there he was, with his collared shirt untucked and a burger on his tray, talking to—ugh, Genevieve Reaser.

A couple of days ago, in the hall bathroom, I was innocently brushing my teeth, and Genevieve had come in with her face wash and cheerfully informed me that "Jesus wants us to be ancestors of our future happiness by staying positive." I'd told her that Jesus wanted her to wait her turn for the sink.

I watched as Genevieve led Lane back to her table of prayer-group disciples. What a grim crowd. But it was always kids like that who volunteered to be tour guides.

"What's with you?" Nick asked.

"Nothing," I muttered. "I know him, that's all."

"Uh-oh, typhoid Sadie."

"Shut up. I meant when we were kids."

"Even worse." Nick smirked, shoveling a spoonful of sweet potato fries onto his plate.

"Hey, Nick, do you know what it would say under your photo in a high school yearbook?" I asked. "'Most likely to be friend zoned.'"

"Funny," Nick grumbled. "Sharpen that wit of yours any more and someone might think you actually have a point."

I shot him my most serene smile.

The truth was, most of us weren't in high school yearbooks. We were the ones who'd faded away, who hadn't come back in the fall. Who might never come back. Because TB wasn't like cancer, something to be battled while friends and family sat by your bedside, saying how brave you were. No one held our hands; they held their breath. We were sent away to places like Latham to protect everyone else, because it was better for *them*.

Maybe we should have anticipated it. The return of old things, the way history was starting to repeat itself. Spanish influenza came back first, in 2009, although we called it swine flu. Then whooping cough reappeared. Then polio. Then there was a meningitis outbreak at Princeton, some weird strain no one had seen before, which made the government import an emergency vaccine from Europe. Then Ebola. In the middle of this, a new strain of tuberculosis caught on, developing a resistance first to the drugs that had treated it, and then to the vaccine that had prevented it. And then it caught us. I know you're supposed to phrase it the opposite way, with patients catching the diseases, but that's never sounded right to me, as though, instead of catching TB, I could have missed.

Dinner was strange that night. Marina had been right; something was unmistakably off, and everyone else was starting to sense it. I could feel the dining hall playing a giant game of Guess Who.

"Was anyone supposed to go home today?" Marina asked.

"I don't think so," Nick said.

Marina's boyfriend, Amit, had gone home in July. And it had been two months of radio silence, while Marina sent emails that were never returned and waited for a phone call that never came. Lately, when she saw someone celebrating their last night, or packing their things into their parents' car, she went all mopey. And I didn't blame her.

"Bet there's a lockout tonight," Charlie said, glancing up from his notebook long enough to register the weirdness.

"Boys or girls?" Marina asked.

"I'm not the oracle of death," Charlie told her. "I can't be *that* specific."

"It's not specific," I said. "You have a fifty percent chance of being right either way."

Then Nick started telling this story about how he'd accidentally farted in yoga that afternoon and had blamed it on this awful girl Cheryl. And before I knew it, dinner was ending.

We had these tall metal tray returns, the kind that are always full when you get to them, so it takes forever to find a slot for your tray. Miraculously, there was an open slot right in the middle. I shoved my tray in, and at the same moment, so did someone else, from the other side.

Our trays banged, the sound startling me. Mine came shooting back, and I managed to catch it before the plate slid off.

"Sorry!" someone called. It was a boy's voice. "Did I get you?"

"Colonel Mustard, in the dining hall, with a tray," I said. "That's how I died, if anyone asks."

"I'll let them know," he promised, popping his head around to my side.

It was Lane.

"So that's the murder weapon," he said mock-seriously, nodding toward my tray. "Here, let me."

His voice was low and gravelly, with just a hint of California to it, and the way he was staring at me was disconcerting. He couldn't stop staring at me.

Maybe he wouldn't recognize me. Maybe the makeup and dry shampoo and skinny jeans had made me just another stranger in the dining hall.

Before I could say anything, he took my tray and slid it onto the return.

"Thanks," I murmured, relieved he hadn't made the connection. But then, who thinks you're going to run into someone you know on the downward slope of your own precarious fate?

"Sadie, right?" he said, smiling. "We, uh, went to camp together."

Damn it.

"We did?" I frowned like I couldn't place him. I knew that trick, at least. If you pretend not to remember someone, you immediately have the advantage.

"Camp Griffith," he prompted. "I was in 8B. I don't know if you'd remember me."

How could I forget? He'd been horrible to me at summer camp. Unforgivably horrible. I had every right to dump the nearest tray over his head. And now he was acting like he thought I'd be pleased to see him.

"Lane?" I said, pretending it had just dawned on me.

"Yeah."

I waited for him to say something. To apologize, or at least bring it up. But he just stared at me expectantly, with a grin that made him look like a kid, like he had when we were thirteen, with his badminton racket and cargo shorts.

"You got tall," I said, which was idiotic, but too late to take it back.

"And sick, although I can see why you'd say tall." He shrugged, still smiling. "Sorry, again, about the tray."

"The *tray*?" I said, thinking I hadn't heard him correctly.

"You can give me a strike or something for failing the tray return. I hear they're worth collecting."

"Why?" I asked. "Planning on skipping the social?"

"Aren't you?"

He grinned like it was a private joke, but if it was, it wasn't funny. He didn't get to make jokes about missing dances. Not to me.

"I don't know," I said coldly. "Maybe I'll *change my mind*."

All of a sudden, I was furious. Furious that he was here, that he was talking to me the way he never had when we were thirteen, that his acting nice was somehow fifty times worse than his being the asshole I was expecting. I didn't need his pity. I didn't want him feeling sorry for me and putting away my tray for me like I was too weak to lift it myself.

Before he had a chance to respond, I walked away as fast as I could, not caring how my pounding heart would read on my med sensor.

The summer I'd known him had been the worst of my life. The summer of the divorce. The summer my parents had shipped my little sister away to Aunt Ruth's and packed me off to camp at the last minute, so they could fight over selling the house without having to moderate the volume.

I was sent away for eight weeks, which would have been bad enough if the girls in my cabin hadn't all known each other for years. They weren't a cabin, they were a clique. And this one girl, Bethie, was the ringleader.

I had a pink Disneyland sweatshirt, and the first week of camp, she asked to borrow it. I was sitting on the porch reading a Diana Wynne Jones novel, and I was so immersed in the story that I didn't even hear her ask the first time around.

"So can I have it?" she demanded impatiently, like it was me who was inconveniencing her. I was suspicious of what she meant by "have it," so I said no. It's funny how small moments can ruin everything.

Later that afternoon, I was reading on my bunk while Bethie held court in the cabin. She'd gotten this box of tampons from the commissary, and her friends were wetting them in the sink, then launching them at the ceiling and laughing. The tampons stuck there, twenty feet up, their strings dangling like little mouse tails.

When our counselor came in, she took one look at the ceiling and demanded to know who had done it. Bethie blamed me, and her friends backed her up. Which was how I got banned from the coed rafting trip that weekend.

It would have been awful enough to stay behind during one of the few off-grounds trips, but then one of the boys asked where I was. And Bethie told him I hadn't come because I was on my period. According to her, I got super-bad ones. Really heavy, "like Ragú."

Of course no one questioned how Bethie, who I'd only

met last Sunday, knew the intimate details of my menstrual cycle. When the bus came back from the rafting trip, everyone on it called me Ragú. Even the boys. Especially the boys.

No one in my cabin would sit next to me, or swim near me, or use the toilets after me. The girls dumped my shampoo and crammed my bathroom cubby full of sanitary napkins. Whenever I put on my swimsuit, they talked really loudly about how sharks can smell blood. Every time they did it, I'd squeeze my eyes shut and I'd write "Don't cry" on my leg with my finger like I was casting an invisible don't-cry spell.

I had a camera with me, so I started spending all my time doing photography. I'd sign into the arts and crafts cabin, where they never checked, and then I'd go into the woods. I'd take pictures of birds, or spell out words with rocks and photograph them. So while my cabin was hell, at least I had a sanctuary.

And then, one day, I felt someone watching me. It was a boy, from 8B, with floppy brown hair and the cool kind of braces, the ones everyone called "invisible" even though they were really just clear. He was holding a badminton racket and one of those plastic balls that looks like a Snitch, which I guessed was the reason he'd come into the woods. He stood there a minute, where he thought I couldn't see, and then he was gone.

I saw him a couple of days later in the same place. And

again the day after that. Always just for a minute, like a deer pausing in the woods. He never got closer. Never said hello.

I hoped he wouldn't tell anyone where I was. I didn't want the girls from my cabin to show up and ruin it. And I didn't want those awful boys to come laugh at me. They were always asking really crudely if any girls wanted to go to "the rock" with them, which was this urban legend at camp, this hookup spot.

I was a little nervous that this boy from the woods knew where I went all day, so one night, after dinner, I asked one of the nicer girls in my cabin about him.

"Lane Rosen," she said. "He's kind of a nerd. Why, do you *like* him?"

"No," I said. "I was just wondering."

She'd made it sound threatening, as though I wasn't allowed to like him. And I didn't. I'd only wanted his name.

A couple of days later, everyone was swimming in the lake. It was sweltering outside, over a hundred degrees, so I'd gone into the water to cool off, even though I usually just watched from my towel.

"Stay back!" one of the girls shrieked when I swam too close. "Sharks can smell blood!"

"We're going to die!" her friend added, pretending to be terrified.

It was so unfair. I didn't even *have* my period yet.

And then Lane, who was floating on one of those inner tubes nearby, pushed his sunglasses into his hair and sighed.

"That's the stupidest thing I've ever heard," he told them. "We're in a lake. There aren't any sharks."

After he said that, I thought maybe he wouldn't tell anyone about the woods. I thought maybe he was nice, even though I always saw him with that foul group of boys. I thought maybe he was different.

I'd never been so wrong.

The next weekend was the lower-seniors dance, and the girls in my cabin wouldn't shut up about it. They practiced their hair and makeup in the bathroom for days. They acted like it was a formal prom, not some lame thing with bug juice and a disco ball and the horrible boys from 7B and 8B.

"Has anyone asked you yet?" they'd say, giggling, and then discuss which boys they wanted to make out with.

Back home, I went to the K–8 school down the street, so I could walk my little sister. The neighborhood kids who went to the actual middle school called where I went "baby school." I hadn't understood what they'd meant until camp, where I suddenly felt years younger than everyone else in my grade. I had lip balm and pastel panties, while they had lace thongs and eyeliner.

The night before the dance, this girl Meghan from my cabin caught up with me on the way to dinner.

"I'm supposed to give you this," she said.

It was a note, folded into one of those footballs, with my name on the front in cramped boys' handwriting. I unfolded it. The note asked if I would go to the dance with him, and if yes, he'd pick me up at my cabin. It was signed Lane Rosen, from 8B.

I couldn't believe it.

"Well?" Meghan asked.

"Did you read it?" I asked.

"Duh, I don't have to. He likes you. Or maybe he just waited too long and you were one of the few girls left."

I put the note into my pocket, trying not to grin.

"And he said to give you these," Meghan told me, producing a pair of sunglasses from the pocket of her hoodie.

They were Lane's Ray-Bans, the red ones he'd been wearing in the pool. I couldn't believe he remembered. Bethie had "accidentally" stepped on my sunglasses at the lake the other day and had broken them.

Lane had seen. Everyone had. And now he wanted me to have his sunglasses. He'd been watching me in the woods because he liked me. Maybe, if he thought I was cool, the girls in my cabin would finally leave me alone.

The night of the dance, I got ready early and sat on my bed reading while everyone else jostled for the mirror. Finally, the first boy arrived. It was this buzz-haired guy, Zach, who'd asked Bethie. She sashayed off with him, and the rest of the girls rushed to make last-minute touch-ups before their dates arrived.

And their dates did, in a trickle, the boys wearing short-sleeved button-ups and khakis and looking underdressed in comparison to the girls in their strapless dresses. I was the last one left, so I took my book out to the porch to wait.

I waited a long time, and Lane never came.

Just as I was about to go inside, this girl Sarah came back to the cabin.

"Note for you," she said, handing me a folded thing with my name scrawled across the front.

I tore it open. *Sorry,* it said. *Changed my mind.—Lane.*

Something in my face must have given it away.

It had been a joke all along. A cruel prank he wanted to play on me to show everyone he wasn't interested in the weird, nerdy girl who kept asking about him.

"God, I'm so stupid," I whispered, half forgetting that Sarah was there.

Sarah sighed.

"News flash," she said, "boys suck. It's why our cabin sticks together. It's like, we've known these boys for years, and they're all pigs. Most of them have girlfriends back home."

I could feel the tears bubbling up, my chest constricting so tightly that it hurt to breathe. Wordlessly, I turned around and ran back into the cabin, and for the first time that summer, I let myself cry.

Standing in Latham's dining hall with him, four years later, had made time melt away. I was back there again, thirteen years old and sobbing in my best dress, alone on my bunk with the meanest note a boy had ever written.

And I didn't want to be. I'd spent a long time walking away from that summer, that loneliness, that version of myself. And then Lane Rosen had found me by the tray return, and it turned out all the walking I'd done had been in a circle.

CHAPTER FIVE

LANE

AFTER DINNER, AS I walked across the grounds back toward the cottages, I had to admit, Latham was beautiful. The dorms looked like fairy-tale ski lodges, and the lake glittered, and the classical revival buildings felt exotically collegiate. Even the stone benches along the pathways were charming. We might have been anywhere. Any place where grades mattered and students had bright futures, instead of, well . . .

I'd thought Sadie would be happy to see a familiar face, but she'd reacted as though I was a ghost. I supposed the fact that I'd almost impaled her with a cafeteria tray hadn't made me particularly endearing. I'd only wanted to say— well, I wasn't sure. It wasn't like I knew her. But I wanted to. Sadie and her friends seemed interesting, and anything was better than sitting at Genevieve's table, which I was start- ing to suspect was a faction of an overeager prayer group I really didn't want to join. I mean, it's not like you can pray for something to un-happen.

I touched my med sensor to the scan pad outside my dorm, but it flashed red and beeped, refusing to open.

"Come on," I muttered, scanning again.

It stayed locked.

I scanned again, and again. Still locked.

"You've got to be kidding!" I cursed, banging my fist against the scan pad.

I don't know why, but that stupid red light got to me. I couldn't do anything right. I'd been ditched by my tour guide, and then Sadie couldn't wait to get away from me. I'd failed breakfast, and now I was going to fail the goddamned front door.

Suddenly, everything that had happened over the past twenty-four hours came crashing over me in this horrible wave. I gave the door a frustrated tug, but it was no use.

"Dude, calm down. We're locked out," someone said.

It was the punk kid from the woods. He was sitting on the porch, his back against the railing, a Moleskine notebook propped over one knee. He looked frail and exhausted up close, not so tough after all.

"What?" I asked.

"Locked out," he repeated, gesturing toward the crowd of people standing around.

I'd been so lost in my own misery that I hadn't realized. No one had gone inside. It looked like half the dorm was congregated around the porch, their expressions ranging from resigned to upset.

"What's happening?" I asked. "Fire alarm?"

The punk kid snorted.

"Someone checked out. They're doing housekeeping." He said it darkly, like he'd deliberately chosen the wrong words. When he realized I didn't get it, he sighed. "You know, cleaning out his room for the next lucky occupant."

"Someone *died*?"

"Oh, you get used to it. Just wait until they bring the body out." He nodded toward the front door.

I must have looked freaked, because he laughed, coughing a little.

"Nah, I'm messing with you," he said, and then added, "They have tunnels for that."

I didn't know whether I believed him.

"So we all have to stand around until his stuff is removed?" I asked.

"Pretty much."

He went back to scribbling in his notebook while I stood there in shock. Someone had died. I mean, I knew it happened at Latham, but I hadn't expected it on my first day. It felt so . . . sudden. Like I was being thrown headfirst into the deep end of tuberculosis before I'd even gotten used to the water.

"Who was it?" I asked.

"Grant Harden," a wiry, mustached kid said. "Wasn't

at breakfast. Went to the medical building and never came back."

I couldn't believe it. Grant. He was supposed to show me around.

My tour guide hadn't ditched me. He'd died.

After the nurses let us back into the dorm, I watched in shock as people staked out places in the common lounge, turned on the television, and set up board games like nothing had happened.

I went back to my room and collapsed onto my bed, listening to the noises in the hall. The walls of my room felt so close, so claustrophobic. And so thin, like there was nothing between me and the hallway except a flimsy sheet of cardboard, and I had no privacy at all.

I was shocked that everyone could bounce back so fast, that Grant's death had been cleared away as quickly as his belongings. All I knew was that I didn't understand Latham, and I wondered if I ever would.

"*Start as you mean to go on,*" my father was fond of saying, but I certainly didn't mean for my life at Latham to continue like this.

No, not my life. Just the next few weeks. Latham was temporary. A vacation. A place to stay while I was contagious, so my parents wouldn't get fired, and so my mom wouldn't panic every time I coughed.

The whole Grant thing was an anomaly. A weird twist in the fabric of the universe. But then, so was my being sick.

I'd caught TB somewhere. It was random and unfair, and if I'd just taken Spanish instead of science, volunteered at the clinic on Tuesdays instead of Wednesdays, seen a different movie, taken a different seat, I'd be at home, eating pizza for dinner and working on my Stanford application.

Thinking of it like that helped. As long as I was here, the plan was not to care. To keep my head down, do my work, and get through it.

I didn't need to play nice, or to make friends. I needed to stay on track, get better, and go home. I took a couple of deep breaths, which actually sort of hurt, put on some appropriately gloomy music, and started to unpack.

My mom had packed my suitcase for me, and even though I'd made pretty specific requests, she'd still grabbed the wrong jeans and, like, five of these polo shirts I never wear. Instead of my favorite T-shirts, I had a stack of every unwanted Hanukkah gift, my name freshly scrawled across each label for the laundry. Fantastic. I put all of it into the wardrobe, and then I stacked my Harbor coursework, my college guides, and my SAT books on my desk.

I tried to unpack slowly, so I could avoid the inevitable phone call home, but calling your parents is just one of those things you can't put off forever.

It was seven thirty, and they were probably sitting on the sofa grading papers, with the news on in the background. I could picture my father with his herbal tea and Chapman sweatshirt, my mother in her purple slippers and reading glasses, sipping decaf, the careful way my parents used coasters, as though they were guests in someone else's home and didn't want to offend. They were big believers in routine, in getting things done. *"When you feel like quitting, do five more,"* my dad always said. Most of his catchphrases were motivational insults.

I stared dubiously at the ancient landline on my desk, knowing resistance was futile. And then I picked up the thing and dialed.

Of course my mom answered on the second ring, sounding way too concerned.

"Lane, sweetie, how are you?" she cooed. I said I was fine, and she plunged on, talking about how Dr. Barons had uploaded my new X-ray so she and dad could see it, and how she thought it looked much better than the last one, and my dad agreed.

The thought of them staring at a picture of my insides on their iPads was pretty embarrassing, and I tried not to imagine the two of them discussing it over dinner like they'd done with my SAT scores.

There was an awkward silence, where I guessed my mom was waiting for me to say something about my doctor's appointment, but I had no idea what.

"How was the drive back?" I asked instead, trying to change the subject.

"Oh, fine," Mom said. "Not too much traffic."

An uncomfortable pause again.

"Hold on, let me get your father," my mom said. "I'll put you on speaker."

Then she and my dad took turns asking Concerned Questions about what I was eating, and if there were enough pillows on my bed because they could always send more, and if I was running a fever, and how I was sleeping, and how were the nurses, and did the doctor say anything at all about how he thought I was doing. It went on forever.

"Did you ask your teachers if you can do the AP work you brought with you instead?" my dad asked.

"Um," I said, glancing at the stack of textbooks and assignments on my desk. It was more like a tower, actually. I'd meant to ask, but I'd been so thrown by everything that I hadn't gotten the chance.

"It doesn't matter," my mom said soothingly, and my dad cleared his throat like he disagreed. "I mean it, sweetheart. I don't want you to tire yourself out."

"No, I'm sure it's fine," I said. "I'll ask them tomorrow."

Then my dad told me to "Hang in there, bud," and I said, "You too," which was completely the wrong thing. But too late. There was an awkward chorus of "I love yous," and, thankfully, it was over.

I felt entirely removed from my old life in that moment, a million miles from the band posters on my walls, and from Loki, my black Lab, and from everything that had defined me for so long. My parents never used to worry how I was sleeping, or if I wanted more pillows. They never used to tell me not to tire myself out back when I was pulling all-nighters over my physics exams. They'd just ask if I felt prepared, and then, after I got my grade, they'd ask what I could do to improve my score on the next one.

I was used to my parents. To our cadence, and our lives. I just hadn't realized quite how much my getting sick would turn us into strangers, our usually predictable conversations becoming distant and unfamiliar.

I picked up the phone one more time and called Hannah, which was my reward for talking to my parents. Hannah and I had been together for five months, since the Model UN trip to San Francisco. The amount of time surprised me. It sounded so significant, when in actuality we'd barely even started.

"Hello?" she said tentatively.

"Congratulations, you've won a romantic trip for three to Sea World." I tried to disguise my voice.

"Lane?"

"Yeah, it's me," I said. "Sorry about the weird number."

"It's fine, although I'm devastated I won't be taking my two favorite lovers to Sea World."

"Wait, you have more than two?"

"You don't know me." Hannah giggled.

It felt so good to talk to her, to joke about things that didn't matter. I leaned back in my chair and closed my eyes, for a moment letting myself pretend that I was somewhere, anywhere else.

"So what's going on in the Harborverse?" I asked.

"Oh God, everything."

Hannah had this wonderfully energetic voice, which always reminded me of a steam engine, barreling full force ahead. So I listened as she talked about the weekly quizzes in AP Bio, and how freaking unfair it was that six of them got picked at random to count for most of her grade.

"If I fail, like, one quiz and then do perfectly on the rest I'd still get, like, ninety percent. It's precarious. I'm going to stress eat an entire pizza over this every Thursday night, I can just tell."

"You'll do fine," I said.

"Maybe." She sighed. "Except it's on a curve, and everyone's fighting for second now that . . ."

She trailed off, embarrassed.

"Now that I'm out of the picture?" I supplied.

Hannah didn't say anything. She didn't have to.

"I'm coming back, you know," I said.

"I know," Hannah said quickly. "Forget I said anything."

We lapsed into silence for a moment. I wasn't used to talking on the phone. Not with Hannah. We texted, sure. And we stayed on Skype for hours sometimes, leaving it running in the background while we reviewed for exams. But this was different. This wasn't keeping each other company. It was keeping in touch. Being long-distance, as opposed to past tense.

"How is it there?" Hannah asked. "Really?"

"Fine."

"And you're feeling okay?" She said it in this mom-ish voice, and I shut my eyes a moment, as though that would erase it.

"Yeah, I'm great," I said. "There's only four classes. We mostly get to lie in bed and watch movies."

"Sounds nice."

"Well, I'd say 'wish you were here,'" I joked.

"Lane?" she said tentatively. "Can I ask you something?"

"You can ask me anything."

Although she hadn't asked me much of anything recently. It was like she was afraid. Afraid of answers she didn't want to hear. That was why she acted so cheerful and talked about her classes, the ones I should be in. It had to be.

"You know how I'm applying early action to Stanford?"

Almost everyone in our group was applying early action to Stanford, so I said yeah.

"I was wondering if you'd read over my admissions essay?" she asked.

I didn't say anything. I couldn't say anything.

"Just to proofread and see if I'm on the right track, or if it's obvious that I used a thesaurus. That kind of thing. You were always better than me in English, so . . . ," she trailed off, waiting for me to respond.

I knew I was supposed to agree to it no problem. Because that was what we did, Hannah and me. Back in sophomore year, I'd outscored her on every English quiz, and she'd beaten me on every precalc, so it only made sense to partner up in chem. And, eventually, in other things. I used to joke that we were "lab partners in crime," because instead of staying nemeses, locked in a battle over class rank, we'd become a team, fighting to succeed at the same thing.

"I just started it, but can I send a draft this weekend?"

"Sure," I said hollowly. "Email it over whenever."

My voice caught in my throat, and I started coughing. I pressed the receiver against my jeans, so Hannah wouldn't hear how bad it was.

"You okay?" she asked.

"Fine," I said hoarsely.

"Promise?"

"I'm fine," I insisted.

"You'll get better soon," Hannah said, like she had some authority on the matter. "And then everything will go back to normal."

"Right," I said. "Normal."

Except Latham was my normal now. And being healthy, being okay, wouldn't feel normal at all. It would feel incredible.

CHAPTER SIX

SADIE

FRENCH WAS ONE of the better classes, which wasn't saying much. We had it with Mr. Finnegan, who was about thirty-five and was married to one of the hall nurses. When I first arrived at Latham, Finnegan had been new, and eager, and actually sort of good. He'd let us read poetry and listen to French music instead of doing insipid exercises about Janine and Paul going to the store to buy a baguette. But Latham had gotten to him. Too many cross-outs and add-ins on his attendance sheet. Too many kids having coughing fits when he called on them, even though half the time they were faking it because they didn't know the answer. Lately, Finnegan had begun sticking to the textbook, and had mostly put away his playlists.

My friends and I all took French together, which was how we'd met. We were sitting in our usual seats by the windows when Lane walked in. Nick was in the middle of some story about this care package his mother was sending, which promised to be the worst thing in the world. "Underpants and caffeine-free tea bags," he predicted. "And newspaper clippings about my cousins."

And then Lane was there, hovering awkwardly in the doorway, wearing another button-up shirt and cardigan, which shouldn't have annoyed me, but it did. That was *our* thing, my friends and me. While practically everyone else shuffled around in their sweats, we were the ones who still got dressed in the morning and carried school bags. I knew it was just an illusion of normalcy, but it was our illusion, not Lane's.

Mr. Finnegan walked in then, carrying a travel mug of coffee. Watching him take a sip was torturous, since all we got was weak, generic tea.

"*Un nouvel étudiant!*" Mr. Finnegan said, spotting Lane.

I noticed he didn't comment on the lack of Sheila Valdez, who'd decided to take a sick day that morning and was laid up in the nurse's station, enjoying trashy magazines and a dose of Vicodin.

Lane asked where he should sit, but Finnegan shook his head and made him stand up in front of everyone and have a conversation in French. First-day torture. I'd hoped Lane would stumble, but he hardly seemed fazed, speaking with Finnegan in rapid, flawless French.

God, I hated him. I hated his pretentious button-up and

the way he smirked after he answered each question and Finnegan said "*Bien*," because he didn't need any grammar corrections.

My French never sounded like that. I had to pause and mentally conjugate each verb, starting with *je*. Of course Angela Hunter and her clique of brainless Frenchie girls all stared at him lovingly. They didn't know he was a jerk. They just knew that, with 150 of us at Latham, a new boy had miraculously appeared. A cute boy, who hadn't yet proceeded to pull out a handkerchief and noisily hack up blood.

That day, we were working on a unit that was supposed to help us in case we got sick in France. I knew we were just going through the textbook, but it still annoyed me.

In the exercises, no one ever had anything worse than flu. It was always a cold, a cough, a headache. Something that could be fixed with Tylenol or a bandage. Something you wouldn't really go to the hospital for, particularly in the middle of a European vacation.

"I'm going to pair you up," Finnegan said. "You'll come to the front of the room and put on a short skit about going to the hospital. One of you will be the patient, and one of you will be the doctor. Let's start with . . . Genevieve and Nikhil. Nikhil, you're the patient. Genevieve, you're the doctor."

Nick gave me a look of pure mourning over that one. Genevieve hated us. She said that Nick and I did the devil's bidding, since we ran Latham's black market. We supplied everyone with a liberal sprinkling of booze, junk food, and condoms, sneaking everything in through twice-a-month collections in the woods. We left a list, and our guy got what we wanted, although he charged a fortune. Nick and I didn't really take a cut. It was more about the mischief, about doing something that undermined Latham's system. And so Genevieve, despite having cornered me by the laundry chute last month to order five boxes of Milk Duds, was convinced that we needed to get us some Jesus.

Nick shuffled to the front of the room, where he melo-dramatically informed Genevieve that, *Zut alors!* He had a terrible stomachache.

Genevieve, who spoke awful French, asked if it hurt.

"Yes, because it's a stomachache," Nick said incredu-lously, while everyone collapsed into giggles.

"Shhhh!" Mr. Finnegan warned.

"Do you eat something?" Genevieve asked.

"*Qu'est-ce que vous avez mangé?*" Mr. Finnegan cor-rected, and Genevieve repeated it in the right tense.

"Twenty hamburgers I found in the trash," Nick said, clutching his stomach in fake agony. "Help me, Doctor!"

And then he very loudly pantomimed throwing up all over the floor.

"Eewwww!" Genevieve screeched, looking to Mr. Finnegan.

"*Continuez,*" Mr. Finnegan instructed.

"You are pregnant," Genevieve informed Nick, at which

point Mr. Finnegan sighed and told them they could sit down.

The next few groups weren't nearly as bad. Marina and Charlie got a lot of laughs after Charlie did a flawless impression of Dr. Barons and asked her to rate her pain on a scale from one to ten.

I suppose I knew what was coming, because I didn't even blink when Mr. Finnegan called, "Lane and Sadie."

"I'll be the doctor," I said, because there was no way I was letting Lane diagnose me with God-knows-what in front of everyone.

Lane shrugged like he didn't care. His hands were in the pockets of his jeans, and I could see a leather belt peeking out from under the hem of his shirt. Honestly. A belt. At Latham.

"*Où est-ce que vous avez mal, monsieur?*" I asked.

"*Alors, j'ai toussé depuis une semaine,*" said Lane.

Ugh, he was being so flowery about it. So show-offy. We could do the whole thing in present tense, but he was conjugating in the *passé composé*.

"*Et vous avez de la fièvre aussi?*" I asked, a plan beginning to form.

Lane confirmed that yes, he coughed and he had a temperature.

"Have you coughed up any blood?" I asked, in French.

Lane paused, staring at me in panic.

"*Et voilà,*" I said, pointing at his shirt. "A spot of blood!"

"No, no, that's . . . ketchup," Lane said, trying to deny it. "I think I have the flu."

"*L'infirmière a déjà fait une radiographie, n'est-ce pas?*" I demanded.

And Lane, looking resigned, had no choice but to agree that yes, the nurse had taken an X-ray.

I pulled an imaginary X-ray out of my notebook and pretended to hold it up to the light, enjoying myself immensely. The whole classroom was silent, waiting.

"It's only a little tuberculosis," I said, somehow keeping a straight face.

"*Un peu de tuberculosis?*" Lane repeated, glaring at me.

And that was when I did it.

"Luckily, *monsieur,*" I said, "this is simple to treat with the excellent drugs we have. You are very lucky that you are in France."

That was when Finnegan snapped for us both to sit down. He didn't look happy. Actually, he looked exhausted at the thought of having to deal with me. Which was fine. Lane knew better than to mess with me, and I'd put on a fun little performance for the class, so whatever Finnegan did to me now would be entirely worth it.

"Sadie, what was that?" Finnegan asked.

"I read about how they treat tuberculosis in France with medication that worked on the older strains," I said.

"Is that true?" someone asked.

Finnegan took off his glasses and polished them on the

hem of his shirt. You could feel the discomfort radiating off him.

"No," he said firmly. "Not for two years." He paused, considering it, and then allowed, "Well, only in desperate cases, when the patient requests it. But it was deemed an extraordinary means of preserving life."

"What does that mean?" Angela asked.

Finnegan sighed. He wasn't getting out of this one easily.

"The treatment for the other strains didn't work the same on TDR-TB," he explained. "Doctors couldn't figure out why, but too many patients who were given the medication died from it. And a lot of those people might have gotten better on their own, or at a sanatorium."

Finnegan glared at me, and I stared back at him defiantly. The room was so quiet that you could hear the maple trees outside the window, their leaves rustling in the breeze.

"But it worked on some people, right?" Angela asked.

"The odds of dying from the treatment were higher than the odds of being cured by it," Finnegan said. "And in those cases, where the treatment is worse than the disease, doctors stop offering it."

"Like pneumothorax," said Charlie. "When doctors collapsed people's lungs."

"Sort of," Finnegan allowed.

"Doctors collapsed people's lungs?" Genevieve sounded horrified. "Like, inside their bodies?"

Finnegan put his glasses back on.

"This is a French class," he reminded us.

"Inside their bodies?" Genevieve echoed, scandalized.

"Enough talk!" Finnegan said sternly. "Take out your workbooks! Page forty-three, exercises A and B."

And then, like he'd been doing more and more lately, he left the room.

WHEN CLASS WAS over, I watched Lane approach the teacher's desk.

"Excuse me," he said tentatively. "Monsieur Finnegan?"

"Not now," Finnegan snapped. He recoiled a bit, the way the teachers did sometimes when we got too close and they weren't expecting it. I wondered if Lane noticed.

"Sorry," Lane apologized. He shuffled out of the room, looking dejected.

"Dude," Nick whispered, shoving his French exercise book into his bag. "That TB is curable thing was genius."

"Thanks," I said.

"Too bad it isn't true."

"Too bad you're not really pregnant," I shot back.

He laughed as he sailed out of there.

I was the last one left in the room, and Finnegan didn't even look up from his desk as I slunk out. Whatever. He didn't have to explain all that stuff about the treatment for multi-drug-resistant TB killing people with the TDR strain instead of curing them. He didn't have to tell us that it was a last resort only offered in rare cases. He could have just given me a stupid strike and moved on. He could have yelled at me, like a real teacher would have done in a real classroom. Like he used to, in the beginning, when Nick and I did that presentation about the mating habits of ducks. It was his fault for acting like we were actual students, and slowly taking it back.

Of course Lane was waiting for me in the hallway. He was actually pacing. And he looked furious.

"Sadie," he said, the moment I opened the door.

"Need something?"

"You threw the assignment!" he accused. "On purpose!"

I wasn't expecting that, or the way he seemed to mean it. He looked genuinely distraught that we hadn't been the best in the class.

"It's not a big deal," I said.

"It is to me!" Lane fumed. "*You* may not care about your grades, but *I* do. I can't believe you did that to me on my first day!"

"I thought yesterday was your first day," I said.

Lane glared.

"You know what I mean. We failed that exercise, didn't we?"

"It doesn't matter," I said slowly, wondering why he still didn't get it. "None of this is real. The teachers wouldn't dare to give anyone less than an A. So you can stop worrying about your stupid grade, okay?"

And then I stomped away, toward the dining hall, putting enough distance between the two of us that we wouldn't have to wait in line together, because I didn't know if I could stand it.

CHAPTER SEVEN
LANE

AS FAR AS first weeks go, I was pretty sure my first week at Latham contained a record-setting quantity of suck. No matter what I did, I couldn't seem to get it right.

Everyone else seemed to know exactly what they were doing and where they were going. Everyone else seemed to have mastered the art of blending in. Except for Sadie and Nick's crowd, who made it their business to stick out.

I only had one class with them, so I began to watch for them in the dining hall and around campus. Nick lived on my hall, and Charlie was on the floor below, but I rarely saw either of them in the dorm. My only interaction with Charlie was the frantic ukulele strumming and angry falsetto that occasionally drifted out his window.

The four of them spent a lot of time in the woods, slinking off into the birch trees in a way that was almost secretive, with bags over their shoulders that seemed too full to be carrying textbooks. In the dining hall, they created small amounts of havoc with the nutritionist. One afternoon, when a plate of freshly baked cookies was set out, they ate them while waiting in line, before their trays could be checked.

Which isn't to say that I was overly preoccupied with them. I wasn't. I kept mostly to myself, studying in my room, or in the library, which was unexpectedly amazing; a hold-over from when Latham was a real boarding school. The selection was largely classics, but the study alcoves were fantastic, and I never saw anyone using them.

Everyone else seemed to treat Latham like a vacation. The TV lounge was constantly crammed, and the DVD collection in the library was so heavily checked out that at first I'd thought it had been removed. Graphic novels, magazines, and popular books they didn't carry in the outdated library were passed around like contraband in the dorms. Board game tournaments took over the common room, with Post-it note warnings stuck on top of in-progress games, saving them. The guys on my hall even turned showering into an extracurricular activity, spending so long in there every night that it was lights-out by the time a stall would open up, the water ice cold and the floor slippery.

But the thing about a vacation is that eventually, it has to end. And I wondered why I was the only one who seemed to realize that. While my hall mates played Monopoly in their pajamas, napped during the day, and marathoned TV shows in bed, I sat at my desk and worked.

I tried to approach my teachers about doing the AP

work, but it was difficult to talk to them. They were rarely in the classroom, and when they were, they acted like they couldn't wait to leave. I finally managed to corner my geology teacher about it, but she'd just blinked at me when I brought up working on my AP bio textbook instead and said that I should ask Dr. Barons at my next appointment. I didn't tell my parents, though. I lied that it had been no problem and I was keeping up easily. I didn't want them to worry about it, not when they already had so much else to stress about.

I woke up early to shower, and I stayed up late to study, and by the weekend, it had paid off. I'd done a week's worth of the AP reading and assignments. Plus, I'd taken half of a practice SAT test, since I wanted at least a thirty-point boost when I retook the test.

On Friday afternoon, I was sitting in the library working on a practice SAT math section, even though I didn't feel that great. I was exhausted, and had a slight fever, and my temples throbbed with a headache that wouldn't go away. The hall nurse had given me an aspirin, which was about as helpful as a pat on the back.

I sighed and stared down at my workbook, trying to muster the energy to do another page when all I wanted to do was put my head down on the table and sleep until dinner.

Come on, I told myself, just five more. I'd worked through another two problems when the door to the library opened.

"Are you sure you have it?" a girl whispered.

"God, Sadie, for the last time, *yes*," a boy whispered back.

It was the four of them. Charlie in his Doc Martens and enormous DJ headphones, Marina wearing a funny old dress with billowing sleeves, and Nick and Sadie, bickering. They'd brought their book bags, even though it was Friday, even though classes had ended hours ago. A strange, illicit energy passed between them.

I hadn't run into them in the library before, and I watched as Nick went to the librarian's desk to ask for an internet pass. There was a bank of old desktops in the back of the library, the one place at Latham where you could get online. You needed a pass, though. And even then, you could only use the internet for thirty minutes, once a week. According to the handbook, internet access was "stress-inducing and unnecessary."

Nick chatted with the librarian, and instead of waiting for him, his friends split up, each of them sitting at a different table. That by itself was weird. Why go to the library with your friends if you're just going to sit by yourself?

I was studying near the computer bank, and I couldn't help but watch as Nick sat down at one of the PCs. He opened his bag and took out a little box and some cables. An external hard drive, probably, which was smart. I tried to think if I still had my USB stick. But as Nick plugged it in, I realized it wasn't a hard drive. It was a router.

And then I saw that girl Marina with her laptop open at one of the big tables. She was logging onto Facebook. I couldn't believe it.

I got up and took a walk around the library, pretending to look for a book. Sure enough, Sadie had her computer out, too, with noise-canceling headphones clamped over her ears. And Charlie was on his tablet.

They had internet. All of them. Without using their passes. And I was beyond jealous.

I could feel the librarian watching me like she thought I was going to shove a copy of *Moby Dick* down my pants. So I grabbed a random book and brought it back to my table, pretending that was what I'd wanted.

I tried to turn my attention to my practice test, but it was no use. All I could think about was that router.

I'd never wanted to be part of a group the way I did in that moment. They were out of sync with Latham House, but not in the same way that I was. They acted like we were at any old boarding school, where you rolled your eyes at the rules and snuck off to do what you wanted. And it wasn't just the internet. It was the way, out of everyone, they seemed the least defeated. The least likely to give up and spend the day in bed feeling sorry for themselves. They weren't on vacation, they were off on an adventure.

I wished I knew how to talk to them, but every time I saw them together, they seemed so unapproachable. Sadie most of all. She'd seemed to hate me after I'd nearly impaled her with a cafeteria tray. I told myself that I didn't care. I wasn't at Latham to make friends, and I didn't plan on sticking around long enough to need them. Besides, I had work to do. I didn't have time for adventures.

After a few minutes, a loud group of guys came in, returning DVDs. There was some commotion with one of the cases having the wrong movie in it.

"It was like that when I got it," a guy with a nasally voice complained. "Come on, let me check out another."

"I'm sorry," the librarian said, "but you're at the limit. You need to return one before I can let you do that."

"I *am* returning one!" the guy insisted.

"You need to return what you checked out," said the librarian.

"That's what I'm *doing*!" the guy said. "Do I *look* like I'd own a copy of *Legally Blonde*?"

His friends started laughing.

"Shut up!" he said. "Someone probably switched the cases. Help me look."

The three of them sauntered over to the DVD section and started pulling out cases and opening them.

"Excuse me!" the librarian shrilled. "You can't do that!"

I could hear her heels clicking against the wood floor as she cut a swath through the library.

And then it hit me: Sadie was sitting right near the DVD

section. She wouldn't hear the librarian coming. Not with those headphones on. The librarian was going to catch Sadie on the internet. She was going to discover the router.

I pushed back my chair and ran.

"Wait!" I called. "Mrs., um, Librarian?"

"Just a minute," she snapped.

"It's an emergency!" I said desperately.

She turned. And I had nothing. I tried to think fast.

"A *really big* emergency," I repeated loudly.

I caught Sadie's attention, and her eyes went wide as she snapped her laptop shut.

"Um . . ." I stalled. "There are ants all over the reference section. Someone spilled juice."

It was a lousy excuse, but too late to make up another one. The librarian muttered something under her breath and rushed in the other direction.

I hurried back to my table to pack up, because I didn't want to be there when she realized I'd lied.

I was putting my calculator into my bag when a shadow fell over the table.

It was Sadie. And she looked furious.

"What are you doing?" she demanded.

"Fleeing the scene of a crime." I shouldered my back-pack. "Colonel Mustard, in the library, with the ants."

"That's not cute," Sadie said, following me out of the library. "Just in case you were wondering."

I held the door open for her, and she shot me a look.

"I didn't need your help." She folded her arms across her chest.

"It looked like you did," I told her.

"Well, I didn't."

"Okay." I shrugged. "Whatever."

I started to head back toward the dorms, but Sadie followed me.

"You're not going to tell anyone about the router, are you?" she asked.

"Of course not," I said.

The thought hadn't even occurred to me. But it had clearly occurred to Sadie. I waited for her to thank me, or to say that I could join them next time they pulled an internet heist, but she did neither of those things. And I was tired of her acting like I was this terrible person who needed to be taught a lesson.

"What is it?" I asked. "Why do you have a problem with me?"

Sadie laughed a little, like it was so obvious that she couldn't even believe I was asking.

"Think back to summer camp," she prompted.

"I didn't even know you."

"Then why did you ask me to the freaking *dance*?"

She said it with such force, and such anger, that I took a step back. Her eyes were dark, and her jaw jutted stubbornly, and I knew that whatever she was talking about was the real reason she'd been so awful to me ever since we'd run into each other at the tray return.

"I never asked you to any dance," I said.

"Yes, you did!" Sadie accused. "You wrote me a note, and you gave me your sunglasses!"

"My sunglasses?" I tried to think back, and then I realized: they'd been stolen, along with my headphones. These two guys in my cabin had gotten kicked out for it, too. They'd taken iPods, watches, even cash.

"I waited forever for you to pick me up for the dance," Sadie went on. "And then a girl came with that note saying you'd changed your mind."

"I've never written you a note in my life!" I said, which was the truth. "Someone was messing with you, but it wasn't me!"

Sadie narrowed her eyes at me, like she wasn't sure what was true, and then she shook her head.

"I don't believe you."

"Do you remember the note? The writing?" I asked. She nodded.

I pulled out my notebook with a flourish.

"Well?" I demanded.

One of the things about having a mom who taught third grade was that she'd drilled me on perfect penmanship. She'd made me practice in composition books after school, sitting next to her while she graded papers. I'd hated it, but it had resulted in what Hannah called "Lane Sans Serif."

Sadie stared down at my notebook, her cheeks flushing an even brighter shade of pink.

"I have to go," she mumbled. "Thanks for the, uh, diversion."

I REALLY WASN'T feeling that great, so I spent the rest of that night in bed. I told myself it was just a migraine, but I suppose on some level I knew the truth. I'd been overdoing it. Too much studying, not enough food, too little sleep.

I'd managed it well enough at home, but that was before. Before my lungs turned traitor, and walking laps around the sports field in Wellness made me so exhausted that I plonked facedown on my mattress after it was over.

I felt gross when I woke up the next morning. I was running a fever, which wasn't high enough to bother a nurse over but still made getting out of bed feel like an ordeal. I lay there feeling sorry for myself until I barely had enough time to throw on a pair of shorts and make it to breakfast. Genevieve and John and their friend Angela were trying to sell me on their prayer group again, but I couldn't pay attention.

My head throbbed, and my arms felt so rubbery that it was a miracle I hadn't dropped my tray in line. I felt like I'd pulled an all-nighter, even though I'd gone to sleep around one.

"Well?" Genevieve asked, leaning toward me. "What do you think?"

I hadn't been listening. At all. Instead, I'd been watching Tim cut his pancake into tiny pieces and drop them into his cereal, which was so weird that at first I thought I must be imagining it.

"About what?" I asked.

Angela sighed.

And then I started coughing. I scrambled for my handkerchief. But I hadn't brought it, or that stupid biohazard baggie we were supposed to carry it in, so I grabbed a napkin instead.

When I took it away from my mouth, it was stained with blood.

My mouth tasted disgusting, and the whole table was staring at me uneasily.

The blood thing freaked me out. It had happened twice before, right when I'd gotten sick, but not for weeks now.

"Shit," I said, balling up the napkin. "Sorry."

"Hey, everyone has bad days," John offered. "It's no big deal if you can't make it to prayer group later."

"Wow, thanks, I was really worried about that," I said. I knew I was being a dick, but I didn't care. I couldn't sit there and eat my breakfast while they stared at me with these worried looks on their faces, like my med sensor was about to start beeping.

"I'm not hungry," I said, picking up my tray. And then I went back to the dorm, where, for the first time that wasn't six in the morning, both showers were free.

I stood there for a long time in the lukewarm water, hoping it would bring down my fever, and trying not to panic over the indisputable evidence that I wasn't getting better at all; that, if anything, I was getting worse.

HANNAH CALLED ME that evening. I could hear the excitement in her voice as she asked if I'd gotten her email, and I told her I hadn't checked yet.

"Why not?" she asked.

"Because the librarian hates me."

"What did you do, study too loudly?"

Hannah giggled like it was inconceivable that I could do anything to jeopardize my permanent status as teacher's pet. I sighed, not wanting to get into it.

"I'm not going back there," I insisted. "I'll just give up the internet. I'll go outside or something. I heard there's this thing called the sun."

"Overrated," Hannah said. "Now, go read my essay and call me back, please."

So I went. Thankfully, the librarian gave me an internet pass without even bothering to look up.

I logged on, not knowing what to do first. Because it turns out, when time is precious, there isn't much of a point in reading webcomics or listicles. I didn't have anything important in my in-box apart from Hannah's essay, which I loaded onto my stick to read later.

I had a couple of Facebook messages, mostly of the

"how are things" and "get better soon" variety, from classmates I'd barely ever talked to. And one glance at my wall was enough to thoroughly depress me. Everyone wanted me to know that I was in their thoughts and prayers, except for this kid from math class who was promoting his band's new EP. I loved that, how there was one guy who just wanted me to buy some music, who either didn't know or didn't care what was going on in my life.

For the rest of the time, I clicked through my Facebook photos, trying to see what my life would look like to a total stranger. Most of the pictures were grainy cell phone things, other people's uploads from the Model UN conferences, featuring everyone in the van, in our suits around a conference table, wearing sweatshirts in an Applebee's at one in the morning somewhere near San Diego. I had my arm around Hannah in most of them. There were pictures from junior prom, too. Of Hannah and me in our formal wear, our smiles ridiculously fake as we posed with the Paris-themed backdrop. From the pictures, you'd almost think I had a life beyond making the honor roll.

After my internet session expired, I walked back to the cottages. It was around eight o'clock, and one of the Indiana Jones movies was being screened in the gym. Genevieve and Angela hadn't shut up about it at dinner. Apparently everyone brought blankets and pillows and came in their pajamas. But it seemed like the kind of thing that was only good if you had the right people to go with.

It was eerily quiet outside, and the birch trees behind the dining hall rose straight and white in the distance. I hadn't spent a lot of time outside lately, and I'd forgotten how peaceful it was to be alone in the dark. I walked slowly, breathing in the cool air, and it made the ache in my chest a little better.

I could feel the USB stick in my pocket, and I wondered what Hannah had written for her essay. Maybe about how she wanted to work as a White House staffer, or how she'd moved from Canada when she was fifteen. I had no idea what I was going to do for mine.

When I got back to Cottage 6, I went up to my room and plugged my USB stick into my laptop. There was this awful moment where I thought the file hadn't transferred, and then it opened.

L—Thanks for proofing! she'd put at the top. *You're a rock star.* ☺

It was the smiley face that made me totally unprepared for what she'd written.

At first, I thought it was a joke. Then I was confused. And then I was angry as all hell.

The essay was about me. About how we'd planned to go to college together, but after I'd become "terminally ill," she knew that she needed to live for the both of us. She actually said that. "Live for the both of us," like I was too corpsified to do any living for myself. Like TB was a guaranteed death sentence, and the bedsheet was already being pulled over my head.

It wasn't a college essay. It was an obituary. My obituary.

My phone rang, startling me. I knew it was Hannah. And I knew that whatever I said to her right now would be unforgivable. But I also knew that I didn't give a shit.

"Hi," I said flatly.

"Did you read it?" Hannah asked.

"Yeah."

"And?"

"Honestly? I'm in shock," I said.

"Well, it's a bit embellished for dramatic effect," Hannah allowed.

"Wow, you think?" I said, my anger flaring. "Was the essay prompt to write an obituary for someone you know?"

"I thought you'd be flattered," Hannah said.

"Flattered? That I, how did you put it, was grateful for the days you sat by my hospital bed, helping me through the pain?"

It was quiet on her end of the line, but I could still hear her there, pop music playing softly in the background.

"I wasn't trying to exploit you," she said.

"Your words, not mine."

"Lane—"

"No," I said. "I don't care, and I don't want to hear it. Because the thing is? I'm not *dead*. I'm not *dying*. And here's another thing I'm not, while we're at it. I'm not your boy-friend anymore."

I slammed down the phone, which was oddly satisfying. Much more than stabbing angrily at the screen of my iPhone.

I kept repeating what I'd said to her over and over again in my head. That I wasn't dead. And I wasn't dying. No matter what Hannah had written in her essay.

The odds were 80 percent that I'd walk out of Latham before the end of the year with an arrested case of TB and a doctor's note permanently excusing me from gym class. I'd thought Hannah knew that, or at least that she understood the difference between terminal and incurable. I'd thought she understood a lot of things. And I thought I had, too.

I'd been so stupid. It was never going to work out with Hannah and me. Staying together while I went off to Latham was a joke. We'd been humoring each other, but it wasn't funny anymore. I didn't know if she'd sent me that essay because it said what she was afraid to tell me—that she wanted to move on. Or if she'd genuinely wanted me to have it, like some fucked-up tribute.

At least I got some small satisfaction from knowing how awkward it would be for her when I returned to Harbor, and to her classes. And when she saw me around campus at Stanford—if she even got in. I hoped that sob story of an essay ruined her chances.

I'd done so much of her English homework. Come up with her essay topics, helped her put together the outlines, proofed every one of her papers, even the two-page weekly responses. I'd carried us through physics for the entire thermodynamics unit because she was too stressed over the SATs to prep for labs. And I hadn't minded. I'd been happy to help, because it meant I had someone to spend time with, instead of studying alone in my room. Instead of being the guy everyone hesitated over before inviting me to things, because no one really wanted to hang out with their hard-ass history teacher's kid.

I read her essay one more time, just in case I'd overreacted, just to make sure it really was as bad as all that.

It was worse.

I took the stairs down to the common room and let myself out of the dorm. It was cool outside, the whole world vibrating with the low hum of crickets, or maybe cicadas. I could never tell the difference. I stood there for a minute, not knowing what to do or where to go. Latham still felt so wrong, like I was living someone else's life, because this couldn't be mine.

I could see the gazebo in the distance, so I walked out there through the wet grass and sat on the steps, feeling totally out of sync with the universe. I stared up at the stars, which were dead things, and the trees, which were silent and ghostly, but alive, and I tried not to think about what Hannah had written in her essay.

I didn't cry, because I was scared that if I started, I'd never stop. I could feel everything straining inside of me, like strings stretched so tightly that maybe it wasn't the crickets that were humming at all. Maybe it was me.

After a while, there was a rustling in the woods. The sound of footsteps. I glanced up, wondering who else would be outside.

I could just make out the shadow of a girl. She crept across the grass with a heavy backpack, a knit cap on her head.

And then she stopped, staring at me.

"Lane?" asked Sadie.

CHAPTER EIGHT

SADIE

I HATED WHEN Nick didn't come with me, and he hadn't that night. He'd backed out at the last minute, claiming he was tired, so I'd gone to meet Michael myself.

It was always unnerving to be alone in the woods after dark. I wasn't afraid of whatever animals lurked behind the trees. Mostly, I was scared I'd get lost. That I'd wander out the wrong side, into town, shivering and terrified, and everyone in Whitley would act like I was Frankenstein's monster.

That didn't happen, though. Michael was there in our meeting place just like he'd promised, a lit cigarette dangling from his lips.

"Those things will kill you," I said, handing him the envelope.

He crushed the cigarette under his boot and shrugged.

"I didn't realize you'd ridden here on your high horse," he said.

"His name is Applesauce, and he's a palomino." I

motioned toward the bags. "This everything?"

"Sure is," Michael said, counting out the money. He put on a tough act, like he was some thug drug dealer, instead of a Starbucks barista. "What happened to your bodyguard?"

"He's taking a sick day."

God, I was going to kill Nick. The bags looked heavy, and I didn't know how I was going to carry all of them back without him.

Michael's cell phone vibrated, and he pulled it out, checking. He made a face. "Gotta head back, but it was a pleasure doing business with you, sweetheart."

I hated when he called me that.

"The pleasure's all yours," I said, and somehow managed to cram everything into my backpack.

"What a shame."

He smirked at me, and the leaves crunched under his feet as he walked away. I clicked my flashlight onto its highest setting, heading in the opposite direction.

I WAS HALFWAY across the grass when I saw Lane sitting in the gazebo, looking miserable. At first, I thought I was imagining it. That the shadows were up to some new trick, making me see boys in the dark. But when I got closer, I saw that it really was him, hunched and upset and sitting on the steps.

"Lane?" I called.

It was just the two of us outside. Everyone else was at

the movie night, or in the cottages, or asleep. And I wondered why he wasn't any of those places. Why he was leaning against the peeling paint of the gazebo, looking like the universe had just punched him in the gut.

"Hey," he said.

"Bad night?"

"That would be an understatement."

My backpack was heavy, and I'd had to walk pretty far through the woods wearing the thing. I was exhausted, and all I wanted was to get back to the dorm, take off my boots, and climb into the shower. But I couldn't leave him there.

He'd been nothing but nice to me, and then I'd stomped all over him, trying to put out the embers of a fire that had never existed. Yesterday in the library, I wouldn't have blamed him for sitting back and doing nothing when Mrs. Hogan nearly caught us stealing internet. But he'd run up and distracted her, making up a dumb story to save me.

Even after the way I'd acted. Even when he didn't have to.

"Move over," I said.

I shrugged out of my backpack and sat down next to him on the steps. We stared out at the woods. The trees. The sky. All of the things that didn't belong to Latham, that weren't put here behind iron gates for us to cough over.

There was barely any space between us, and I hadn't quite realized how intimate it would be, sitting there together in the dark. I'd interrupted his solitude, and I could feel him wondering why.

"I used to come to this gazebo a lot," I said. "Back when I first got here. It felt almost magical, like if anything at Latham could transport you somewhere else, it was probably this."

"I thought you hated me," Lane muttered.

I guess I deserved that.

"False alarm," I said. "It turns out that what I really hate is TB."

"Yeah, me too."

His shoulders were slumped, and the stubble that shadowed his jawline looked more defeated than deliberate. Up close, I could see that his jeans were too loose, and the belt I'd made fun of was actually necessary. He looked exhausted, like he hadn't slept for days. And I had no idea what to do, or say, or how to apologize to this strange, sad boy who was so different than I'd imagined.

"I only hated you because I thought you were an asshole to me when we were thirteen," I said, all of it spilling out in a clumsy, unplanned mess. "It was stupid, and dumb, and if I'd thought about it for two seconds, I would have realized that the girls in my cabin had faked the whole thing. So I'm sorry. I was horrible to you, and you didn't deserve it, and you still saved me from Mrs. Hogan."

"Who's Mrs. Hogan?" he asked, coughing a little.

"The librarian," I said.

He nodded, filing away the information.

"How long have you been here?" he asked.

"Fifteen months. Maybe sixteen, depending on whether it's October yet, or if I only think it is."

"It's October fourth," he said automatically.

"Got the weather forecast for me, too?"

"Sorry." He shrugged. "Hey, can I tell you something?"

I said sure, expecting the same panic attack that everyone had in their first few weeks at Latham, about not wanting to die here. I braced myself for a conversation so predictable you'd almost think it was a symptom of tuberculosis.

And then he told me how his girlfriend had written his eulogy as her college admissions essay. I hadn't been expecting that, at all. But then, nothing about Lane was what I expected. He was familiar and unfamiliar, like a song I'd heard a different version of, and whose lyrics I couldn't quite remember.

I sat there as it poured out of him, what she'd written, how she hadn't even seemed sorry, and how fucked-up it was that she saw him like that. I hadn't known any of that was going on with him. Sometimes I forgot that everyone who arrived here left behind their actual lives, often in a hurry, and frequently unfinished. And when I thought about how I'd acted all week, like he owed me this big apology for even existing, I felt even worse.

"She doesn't know what she's talking about," I said.

"Yeah, but that doesn't make it suck any less." Lane sighed. "I'm just so *tired* of everyone going on about how I'm sick, and how sorry they are. I can't remember the last

- 94 -

time anyone had a normal conversation with me."

I couldn't, either. I was so used to it that I hardly even noticed. If a stranger on the street had asked me to rate my pain on a scale of one to ten, I probably wouldn't have blinked.

"Do you know what my mom talks about?" I said. "Ice baths and miracle herbs. She seriously calls them that. 'Miracle herbs.' And I'm like, I'm sorry, but if there *was* some miracle out there, I don't think they'd sell it in Whole Foods."

Lane snorted, and I went on, encouraged.

"So yeah, talking to people? Totally depressing. We should off ourselves right now, so we can be done with people caring how we feel."

For a moment, Lane thought I was serious. Then he realized I was full of shit, and he laughed.

"When you put it that way," he said.

"Your ex-girlfriend cared about you. She cared in a shitty way, but that's why it took her so long to say anything."

It was cold out, and the wind picked up then. I pulled my hands inside the sleeves of my sweatshirt, shivering.

"Ex-girlfriend," Lane mumbled. "That's so weird."

He was quiet a moment, lost in thought.

"What?" I asked.

"Oh. Um. I was just thinking how having an ex-girlfriend is one of those things that isn't true until someone says it. Like, we all had TB before we were diagnosed. We just didn't know we did. But breaking up isn't like that. Being single is something you're aware of the moment it happens to you."

"Or if you're like me, being single is a chronic condition since birth." I said it like I was joking, even though it wasn't funny.

"Wait, so you and Nick aren't . . ." He sounded surprised.

Everyone assumed Nick and I were a thing. Everyone. But as much fun as Nick and I had hanging out together, I had zero interest in going there.

"Nick?" I made a face. "God, no. He's practically my brother. We're partners in crime."

Lance winced at my joke, like it dredged up something painful.

"Hannah and I used to call ourselves 'lab partners in crime,'" he explained. "Before she decided to eulogize me for shits and giggles."

He leaned forward and propped his chin on his hand, looking tremendously sorry for himself.

"It'll be okay," I said.

"Will it?" Lane murmured, like he didn't believe me.

"Here's a secret," I said. "There's a difference between being dead and dying. We're all dying. Some of us die for ninety years, and some of us die for nineteen. But each morning everyone on this planet wakes up one day closer to their death. Everyone. So living and dying are actually different words for the same thing, if you think about it."

I'd thought about it for a long time, even though I'd never

said it out loud. Nick and I joked around a lot, but I didn't confess anything serious to him. We weren't that kind of friends. I didn't have that kind of friends. The ones you could talk to, without being afraid someone would cut in with a witty remark, trying to get a laugh, and ruining the whole thing. But there was something about sitting on the steps with Lane that made it feel okay to let the darkness spill out.

"So basically, I'm saying the glass is half-empty of TB, and you're saying the glass is half-full of it?" he asked.

That was a clever way to put it.

"Pretty much," I said.

"Awesome. I was looking for a new metaphor about being sick." Lane gave a hint of a smile.

"My personal favorite is the one about the invisible hand of tuberculosis trying to grab hold of us all."

"Show me on this doll exactly where the invisible hand touched you," Lane said, his voice serious.

We laughed. He had a nice laugh, a sort of embarrassed chuckle. Unlike mine, which was completely silent, as though someone had turned off the volume.

I shivered again and balled the sleeves of my sweatshirt in my fists, but it didn't help.

"It's getting pretty cold," I said. "We should head back."

We climbed to our feet, and I shouldered my giant backpack. I could feel Lane staring, but thankfully, he didn't ask me about it.

We walked back to the dorms together in silence. Not

the awkward kind, but a nice, contemplative silence. Usually, spending any amount of time with someone was a forcible reminder of how much I'd rather be alone. Even my friends could grate on me sometimes, although I tried not to let on. But talking with Lane felt easy. Nice. Like being alone but less lonely.

"So," Lane said, when we reached my dorm, "thanks for keeping me company."

I shrugged, like it was no trouble.

"Well, fresh air's supposedly good for us," I said.

"Breathing: the miracle cure everyone's been looking for."

He smiled at me. We were at the bottom of the porch steps. Gnats swarmed the light above the screen door, and the ancient glider creaked softly. It felt like we were waiting for something, but I didn't know what.

And then the quiet evaporated as everyone returned to the cottages, surrounding us with a maelstrom of laughter, and conversations, and coughing. The movie had ended. A couple of girls from the second floor pushed past us without apology, and suddenly, standing there felt unbearably awkward. So I told Lane I'd see him around, and then I went inside.

CHAPTER NINE

LANE

I LIKED SADIE'S theory about living and dying being the same thing, and I wanted to believe it. But the thing was, although I might not have been dying, I wasn't really living, either. I was doing what I'd always done: keeping my head down, working hard, planning for the future, and trying to ignore the present. Like Harbor, Latham was someplace to get through on the way to somewhere else.

I had an appointment with Dr. Barons on Sunday, and when he pulled up my vitals on his tablet, I could tell I was in trouble. He stared down at the screen, his expression dismayed.

"Lane, buddy, what's going on here?" he asked.

"Nothing."

I tried to look innocent, like I didn't know what he was talking about, but I had a pretty good idea. I still wasn't feeling that great, although it was nowhere near as bad as it had been on Saturday morning. I'd been so focused on keeping up with my schoolwork that I'd ignored my test scores—the ones I couldn't study for. I'd overdone it, and now Dr. Barons was going to . . . what? Give me a strike for being sick?

"How are you feeling right now? On a scale of one to ten?"

Four, I thought.

"Two," I said.

"I wish I believed that." Dr. Barons frowned, and I shifted uncomfortably, hating that he could tell. "But you've lost weight, you're running a fever half the time, and you're barely sleeping."

He said it like I was this grand disappointment, as though having a fever was as shameful as flunking an essay, or forgetting to do my homework. I'd read enough about TB to have its list of symptoms memorized: cough, fever, fatigue, chest pain, chills, loss of appetite, coughing up blood, weight loss.

"Right, but all of that's normal," I said. "It's in the pamphlets or whatever."

Dr. Barons shook his head.

"New symptoms are always worrying. You should be getting better at Latham, not worse."

I hated that he was right, that I wasn't okay, and this wasn't some bullshit checkup. I didn't want to be at Latham, but more than that, I didn't want to need to be here.

I kept quiet, and Dr. Barons sighed.

"I don't want to have to update your parents with news like this," he said, "when earlier this week, it looked like things were on the mend."

"They are," I insisted. "I am."

And then I fucking started coughing, right there in his office. It was the air-conditioning, cranked up so high that I was shivering even in my Stanford hoodie. I took out my handkerchief just in time, and Dr. Barons watched me, his face eerily calm, and his gaze unnervingly sharp. I didn't cough up blood or sputum or anything, but it still sounded pretty rough.

"A decline like this worries me," he said, taking a stylus out of his lab-coat pocket. "So what we're going to do is make a couple of preventive changes. We'll add you to the monitor list so a nurse will check on you during rest periods to see if you need anything. And I'll put you down for a sleeping pill every night at eight."

I stared at him in horror.

"You can't do that!" I said.

This couldn't be happening. I didn't need some nurse hovering over me and forcing me into bed when it was still so early. I'd never have any privacy, or get anything done.

"I can fix it," I promised. "Honestly. I didn't realize it was that bad, or I would have eased up."

"Exactly. You were just trying to keep up with the schedule, but it was too taxing. So we'll make some accommodations and see if we can stave this off before—"

"That's not what I meant!" I interrupted. He had it all wrong, thinking that *Latham* was too much for me to handle, that I'd gotten worse from a couple of bullshit classes and nature walks. I'd been planning to ask him about doing my AP work, but now that I had to admit what was really going on, I knew he'd never allow it.

So I confessed everything. How I'd been studying during the rest periods. That I wasn't having trouble sleeping, I was staying up to work. And sure, I wasn't feeling great, but I hadn't realized it had gotten *that* bad. I just didn't want to lose everything that I'd worked so hard for. I didn't want Latham to ruin my perfectly planned-out future.

After I finished, Dr. Barons was quiet for a moment. I could feel his disapproval hovering there like a giant doom cloud. And then he sighed.

"Lane," he said, "I don't think you understand how serious this is. I'm not suggesting you slow down, I'm insisting that you stop. You're not at a school, you're in a medical facility, and you need to get with the program. Immediately."

I'd never seen an adult look so angry at me, or so disappointed. I was actually being scolded—for studying. In the weirdness of Latham House, where it was easier to fail your meals than your classes, I'd gotten it wrong once again.

"Can I trust you to do that?" Dr. Barons pressed. "Or do I need to transfer you to the hospital wing for round-the-clock care? Because I'm going to be blunt here, Lane. If you keep going like this, that's where you'll wind up."

It hit me then, as I sat on the crinkled paper of the exam table, how monumentally stupid I'd been. When I'd arrived at Latham, I hadn't felt that sick, so I'd figured I wasn't. And then I'd seen how easily that could change. I could either get better, or I could keep up with my old classes from my old life. I couldn't do both.

Everyone else had known that. And I should have, too. I just hadn't wanted to admit it, because admitting it meant acknowledging the possibility that the odds might not be in my favor. And that possibility was terrifying.

I wasn't surrounded by sick kids, I was one of them.

"Yeah," I said hollowly. "You can trust me."

"Good."

Dr. Barons smiled, and I tried to smile back, but I couldn't think of anything to smile about.

"Is there any way we could forget about the sleeping pills and nurse checks?" I asked. "I'll go to sleep at lights-out and everything. I swear."

The doctor considered this, staring at my chart.

Please, I hoped, putting it out there into the universe for any deity that might be listening, I'll do the stupid nature walks and yoga if he just grants me this one thing, if he lets me keep some small measure of dignity in this place.

"All right," he said. "We'll hold off for the time being. So long as I see an immediate improvement."

"You will," I promised, relieved.

"Fantastic." Dr. Barons put away his stylus. "Oh, and Lane? Your hall nurse will come by shortly to collect any study materials that might be in your room."

Of course she would. Because it wasn't enough that I had to be here, now I had no escape. I was completely severed from everything.

So fine, I'd play by Dr. Barons's rules. And once I got this TB thing under control and went home, I'd try to figure something out. But I'd rather get well enough to leave than stay sick enough for Dr. Barons to keep me here.

Just the thought of what it would mean to follow the schedule taped above my desk overwhelmed me. It would mean that just like everyone else, I was a patient here. One who was expected to endure an endless stretch of hours every afternoon, with no internet and no phone and no friends and nowhere to go and nothing to do except lie in bed and wait. I saw now why everyone crowded the TV room, and read graphic novels, and ransacked the DVD shelves, and saved their board games.

Classes ended before lunch, and the teachers didn't assign homework. It was like Sadie had said—they wouldn't dare to give us less than an A. I thought about Sadie's group, with their contraband internet, their mystery trips to the woods, the way I never saw Nick or Charlie hanging around the TV lounge in their sweatpants.

When I'd first arrived, I'd thought they were troublemakers and that breaking the rules was wrong. But now, the idea of getting in trouble sounded appealing. Being yelled at for something that wasn't on my medical chart would be great. I was sick of being perfect, and maybe it was okay not to be, just for a while, just at Latham.

Maybe I could be a different version of myself here, one who didn't feel enormously guilty for watching a movie on a school night. Someone with a hobby that did nothing for my résumé. Someone with friends, not just a friend group.

When Sadie had joined me in the gazebo and we'd sat there talking about everything, I'd been so lost in my own misery that it hadn't quite dawned on me how amazing it felt for someone to understand, someone who was going through the same thing. Sadie had made Latham seem like a common enemy to be laughed about, and for the first time in months, I hadn't felt panicked, and I hadn't felt alone.

I'd gone about my life here all wrong. I saw that now. And I was determined to fix it.

HAVE YOU EVER driven somewhere with the GPS on and you decide to stop off for a coffee or something? The GPS keeps giving you directions to your destination, keeps making this rerouting noise at every turn, like you've done something wrong. And suddenly, instead of blindly following what your GPS says, you're actively ignoring it, and getting angrier and angrier at the stupid machine for telling you to turn right.

I'd always thought of myself as the passenger in this scenario, but as Nurse Monica went through my belongings, taking away my binders of makeup assignments, and the books on my desk, and even my college brochures, I realized that I was the GPS.

I was the one who hadn't understood about the detour, and who kept stubbornly trying to get back en route. I'd been rerouting at every turn, when the only thing to do was to stop protesting and go off course.

I HAD MY chance to fix things in French class on Tuesday. We were working silently at our desks again, and I kept glancing over at Sadie and her friends. I'd been trying to figure out how to approach them all morning, because I didn't think I could stand another meal at Genevieve's table.

Mr. Finnegan wasn't in the room. He'd come in for about two seconds, written an assignment on the board, and instructed us to work silently until he returned. Which, if last week was any indication, would be right before class ended.

Back at Harbor, my honors French class had alternated between Socratic-method verb conjugations and sitting in the computer lab with headphones on, doing dictation. The whole thing was a nightmare.

Latham's version of French, a catchall combined class for anyone with the basics under their belt, felt like a total joke in comparison. We'd moved on from hospital visits to office jobs. I couldn't figure out why we were going over this stuff, other than to keep us busy. To top it all off, the textbook was ancient. There was an entire dialogue about sending a fax.

I flipped to the front of the book and took a look at the publication date. The book was a relic of the early nineties, stamped with a fancy seal proclaiming it PROPERTY OF THE WHITLEY PREPARATORY SCHOOL LIBRARY. I guessed someone had found a stack of them gathering dust and figured we could mend and make do.

The assignment was easy, and I finished pretty quickly. I wished I'd brought a book, or something else to work on, but it's not like I had too many options after Nurse Monica had ransacked my room. So I sat there double- and triple-checking my answers and glancing over at Sadie.

Her desk was beneath a window, and the sunlight caught the gold in her hair. She had on this striped sweater, which had slipped off one shoulder, revealing the pale wing of her shoulder blade. She bent over her work, tapping her pencil against the textbook, this wonderful smile on her lips, like she was silently laughing at the assignment.

And then Nick leaned across the aisle and dropped a folded note onto her desk. She opened it warily, and they whispered about something. Nick leaned back in his chair with a smirk.

I watched as Sadie stood up, gathered her assignment, and walked to the front of the room. Everyone stopped what they were doing, unsure what was happening. And then Sadie put her things down on the teacher's desk, next to Finnegan's travel mug. She smoothed her hair, an expression on her face like she was about to pull the best prank in the history of Latham.

"*Bonjour, classe,*" she said, plucking a whiteboard marker from the tray and uncapping it. "Everyone take out a different colored pen and we'll go over the assignment."

We all looked around, confused. Only Nick and Charlie were laughing, like they knew the drill. Marina shook her head and put away her graphic novel with a grin.

Finnegan hadn't mentioned anything about correcting the assignment. He still hadn't handed back any of our work from last week's classes.

"Exercise A. The answers are: *le bureau, l'ordinateur, l'imprimante, l'agrafeuse,* and *le classeur,*" Sadie went on, writing each answer on the board. "Does everyone have that?"

"*Oui, madame,*" Nick called, trying not to laugh.

Everyone still looked confused.

"What are you doing?" Genevieve asked.

"*En français, Mademoiselle Reaser,*" Sadie chided.

Genevieve muttered something under her breath and slid down in her seat, folding her arms.

"Exercise B," Sadie went on. "We'll do this one together.

Let's go down the rows, starting with Charlie. Please read the full sentence out loud."

"*Avez-vous pris des notes pendant la réunion?*" Charlie read, sounding bored.

As everyone down the rows read their answers to the assignment, I tried to figure out Sadie's game. We'd gone over the homework like this every day at my old school. It was just . . . normal. Just school.

Which must have been the point: to do something so normal that Mr. Finnegan would feel ridiculous getting upset over it. It was an interesting idea. A way to screw with the teacher that didn't actually cause any trouble.

"Section C," Sadie said. "Angela, I think it's you?"

"*J'avais une pièce de papier,*" Angela recited.

"*Bien.*"

"Wait, that's wrong," I said, without thinking.

Everyone turned to stare at me.

"It's *une feuille de papier,*" I said, trying to play it off. "It's idiomatic."

"Is it now?" Sadie grinned. "Well. I think we've got ourselves a new substitute teacher. *Levez-vous.*"

She motioned for me to come to the front of the room, and I shook my head. No way was I getting up there while we were supposed to be working quietly in our seats. What if Finnegan came back? What if everyone hated me and started yelling for me to shut up and sit down? The ways in which this could go wrong were endless.

But Sadie held out the marker, waiting. The whole room was watching. Even the kids who'd been gaming on their tablets. I wished I could take back my stupid grammar comment, and possibly disappear. But Sadie and her friends were staring at me, and I realized with a sudden jolt that this was it. My chance to join their rebellion. My way into their circle. I'd been hoping for something more subtle, like making witty conversation in the lunch line, possibly about the milk cartons, but too late now.

So I sighed and stood up, hoping I wouldn't regret it.

"*Classe*, say *bonjour* to substitute teacher Lane." Sadie pressed the marker into my hand with a smile.

"*Bonjour, Lane*," Sadie's friends called back, enjoying themselves immensely.

And then she went back to her seat and left me there.

I stared down at the textbook that was old enough to buy beer, trying to muster my nerve. I never did this sort of thing. I volunteered to pass back exam booklets, and I went to school sick so I wouldn't lose out on the perfect attendance award. I followed the rules because that was why rules existed, to be followed.

At least, that's what I'd always believed. And now I was standing at the front of the room, not because the teacher wanted me to, but because Sadie had dared me. Because it was worth getting in trouble if it meant I didn't have to sit at Genevieve's table anymore.

There was no such thing as an honor roll here, and no clubs that the teachers liked best. So I set my textbook on the desk and did an impression of my dad.

I'd been stuck in his history class in the ninth grade, along with the other kids in the honors program, who couldn't stand him. He was strict, and a tough grader, and he didn't let anyone pee, even though his class was right after lunch. But mostly, he did this thing where he hit the board with the marker to stress his point, making eye contact with a specific student while he did it. No one whispered in his class. He was that terrifying.

"*Répétez, plus vite,*" I insisted, smacking the board with the marker and glaring at Angela.

She giggled nervously and gave the correct answer.

"*Exactement,*" I said coldly, writing it down.

Angela sank down in her seat, pouting, and Genevieve shot her a sympathetic look. Sadie and her friends were in hysterics. Some of the other students were grinning. I went on, encouraged, and somehow managed not to break character. In middle school, I'd taken a drama class where we played improv games and acted out two-page scenes. I'd wanted to sign up again in high school, but it would have ruined my class rank if I didn't take a weighted elective, so I'd picked up AP Art History instead.

I'd forgotten how much I enjoyed stuff like this, how fun it was to step outside myself. I was on the second-to-last question when the laughter went totally quiet. Something was wrong, I could feel it. I turned.

Finnegan stood in the doorway, staring at me, unsure what was going on. And to tell you the truth, I hardly knew, either.

It wasn't like the room was in chaos or anything. Far from it. The board was filled with neatly numbered corrections, and everyone was in their seats, quietly marking their answers, while I ran the class like Professor Snape was my spirit animal.

"*Qu'est-ce qui se passe là?*" Finnegan demanded.

"*Rien,*" I said, putting down the marker. "Sorry."

I hurried back to my seat, my heart pounding. Finnegan had caught me goofing off, and now I was going to catch hell. I expected him to yell, or send me to some administrative office, or kick me out, but he just shook his head, like he wasn't paid enough to deal with this kind of thing.

He stared at the uncapped marker I'd left on his desk, and at the board, with Sadie's cursive scrawl and my neat printing, a pinched expression on his face like he didn't want to touch anything we might have used.

"Someone erase this," he said, motioning toward the board. "Genevieve."

Genevieve flounced to the front of the room and started wiping the board.

"Everyone pass forward your work," he said. "Then go to lunch. Sadie, stay behind, please."

I tore my assignment out of my notebook and passed it forward, glancing over at Sadie. She shrugged, like it was no big deal, and I wondered why Finnegan hadn't asked me to stay behind as well. I'd been the one at the board, the one screwing around instead of working in my seat. On the grand list of detention-getters, my name should have been at the top.

I was thinking about this while I packed my bag, and then I looked up and found Nick, Charlie, and Marina standing around my desk. They were all staring at me like I'd gotten away with the biggest prank ever, which I suppose I had, since Finnegan had let me go without even a warning.

"Dude," Nick said. "That was terrifying. I was having flashbacks to my geometry teacher."

"Thanks, I guess?" I shouldered my bag and stood up, following them into the hall.

"I thought you were going to start taking points from Ravenclaw," said Marina.

"Gryffindor, and don't tempt me." I gave her my look of doom.

Marina giggled.

"You're the one who ran interference for us with the librarian, right?" she asked.

"Oh, yeah." I was surprised she remembered.

"That was really cool of you," said Nick. "Thanks."

"It wasn't a big deal," I mumbled, a little embarrassed.

But something about the way they'd phrased it stuck

with me. They thought I'd done it for them, when the whole time I'd been so focused on the librarian catching Sadie that I hadn't thought about anyone else. It was strange to realize they'd all been there.

"Do we really have to wait for Sadie?" Charlie asked, glancing impatiently down the hallway.

"Well, that *would* be the nice thing to do," said Nick.

"Good thing we're not nice." Charlie grinned.

"No, we really aren't," Nick said mock-seriously.

"Speak for yourself, because I'm darling," said Marina.

"You're the worst," Nick told her. "You steal everything clever we say and use it in your fan fiction."

Marina shot him a look.

"It's not stealing, it's recycling," she said. "And whatever, you love it."

"You know what *I* love? Beating the line," said Charlie.

"Dude, there are, like, five hundred better ways to phrase that." Nick laughed.

I'd never heard anyone talk the way they did, like you got a gold star for each clever remark. It was smart, but not show-offy smart, like the guys from Model UN, who always tried to prove that they knew more than you about some obscure topic they'd Wikipedia'd. This was more like seeing how self-deprecating you could be while still making everyone laugh.

They all began to walk away, toward the dining hall. I hesitated, unsure if I was supposed to follow, and after a couple of steps, Nick turned back around.

"Aren't you coming?" he asked, like he'd expected me to join them all along.

"Yeah," I said gratefully, catching up. "Of course."

CHAPTER TEN

SADIE

THE WHOLE THING was Nick's fault, really, so if Finnegan should have kept anyone after class, it was him. But Nick got away with everything, while I always got caught. I could hear him and Charlie and Marina laughing out in the hallway as I approached Finnegan's desk.

"You wanted to talk to me?" I asked.

Finnegan sighed, looking all martyrish, like he deserved a medal for spending more time with one of us than he absolutely had to.

"Yes, Sadie, I did," he said. "I know you were the one responsible for today's . . . excitement."

He actually called it that—excitement. Way to be over-dramatic.

"What's so exciting about grading our work?" I asked.

And then he launched into this totally bullshit speech about how correcting the assignments in class puts unnecessary pressure on everyone, and doing your best was enough without stressing over your grade, and how I'd been at Latham long enough to know that.

"I don't want anyone getting sick because of the French homework," he said.

"You mean dying," I corrected. "Because we're already sick."

Finnegan gave me a watery sort of smile, like he preferred tiptoeing around the subject.

"Yes," he clarified. "I mean dying."

The word floated there in silence, neither of us knowing what to do now that he'd actually said it.

"Wow, thanks for protecting us from dying of French homework," I said sarcastically. I was already in trouble, so what did it matter if I kept going? "It's supercool of you to care so much."

"Sadie—"

"I mean it, thanks for teaching us how to tell the doctors in Paris that we think we might have a cough. That'll be useful, when we're not even allowed to get on an airplane."

I hadn't planned to go off on him, but I'd been up half the night listening to Natalie Zhang's crying through our shared wall. She did that sometimes, but never as badly as last night. I should have asked the nurse for a sleeping pill, but I'd stupidly suffered through it and had been in a terrible mood all morning. Sometimes I got so tired of Latham House that I wanted to scream.

"You know that scientists are working on—" Finnegan

began, but I didn't want to hear it.

"Developing a cure," I said flatly. "Yeah. So I've heard. Twice. And each time we get excited over rumors about some new medication, and then it turns out the doctors faked the data, or the drug doesn't work. So I'm not exactly getting my hopes up."

"I don't know what to tell you, Sadie. I want a cure as much as you do, and one day it'll happen. But until then, we're all stuck here."

I couldn't believe he'd said that. The "we" part.

Nick had this theory that our teachers were all exposure-positive and couldn't get hired anywhere else, even though there was, like, a 90 percent chance they'd never get sick. I'd always told him that was just a rumor, but something about the way Finnegan talked about being stuck made me think it might be true.

"But you're *not* stuck here," I said, "because at the end of the day, you get to go home, and go to restaurants and movie theaters and airplanes and not have anyone get worried that *French homework* might kill you."

He didn't deny it.

"I'm late for lunch, and the line's going to suck," I said. "And for the record, the grading papers thing? Nick started it. Not me."

"I very much doubt that," he said, shaking his head. But he let me go.

It was so annoying. Nick never got in trouble. He was

too geeky, too eager, too out-of-his-way friendly with the adults. They never understood that he was making fun of them, pushing them to be nice and make conversation when they'd rather back away. No one believed that I wasn't dragging him feetfirst into our misanthropy, that actually, we egged each other on.

Of course my friends hadn't waited for me after all. They'd taken advantage of the early dismissal and had gone through the line before it was enormous. Meanwhile, I was stuck at the back of it. I picked up my tray and glanced toward my table with a sigh. Everyone was already there.

But something was different. I looked again, and sure enough, Lane Rosen was sitting at my lunch table. I'd been gone for, like, two minutes, and somehow, in that amount of time, my friends had adopted him.

It was strange, seeing him there, laughing at something Nick was saying, which was no doubt juvenile and only half as funny as he thought. But it wasn't a bad kind of strange, just different. I hadn't thought ahead to his finding a group and making friends.

After we'd talked that night in the gazebo, sitting in the dark and splitting a side order of existential crisis, everything had felt different. He wasn't this grown-up version of a thirteen-year-old nightmare anymore, he was the new kid, with the perfect handwriting and clever remarks and sheepish grin, who never left his room and barely talked to anyone. I'd seen him sitting at Genevieve's table, looking miserable, and had considered inviting him over, but I hadn't known what to say, or how my friends would react.

And now they'd gone and casually invited him over for me. Or, I guess, not for me. They'd just gone and become friends with the guy who'd created a diversion in the library and taken my dare in French class, which, to be honest, I was still surprised about. I hadn't thought he had it in him. And now there he was, sitting at my table.

Oh God, what if they were talking about me? What if he was telling them embarrassing stories about our summer camp days? I fretted over it while I was stuck in the endlessly slow lunch line, behind a couple of sophomores who couldn't make up their minds whether they wanted potato wedges or sweet potato fries.

And then, finally, I was through. I'd been so impatient that I'd grabbed a normal, boring lunch, and Linda got all smug about it, congratulating me on "making healthy choices."

When I got to my lunch table, it was like arriving late to a party. Not like I'd ever been to a real one, seeing as how I'd been Lathamized in the spring of my sophomore year, but it felt like everything had started without me.

Charlie had already finished his lunch and was scribbling furiously in his notebook. Marina was leaning back in her chair, nibbling on a fry while she eavesdropped on the clique of overly dramatic girls at the next table. And Nick was busy carving his veggie burger into some sort of art piece while Lane shook his head over it.

"Hi," I said.

Lane looked up at me with this huge smile, and I wished I'd said something cooler than "Hi," but too late.

"Sadie." He said my name like I was exactly the person he wanted to see most. "Sorry if you got in trouble with Finnegan."

"It's not a big deal." I shrugged, playing it off. "Although, Nick, you know your theory on the teachers being exposure-positive?"

Nick was concentrating so hard on carving up his burger with the dull plastic knife that he was like, "Mmmn?"

"Are you even listening?" I grumbled, putting down my tray.

Lane had taken the seat across from mine, which was usually empty. I was used to us being four people, with plenty of room to spread out. The table felt fuller with him there, and more cramped, with just the one empty seat.

"What?" Nick whined.

"Forget it," I said. "You suck."

He did, too. I still hadn't forgiven him for backing out of our collection with Michael on Saturday night. At least he'd distributed his half, but still.

"You say that, but only because you haven't yet feasted your eyes upon the genius of my latest invention," Nick bragged.

He held up his tray in triumph. It didn't look all that impressive to me. Basically, he'd cored his veggie burger.

"What is it?" I asked.

"I call it the nutburger! It's a portmanteau."

"It's portmanterrible," I said, snorting.

"I *told* him that," said Marina. "It's twenty percent less burger and twenty times more pretentious."

"Whatever, it's awesome," Nick said, taking a bite.

Mustard and ketchup oozed out the middle of his nutburger and plopped onto his plate.

Marina giggled.

"Your prototype needs work," Lane said.

Because he was sitting across from me, we kept accidentally making eye contact. He'd smile a little and then glance away. It happened, like, five times, and whenever it did, I felt all fluttery. Lane's eyes flicked up and met mine for a sixth time, and then he grinned into his lunch tray.

I'd remembered his eyes as hazel, but they were actually green ringed with brown. He had those long, thick eyelashes, too, the kind that I couldn't even get with mascara. There was color in his cheeks, and he looked less exhausted than he had last week. Now that I wasn't still seething over the summer camp debacle, it was easy to see why the girls in my French class were so interested.

Of course he'd had a girlfriend back home. I bet he was one of those drama club guys the girls all secretly had crushes on. Or maybe class council. I couldn't place him. There was the flawless French, the preppy clothes, and the neat hand-writing, and then there was the easy way he laughed, the witty comments, and that evil substitute teacher impression. It was like he thought he should be one thing but secretly was another.

Ugh, I wasn't this girl. This blushy girl who couldn't handle sitting across from a boy. Admittedly, a cute boy. Who was staring at me like he thought I could read Morse eye contact. I took a bite of my burger, hoping that would quelch the flutter.

"So, Lane," I said, "how come you're not sitting in the Bible Belt anymore?"

He made a face.

"I was sort of dying over there."

"Well, now you can be sort of dying over here," Charlie said dryly.

Lane laughed, and then looked embarrassed about it.

Charlie went back to writing again, and Marina tried to read it over his shoulder, being super obvious.

"Stop," Charlie muttered, edging his notebook away.

"Ugh, you're no fun." Marina pouted for a moment, and then her face lit up. "Lane, you knew Sadie from before, right?"

"A little," he allowed.

I tried to shoot Marina telepathic signals to shut up, but it didn't work, probably because I don't have super-powers.

"So, what's the story with you two?" she asked. "Sadie won't tell us anything."

If I could have kicked her under the table, I would have.

"There's nothing to tell," Lane said, and I breathed a sigh of relief. "We were thirteen and went to the same summer camp. I pretty much thought girls had cooties back then."

"I *do* have cooties," I said, and Marina almost choked on her juice.

"Can we *please* call it that from now on?" asked Nick.

"Sure," I said. "I can just picture the final Facebook statuses. 'She fought a heroic but ultimately unsuccessful battle against a grave case of cooties.'"

"Our little angel has gone on to a better place, a place free from cooties?" Nick suggested.

"Oh my God, stop." I was cracking up. We all were. But it wasn't funny. Not really. Being at Latham had warped our sense of humor, until there we were, calmly eating our burgers while composing fictitious final Facebook statuses for hypothetically deceased teens.

"That's why I deleted my Facebook," Charlie said. "Preemptive strike."

None of us knew what to do with that. Charlie was the sickest of anyone in our group, and he was both the most and the least sensitive about discussing the future, and the possibility of not having one.

- 124 -

"I'm surprised Latham doesn't block the site," Lane said, and we all stared at him in horror. "My high school blocked almost everything good on their computers."

"Shhh, don't let them hear you!" said Nick. "Here, toss some salt over your shoulder."

Nick held out the saltshaker, and Lane took it, playing along.

"There," he said, throwing a pinch over his shoulder. "Happy?"

"The internet gods require more sacrifice," said Nick. "Quick, hop on one leg and touch your nose."

"The internet gods require a sobriety test?" Lane asked, and everyone laughed.

It was interesting the way he changed the dynamic of the table. How much louder our laughter sounded, and how the five of us seemed to fill the space more. Watching him and Nick was fascinating. There was something that clicked about the two of them, like they'd been friends forever. Watching them goof around made all the ways that Nick annoyed me somehow seem entertaining. But Lane added another element I hadn't expected. Suddenly, our group felt disastrously coed.

When I went to bus my tray, Lane followed me.

"Can you try not to kill me this time?" I teased.

"Even if it gives you an awesome final Facebook status?"

I laughed.

"I deleted mine, too," I admitted.

It had been too depressing, getting all those messages from classmates who had always ignored me, and it had been even more depressing a month later, when they'd forgotten me again.

"You're all crazy," he said. "I'm keeping mine for bragging rights. And for torturing ex-girlfriends."

"So how's that going?" I asked, finding a slot for my tray.

"It's weird," he said, pausing to gather his thoughts. "I'm not sure. I haven't seen her for a month, so it feels like I'm brooding over something that happened forever ago."

"The Latham Time Warp," I said. "Sometimes a day lasts an hour, and sometimes it lasts a year."

"That must be it. We've fallen through a hole in the space-time continuum."

And then Genevieve sashayed over to the tray return with this sweet yet evil smile on her face.

"Lane," she whined. "Where were you?"

"Oh," Lane said sheepishly. "Um. I sat with Nick."

I tried not to be disappointed that he hadn't said he'd sat with me.

"Angela and Leigh were so worried that something had *happened* when you didn't sit at our table." She said it so dramatically that I snorted, and she shot me a glare.

She had to have noticed Lane sitting at our table, didn't she? I wished she'd leave the whole thing alone, since it was clear Lane couldn't wait to get away from them.

"Nothing happened," Lane said, shrugging. "I just decided to change it up."

There was this awkward silence where I swear Genevieve was waiting for him to apologize and promise he'd sit at her table for dinner, but he didn't.

"Well, our Bible study is always open," she finally said.

"Oh my God, you *do* know he's Jewish, right?" I interrupted.

Genevieve glared at me, and I shrugged.

"Jesus welcomes everyone to his table," she snapped, abandoning her tray on the condiment counter and flouncing away.

Lane picked up Genevieve's tray and added it to the return.

"Do you know who *else* welcomes everyone to their table?" I asked. "Anyone desperate for friends."

He snorted.

"Who are you calling desperate?" Nick interrupted, coming over with his tray.

"Anyone who would date you." I smiled sweetly.

"Whatever, I'm awesome." Nick bused his tray. "We have any plans this afternoon?"

I shook my head.

"Great," he said. "Lane, how are you at first-person shooters?"

"Worse than I'd like."

Nick grinned. "We can fix that."

And then Charlie came over to drop off his tray, and the boys left for the dorms together.

It was rest period, which most of the time I was fine skipping, but that afternoon, I could feel myself starting to drag. Stupid Natalie Zhang and her loud, horrible sobbing. Everyone knew you were supposed to muffle it with your pillow if you didn't want the whole world to hear.

As Marina and I walked back to the cottages, I could see Lane, Charlie, and Nick already scanning into their dorm. Nick was flailing excitedly about something, and they were all laughing.

"The look on your face," Marina said.

"That's just my face. It expresses a range of unprompted emotions."

"Whatever. You're jealous that Nick stole your friend."

"That's ridiculous," I said, because it was. They could go play video games if they wanted.

"Seems pretty on point to me," Marina said, grinning. "Unless, of course, he *isn't* your friend."

I rolled my eyes.

"What else would he be?"

"Who cares, he's adorable."

"You think so?" I asked, a little warily. As much as I didn't want to admit it, I liked Lane. A lot. And if Marina liked him, too, I didn't know what would happen.

"Just because I've sworn off Latham boys doesn't mean

that I can't spot a cute one when he's literally sitting next to me." Marina rolled her eyes. "Besides, I saw the way you were staring at each other during lunch. You two are so completely *Pride and Prejudice*."

"You mean he'll scorn me for my family while convincing my sister's soul mate that he doesn't really love her?" I asked hopefully.

"Exactly." Marina laughed. "But you forgot about the dirigibles. And the talking wombats."

Marina trailed off, and I could tell that she was scripting out the story in her head, one with flying machines and snarky animals and a happily ever after, where no one died, or got too sick to be a perfect love interest.

But we were all too sick to be anyone's perfect love interest here. And it didn't matter how healthy anyone seemed. Any of us could wake up the next morning with blood splattered across the pillow and a hole in our lungs so painful that having a broken heart on top of it would have been unbearable.

And even though I wasn't all that sick on the Latham scale, I was sick enough to know better. I was a stagnant case. I wasn't getting well enough to go home, but my X-rays weren't bad enough for Dr. Barons to be all that concerned. It was like my body and TB had reached a state of equilibrium. Or maybe it was mutually assured destruction, with both sides hovering over the big red button, but neither wanting to push first.

A year ago, it had seemed like a miracle when the lesions on my lungs stopped forming and my blood tests evened out, but you can even get tired of miracles when they're not quite big enough to cure you.

Because the thing about miracles is that they're not answers, no matter how much we want them to be. If anything, they're even more troubling questions. But then, Latham wasn't a place for answers, it was a place for waiting. And I had chosen a long time ago to wait here alone.

"I'm happier alone," I said.

"Nope, I know you," Marina said. "You're just telling yourself that because you don't want to get hurt."

"No one wants to get hurt."

"Well, maybe not, but sometimes it's worth it." Marina shrugged, and I could tell she was thinking about Amit again. "I may have sworn off boys, but at least I tried them."

"Marina!"

"What? Don't you want to? It won't cure you, but it sure makes you feel better," she said, giggling.

"He just broke up with his girlfriend," I pointed out, and Marina sighed like I was missing the point.

"That's what I'm saying! He's so adorable that some girl *continued dating him for weeks* after she found out he was sick."

She grinned, like it was indisputable proof of his cuteness, and I laughed, supposing it was. Leave it to Marina to conjure a silver lining to Lane's horrible breakup story. And as much as I wished she didn't have a point, she kind of did.

When it came to dating at Latham, there were no good options. The boys who stayed cute inevitably went home, and the boys who got sicker just wanted to lose their virginity as fast as possible to any girl willing. By Latham's standards of eligibility, Lane was pretty close to the top. And I was sure half the girls in our French class would be all too eager to take him into the woods and hook up, which was a particular pastime at Latham, in a way that eerily reminded me of summer camp. Except our ticking clock was far more depressing than Camp Griffith's.

I wondered how often Marina thought about Amit, and what his life was like now that he'd gone home. And I wondered if Amit thought about Marina, or the rest of us still at Latham, even though he'd mostly hung out with those RPG-obsessed boys in Cottage 8.

Marina and I scanned into our dorm, and this awful group of girls was already at the table in the microkitchen, painting their nails. They did this super-involved nail art for hours, and stank up the common lounge with their polish remover, and reinforced Nietzsche's theory that hell is other people.

"Show tunes?" Marina asked as we went upstairs.

She kept trying to get me into Broadway musicals, as though hearing her *Spring Awakening* soundtrack for the fifth time would suddenly make me sing along with her, but it wouldn't. Show tunes depressed me. I didn't see the point in listening to songs from musicals I might never see.

"I really want to finish this book," I lied, instead of just telling the truth that I was embarrassingly excited for naptime.

LANE SAT WITH us again at dinner, putting down his tray along with Nick and Charlie. The three of them were in the middle of a ridiculous argument about whether it was sacrilege to put ketchup on hot dogs.

"You *do* know you're eating chicken fingers, right?" Marina asked, looking concerned.

"It's the principle of the thing," Nick told her. "We're having a debate."

"What you're having is chicken fingers," I corrected. "Which go with basically every dipping sauce you can think of."

"That's how the whole thing started," Lane explained. "Hot dogs are exclusionary, but—"

"But the chicken finger welcomes all sauces," Charlie interrupted. "All hail the food of the proletariat, the chicken finger."

And then he shoved an entire chicken finger in his mouth and choked, dissolving into a coughing fit.

Marina rolled her eyes. I was with her. Our table felt overwhelmingly full of boys. It reminded me of those groups from my high school, the ones that crammed too many people around a table and were so unintentionally loud that you couldn't help paying attention. I'd always stared wistfully at those groups across the cafeteria, wondering how they'd happened, and why they always seemed to happen without me. But then, everything always seemed to happen without me.

I was feeling a lot better after my nap, though, and less like I wanted to shout at Finnegan about French homework again. Which reminded me.

"Hey, Nick," I said. "Finnegan said something earlier to go with your ex-pos theory."

"Told you!" Nick gloated.

Lane was like, "Ex-pos theory?" so I explained it to him, and he nodded solemnly.

"It makes sense," he said. "I was wondering why anyone would sign up to, um . . ."

"Be around us?" Nick supplied with a grin.

"Don't make me feel sorry for Finnegan," Marina warned. "I mean, ughhh!"

"I'm not," I said. "I just thought it was interesting."

"Like, maybe they're not terrified of us, maybe they're scared that they could wake up tomorrow and *be* us?" Charlie said.

"No, shut up, shut up, shut up!" Marina said, covering her ears.

Charlie smirked, pleased that he'd annoyed her.

"It's, what, a ten percent chance you get sick if you're exposure-positive?" Lane said.

"Exactly." I shrugged. "You're not contagious, you're not sick, you probably won't get sick, but you stay up all night freaking out anyway. One of my friends back home had that."

What I didn't add was how she'd sent me this horrific Facebook message accusing me of giving it to her, even though we'd been diagnosed within two days of each other, so obviously there was a nefarious third party to blame.

Thankfully, our dinner conversation drifted to other things then, and we got onto the subject of movies. Which, with Marina around, inevitably led to Miyazaki films, her particular passion. It turned out Lane had never seen one.

"Not *one*?" Nick asked incredulously.

"Not *Princess Mononoke*? Or *Totoro*?" Marina pressed.

Lane shook his head.

"That's it," I said. "Tonight we're watching a movie."

So we did. Marina and I went over to the boys' dorm after dinner, which technically we weren't supposed to do, but we'd figured out a way. Marina and I went back to our dorm first and waited for someone to leave so we could slip out after them, avoiding the scan pad.

"How much trouble can we get into for having a girl in our room?" Lane asked as he led us up the stairs.

"Why, are you planning on sneaking a girl into your room?" I teased. "We're going to Nick's room, not yours."

"Right," he mumbled. "That came out wrong."

Marina shot me this knowing look, which I pretended I

hadn't seen. And then Nick poked his head out of his room and was like, "Quick, get in here."

Nick's room was a total nerd cave, even though he clearly thought it was the best thing ever. His posters were things like *Game of Thrones* and *Doctor Who*, and his desk was set up with a video game console and this fancy cinema display. He didn't talk about it much, but I knew his dad was one of those rich tech guys. A lot of kids at Latham were like that, and a lot were on assistance, like Charlie.

I'd brought some contraband snacks with me, and I dumped them on the bed while Nick set up the movie. Lane stared at the bags of sour candy and peanut butter cups like he'd never expected to see junk food again.

"Sadie always has contraband," Charlie explained, opening the bag of peanut butter cups. "It's why we put up with her."

"Oh, whatever." I pretended to be mad. "Nick does, too. He just went to the extra-special preschool where they learned math instead of how to share."

Nick sighed, opened a desk drawer, and tossed a water bottle into the pile.

"Vodka," he said. "What was that about not sharing again?"

"Where did you get this stuff?" Lane asked, which I guess I'd been expecting. There was only so long you could be at Latham without noticing the contraband bags of chips, or the water bottles of booze at weekend movie nights, without asking someone where it came from.

"I'm a coyote," I said. "I help illegal goods cross the border into Latham."

He laughed, thinking it was a joke, and then realized I wasn't kidding.

"What else can you get?" he asked.

"Name it," I said.

"Wait," Lane said. "You do this for real?"

"Nick and I do. We're the kingpins of the black market."

We'd inherited the responsibility about nine months ago, from this kid Phillip, who'd gone home. Which was about the time Nick had inherited an interest in dating me, although I'd quickly let him know that was never going to happen.

"That mixed metaphor was painful," Nick said, wincing.

"How painful? On a scale of one to ten," I prompted.

"Screw you," Nick said, not meaning it. "And seven."

And then we watched *Spirited Away*, which I hadn't seen for ages. It was about a girl who got trapped in the spirit world and worked at a witch's bath house to rescue her parents and get home. I know that sounds like some kid movie, but trust me, it's amazing. I'd forgotten how much I loved it.

At one point, I glanced over at Lane, who was staring at the screen, enthralled. His face was lit up in the glow of the monitor, all sharp angles, and I couldn't help but imagine reaching out and tracing my finger over the curve of his jawline.

I don't know why I did it, but I imagined us at a real movie theater, splitting an overpriced popcorn, our fingers getting tangled as we scooped the last kernels from the bottom. And it was a real date, the kind where he picked me up in his car and we ran into people we knew from school. Except his town was hours away from mine, and I didn't know if he had a car, and we didn't go to the same school, and those weren't even the reasons it wouldn't work. It was just a fantasy. Just a scene in my head of a date I'd never have with a boy who hadn't asked me.

Lane looked over at me and smiled then, and we stared at each other in the dark, across Charlie, who was snoring softly. I wasn't mad anymore about his being friends with Nick. I wasn't mad about any of that. I was angry that Marina was wrong about us being Lizzie and Mr. Darcy, even in some made-up version with wombats and dirigibles. Because if the past year had made me certain of one thing, it was that love stories at Latham all ended the same way: with someone left behind.

CHAPTER ELEVEN
LANE

THERE WAS SOMETHING about having a group of friends at Latham that transformed it. When I thought back to that first day, watching from my window as the four of them slunk back from the woods, they'd all seemed so mysterious and unapproachable.

But as I became a regular fixture at their dining table, they came more sharply into focus. And so did life at Latham House. It was like I'd misread the directions and had been trying to solve an unsolvable equation, when all I had to do was simplify.

Nick began knocking on my door before breakfast, and we'd wake up Charlie, who was usually still in bed and was apparently allergic to early mornings. We'd spend first rest period playing video games in Nick's room, and I'd walk the lake path in Wellness with Sadie and Marina. Then I'd grab a shower and take a nap until dinner. We kept up the post-dinner movie marathon, sneaking the girls into our dorm each night. Marina brought over her selection of Miyazaki movies, which I couldn't believe I'd missed. I wasn't an anime fan, so I'd always figured they weren't my thing, but they completely were.

I remembered how, at summer camp, the first few days had always felt disorienting, and then one morning I'd wake up and everything would just click. That Friday, everything just clicked. I worked on my Dickens packet in English and tried to stay awake during this documentary about the Dark Ages. And then, as we were leaving lunch, Nick complained that his math teacher had brought a travel thermos again and spilled it, making the entire classroom smell like coffee.

"It was like a torture chamber," he complained. "And then, on top of it, we had to do *math*."

"There's no reason we can't have caffeine," Sadie informed us. "I looked it up."

"Except that Latham doesn't want us bouncing off the walls," said Nick.

"Which you do anyway," Marina said, and we all snickered.

"Oh, whatever," Nick grumbled.

I asked why they didn't just smuggle in coffee, and Sadie stared at me like I'd suggested she bring in mung beans.

"Instant coffee?" She wrinkled her nose. "Gross."

"See, that's a coffee drinker's problem," Marina said.

"Meanwhile, I'm perfectly fine with tea bags."

"I love that there's such a rivalry," said Charlie. "It's like, leaf water versus bean water, you know?"

"*Bean water*?" Sadie echoed. "You better take that back."

"Watch out, espresso shots are being fired in the drink fandom," said Nick.

"Can we not talk about coffee, though?" I asked. "Because it's all I can think about. That, and how we don't have any."

Coffee was one of the main things I missed from my old life. Every time Finnegan brought a travel thermos, I practically salivated.

"Actually . . ." Sadie nodded toward the woods, grinning mischievously.

Everyone besides me seemed to know what she meant.

"Oh no," Marina said. "Not again."

"Where's your sense of adventure?" Sadie asked.

"I'll find my sense of adventure when you find your sense of direction," Marina retorted.

"It was one *small* miscalculation," Sadie said. "Besides, I have a compass now."

We were stopped on the lawn outside the cottages, and Charlie started to walk away.

"Wait," Sadie called. "Where are you going?"

"To take a nap," he said, and then snorted. "Where do you think? To get my wallet."

"Does someone want to fill me in?" I asked after Charlie disappeared inside.

"We're going to Hogsmeade," Sadie said. "To get butterbeer."

I was really, really confused.

"There's a Starbucks down in Whitley," Nick explained.

And then it dawned on me what they meant. They were talking about sneaking to *town*.

"No way," I said, crossing my arms.

"Why not?" Sadie asked innocently.

"There are about a hundred reasons why not. Number one, we're *quarantined*. Number two, I'm pretty sure someone will notice. Number three, it's the middle of the aftern—"

"Are you seriously going to stand there and list them all?" Marina asked.

I glared.

"What about these?" I lifted my wrist with the med sensor.

"No problem," Sadie assured me. "They only show your location if the sensor goes off, so the nurses can find you. Dr. Barons doesn't sit there Geotracking us around Latham House."

I stared at it doubtfully.

"I promise it'll be completely fine," Sadie said. "Don't you trust me?"

I wanted to. I really did. But more than that, I wanted to keep hanging out with them. And I had the impression that if I didn't go, their ranks would close, and I'd find myself adrift again on the colorless sea of Latham, with no one to blame but myself.

So I relented, and then Charlie came down from the dorm and we headed off into the woods.

IN THE ALMOST two weeks that I'd spent at Latham, I'd never wondered if there was a way out, or if that way out led anywhere interesting. I figured the woods were followed by more woods, and maybe a highway with a roadside stand where you could buy farm-fresh artichokes, because I'd seen tons of those on the drive up. I'd never once thought that after a mile, the woods would let out into a small town with an old stucco mission and a brightly colored main street. But that's exactly what they did.

I still didn't know how I'd let Sadie convince me to do this. We weren't even supposed to be in the woods during rest period, never mind hiking a mile through them into town. And we absolutely weren't supposed to leave Latham for any reason, particularly something as pointless as getting coffee.

About halfway there, Charlie was looking paler than usual and was having trouble catching his breath, so we stopped to rest. He leaned against a tree, closing his eyes for a moment while we all stared at each other uneasily.

"Maybe we should go back," Marina said.

Charlie opened his eyes and glared.

"I'm fine," he insisted. "Just need a minute."

After a couple of minutes, he joked that he'd photosynthesized some more energy, and we all continued on.

This ball of nerves lodged itself firmly in my stomach the moment Whitley came into view. The town looked like the places my family used to visit when I was little, driving up and down the coast with a guidebook directing us to quaint historic sites, while my father quizzed me on the history.

"You've done this before, right?" I asked.

"Lots of times," Sadie assured me. "It's no big deal. Just try not to cough in front of anyone and it'll be fine."

She dug a handful of cough drops out of her pocket and passed them around. As we unwrapped them, my heart started racing. We were really doing this—going somewhere that wasn't Latham. And as much as I'd protested the trip, I had to admit that I was excited at the prospect.

"In case anyone gets nosy, we're college students," Nick said. "And we're making a pit stop on the drive up to Berkeley. Now push down your sleeves to hide your med sensor."

I dutifully pushed down my sleeves and crunched the rest of my cough drop, and we followed the root-ravaged hiking trail into town.

WHITLEY WAS ONE of those quaint storybook places, nothing like the sprawling suburbia where I was from. I was used to strip malls, not main streets. Even so, being in this tiny out-of-the-way place felt like walking into a huge city after spending time away from civilization.

It was warm out, with just a faint bite of breeze. Early October. The shops had started putting Halloween displays in their windows, and some of the doorsteps already had pumpkins. The lampposts were covered with flyers advertising a Fall Fest in a couple of weeks, which featured face painting and a hayride. There were more flyers, for a corn maze and a haunted house.

"I heard they used to turn Latham into a haunted house," Marina said, reading the flyer. "Back when it was a boarded-up prep school."

"I went to it once," Charlie said. We all turned to stare at him. "When I was six. My cousins brought me, and I got so scared I started crying. My aunt had to wait outside with me."

"That's adorable," Nick said. "You were afraid of the big bad plastic masks."

"I was six!" Charlie insisted. "And that's not why I was afraid. One of my cousins told me that if I was really bad, I'd have to stay there, with all the monsters, forever."

"You're making that up," Sadie accused, but Charlie just shrugged.

And then he started coughing. He muffled it in his sleeve, and thankfully there wasn't anyone walking nearby, but we all still glanced around nervously. I was convinced we'd be caught, that someone would spot us and know exactly what we were and where we'd come from. But that didn't happen. Charlie caught his breath and mumbled an apology, and we continued on.

We passed a pet shop, a little bookstore, and some kind of organic juice place with a sign in its window urging customers to like it on Facebook. I'd spent so long brooding over the fact that I was cut off from everything, and trying to get back to the real world, but now that I had, it felt strange and misshapen. Or maybe that was me. I felt so self-conscious, like I wasn't supposed to be here, and like everyone could tell.

When we reached the Starbucks, Charlie was flushed and sweating. I was pretty sure we shouldn't bring him into a coffee shop, and Marina had the same idea.

"Hey, Charlie, want to check out the thrift store with me?" she asked.

"Sure," he said, brightening.

"Back here in twenty?" Sadie called.

"If we're running late, we'll text you," Marina deadpanned, and for a moment, I believed her.

"Come on, troops," Sadie said, holding open the door of the Starbucks.

Nick and I followed her inside. I'd expected the place to be mostly empty, but a surprising number of people were sitting at the tables with their laptops out. I was wearing my Stanford hoodie and jeans, and even though I was sure we stuck out, I guess we looked pretty normal. Just three clean-cut kids grabbing coffee. No one even glanced up at us.

"So, butterbeer lattes?" Sadie asked.

"I don't think that's on the menu," I said.

"Ah, but it's on the *secret menu*," Nick said, clapping a hand on my shoulder. He went on to explain that Starbucks had a treasure trove of unlisted options, one of which was the butterbeer latte.

"If it's coffee, I'll take it," I said, following Sadie to the register.

This bored-looking blond dude with adult braces was reading something on his phone, and he didn't notice us at first. Sadie leaned across the counter a little bit, examining a packet of cookies.

"Hey," she said.

The cashier glanced up, and I swear his eyes bugged out at the sight of her tight black V-neck sweater. I didn't blame him; I'd been trying not to get caught staring at it all day.

"Um, what can I get for you?" he asked, flustered.

"Five venti butterbeer lattes." She smiled sweetly, as though daring him to say they didn't make those.

The cashier laughed.

"Hey, Mike," he called to the barista. "Can you do butterbeer lattes?"

The barista, this lumberjack-looking hipster dude, shrugged and said sure.

"No one ever orders those," the cashier said, punching it in. "That's awesome."

I held out some money, and he reached out to take it, then stopped, staring at my wrist.

I glanced down to see what he was looking at, and tried not to panic. I'd pushed up the sleeves of my sweatshirt without thinking, and my med sensor was right there.

My stomach twisted, and I winced, waiting for everything to come crashing down.

"Is that one of those fitness bands?" he asked.

I'd never been so relieved in my life.

"Yeah, it is," I said, tugging down my sleeve.

"I've been thinking about getting one," he said, taking the money and counting out my change.

"They're awesome, you should," I said, and then I decamped to the island of napkins and straws, my heart still hammering.

Nick came over and started nervously fidgeting with the sugar packets.

"I *told* you to pull your sleeves down," he said. "Thank God for yuppies and their stupid fitness tech."

I glanced over at the little coffee station, where Sadie was chatting with the barista. He said something sharply and slid the drink carriers across the counter with more force than was necessary.

"Grab some drink sleeves," Sadie said, coming over.

"What was that about?" Nick asked.

"Nothing," Sadie said. "Let's go outside before Michael throws a fit."

"You know the barista?" I asked.

"Long story."

She didn't elaborate, and we brought the drinks outside the store and waited for Charlie and Marina.

"Well?" Sadie asked, after I took my first sip.

I was having a religious experience. Caramel and cream and sugar and caffeine and I didn't know what else, but I didn't care.

"The look on your face," she said. "I bet you're glad we came now."

"Of course I'm glad," I said. "I just had to protest, for the principle of the thing."

"Uh-huh, sure." Sadie smiled into her straw.

Charlie and Marina weren't back yet, and after the second time Sadie checked the time display on her med sensor and sighed, I asked if she thought they'd wanted some time alone.

"Charlie *always* wants time alone," Nick said. "It's why he always skips Wellness."

"I meant, um, with Marina," I said.

Sadie giggled.

"They're just friends," she said. "I mean, Charlie's adorable, but so are the *boys* he likes."

"Boys?"

"I know," Sadie said with a wry smile. "The entire female population of Latham was upset over that one."

I hadn't pictured Charlie as being gay, but now that Sadie had said it, I could see it easily. Suddenly, the One Direction poster above his bed made a lot more sense.

Marina and Charlie came back from the thrift store then, both of them carrying bags. Charlie looked much better, which was a relief.

"What did you get?" Sadie asked, peering excitedly into Marina's bag. "Oh my God, that dress is amazing. We have to use it in a photo shoot."

"Four dollars!" Marina said. "And it has a matching belt."

"I found the theme song to *Cops* on vinyl," Charlie said proudly.

I thought he was kidding, but then he held it up, and sure enough.

We walked back toward the woods, sipping our sugary coffee concoctions, and I was suddenly glad that I'd come, and that they'd invited me. Back home, no one would have thought to include me in something like this, and I probably would have made an excuse if they had, not because I didn't want to, but because I thought I shouldn't.

It occurred to me then how much I'd missed. I'd always told myself that there was plenty of time to goof around later, after I'd gotten into Stanford. But if the past month had taught me anything, it was that the life you plan isn't the life that happens to you. And I was beginning to realize that there was only so long where a trip to Starbucks could be illicit, where there was a campus to sneak away from, and rules to break.

I glanced over my shoulder toward the town one last time, wondering when I had gone from feeling out of sync with Latham to belonging there, because I was relieved to be heading back. Sadie consulted her little compass, and we set off toward Latham. She walked up front, navigating, and I decided to join her. The woods were beautiful that afternoon, the leaves just starting to turn. There were shades of orange and gold and pale yellow, colors I'd seen in movies and photographs but wasn't used to in real life. Some of the leaves had already fallen, and they crunched under our feet.

For a while, Sadie and I didn't say anything, just walked through the woods together, crushing leaves with our sneakers. I kept glancing over at her, in her tight black sweater and jeans, with wisps of hair loose from her ponytail. She was so short that I could see down the front of her sweater, to the little bridge where her pink bra stretched across her cleavage. I swallowed, forcing myself to look away and think about something else, since my heart was already racing from the caffeine.

The woods reminded me so much of camp, of being thirteen and self-conscious about everything. Sadie looked so different than she had back then. But I'd grown eleven inches and could no longer stick a raisin in the gap between my front teeth, so I guessed she could say the same thing.

And then she looked over at me and asked what I was thinking about.

"The last time we were in the woods," I said.

"You mean thirty minutes ago?"

"No, at summer camp. I used to play badminton with Scott . . . Canadian Scott, not creepy Scott who lit worms on fire."

"I was hoping it was the worms one," she joked, and I shot her a look.

"Anyway, he kept hitting the shuttlecock into the woods. And I kept having to go get it. Which sucked. And then one day, when I was looking for the thing, I saw you in the woods taking pictures."

What I didn't add was that I'd been fascinated, and that occasionally I'd missed on purpose so I could chase the shuttlecock into the woods and see if she was there.

"I still take pictures in the woods," she said.

"Can I see them?"

"Lane!" She pretended to be shocked. "You can't just go asking a girl if she'll show you her pictures!"

"Oh, sorry, what was I thinking?" I teased.

"I totally knew you were there, at summer camp," Sadie said. "You weren't very subtle about it. You were like—"

She did an impression of me standing and gawking, and I felt my face heat up.

"Why didn't you say anything if you knew I was there?"

"Why didn't *you*?" she challenged.

I shrugged, not wanting to confess that I'd been ridiculously intimidated by girls when I was thirteen. They'd pranced around torturing me, these magical creatures with tangled hair and wet bikinis and long, tanned legs. I couldn't find shorts that were baggy enough. And it wasn't like the girls were prancing toward me. I'd been short. With braces.

The woods started to thin out, and when I had the impression we were almost back in what passed for civilization, Sadie unzipped her backpack and took out a pen.

"What's your extension?" she asked, and I stared at her blankly. "Your room phone?"

"Um, 8803?"

"Write it down for me?" She gave me the pen and held out her hand.

I took her hand in mine, and as gently as I could, I inked my number across the back of it. She smiled up at me, and then she grabbed my hand and wrote down her extension. I stared at the four neat numbers nestled in my palm, feeling like Sadie had given me more than just her phone number.

And suddenly, we were back behind the cottages, in the same spot where I'd seen them sneaking out of the woods on my first day. Except this time I wasn't watching from my room. I was there, a part of it. A part of everything, I guessed.

The grounds looked the same as always. Peaceful and picturesque and frozen in time. It was a place where there wasn't a point to technology, and a place that ironically existed because we didn't have enough of it to cure us.

It looked like no one had noticed our absence at all. We'd really done it. We'd gotten away with a trip into town. For Starbucks.

"Lane?" Sadie said tentatively.

She smiled at me and tucked the loose strands of hair behind her ears.

"Yeah?"

"We're all going to skip Wellness today."

"Oh." I'd thought she was going to say something else. "How do you skip Wellness?"

"It's easy. You just don't go."

"I think I can manage that," I said.

And then I went up to my room and climbed into bed with a P. G. Wodehouse novel I'd gotten from the library. I tried to concentrate on the book, but I kept flipping it closed to read Sadie's number on my palm. The thrill of Sadie holding my hand in hers while she wrote down her extension hadn't yet faded. So I stared at my palm, grinning, while the theme song to *Cops* drifted faintly through an open window.

It was Friday afternoon, and I was supposed to be walking laps in a pair of gym shorts and sneakers, but I wasn't. And I didn't care. Maybe it was just the caffeine coursing through me, but I felt better than I had in weeks, as though instead of walking those laps, I could have run them.

CHAPTER TWELVE
SADIE

THE FIRST TIME Lane called me, it was Saturday night and almost lights-out. I'd been in the boys' dorm earlier, where we'd watched *The Princess Bride* after Nick had mutinied and insisted on something that wasn't (a) animated, or (b) in Japanese, with subtitles.

I'd just gotten out of the shower and was changing into my pajamas when the phone rang, startling me. I scrambled for it, the cord getting tangled in my T-shirt.

"Hello?" I said, expecting it to be my mom, or maybe my sister.

"Um, hi." It was a boy's voice, deep and unsure, and I thought it had to be a wrong number. Genevieve's dad had called me once, by accident, because her extension was only one number off from mine.

I waited silently to see what this boy wanted, and then he was like, "Sadie?"

"Lane?"

"Yeah, sorry. I forgot these phones don't have caller ID."

I'd never had a call from a boy before. I mean, I had, in eighth grade when Vijay Chandra and I had to do this presentation on the water cycle, and he'd called me over the weekend to practice. I'd gotten the occasional text or DM, but never a call. And never late at night, although it was sad that 8:55 felt late.

"Welcome to the Dark Ages," I told him, "where a ringing phone is always a mystery."

I sat down on the edge of my bed and stared out the window. The view was nothing but woods, which I'd always liked, but for the first time I wished my room was on Marina's side of the hall, where you could see into Lane's dorm.

"So," I prompted.

"So," he said. "I just got off the phone with my parents, and I sort of need a normal conversation right now. I hope that's okay."

I knew what he meant. There was something dreadful about the way my mom always asked how I was doing like it wasn't just some pleasantry and she was actually afraid of the answer.

"No problem," I said. "One normal conversation coming right up. I'll start. Um . . . did you see the new movie that just came out?"

There was a confused moment of silence, and then I could almost hear Lane grinning through the phone.

"Yeah, last night at the IMAX," he said. "I should have

saved my money, it was so overrated. And how about the YouTube video of that animal doing the thing humans do?"

"You're *just* seeing that? Like, fifty people posted it on Facebook yesterday," I said. "Hold on, I'm getting a text."

"It's fine, I should probably open this Snapchat."

We were both laughing.

"There," I said. "A normal conversation."

"It was great. Thank you."

Lane chuckled, then coughed into his sleeve or something, like he thought that would muffle it.

The hall nurse was going to come by soon, so I picked up the receiver and hid it behind my pillow. Then I climbed into bed, the phone cradled against my shoulder.

"It's almost lights-out," I said.

"Yeah, sorry about that. Should we—"

"No, I want to keep talking," I said. "Put the phone in your bed. We'll sneak it."

"Hold on," he said, and there was a lot of banging on his end, and some muttering.

I climbed under the covers and tried to look innocent. I could hear the nurse in the hallway, making her way toward my room.

"Okay, done," Lane said proudly.

"Wow, gold star."

Nurse Blanca knocked on my door then and barged in the way she always did. I thrust the phone under my duvet

- 156 -

and tried to look ready for bed while she pulled up my vitals on her tablet.

"Your heart rate's a little high tonight, honey," she said.

Damn it, Lane. I didn't want the nurse to give me anything, so I tried to think of an excuse.

"There was this huge spider. It was terrifying. But I killed it with my shower shoe," I said, pointing toward the wardrobe with such conviction that for a moment I believed it myself.

"Good for you, honey," she said. "Sweet dreams."

And then she switched off the light.

I waited until I heard her go into Natalie's room, just to make sure.

"Okay," I whispered. "I'm back."

"What was that about a spider?" Lane asked.

"Um," I said.

"Oh, wait, the nurse—" He must have put his palm over the speaker, because I couldn't hear anything for a minute, and then he came back on.

"I almost hung up on you twice by accident," he said. "These phones are ridiculous."

"Yeah, but they'll probably come back into style one day," I said. "We're just ahead of the curve."

"Ugh, I bet you're right. Twenty years from now, all the hipsters will have landlines. Or those other ones, from the black-and-white movies, with the circular dials?"

"And all the girls will wear vintage Ugg boots and complain how they were born in the wrong era," I said, snuggling under the covers.

It was cold out, but the night air felt good. Fresh. Like maybe each breath was helping to fix the mess inside my body. I could hear the leaves rustling, and the insects chattering, and I wondered if any of them were having conversations as wonderful as the one I was having, in the dark, over the phone, with this beautifully strange boy.

"No one thinks they were born into the right era," Lane said. "It's like that movie *Midnight in Paris.*"

"You're a fan of Woody Allen movies?" I asked, pleasantly surprised.

And we spent the next hour whispering into the phones about movies, and books, and music until I could barely keep my eyes open.

I could hear Lane yawning through the receiver.

"Sorry," he mumbled. "Long hike."

"I'm falling asleep, too," I said. "We should probably . . ."

"Wait. Before you go, give me a word, and I'll see if I can dream about it," he said.

I wanted to say, me. Dream about me. Dream about us in a coffee shop, on a real date, and I'm wearing a cute dress, and you're in one of those button-down shirts with the sleeves rolled, and we've both brought books to read, but we can't stop smiling at each other over our cappuccinos, and instead of driving me home afterward, we go to the park and play on the swing set like kids.

"Coffee." It was the first thing that popped into my head.

"That shouldn't be a problem, seeing as how I'm obviously in love with coffee."

"Well, coffee *is* pretty hot," I said.

"That was terrible," Lane said. "Awful. I'm hanging up."

"Fine."

But he didn't.

"And I want you to dream about . . . hmmm." He stopped to think for a moment. "Puppies?"

"Why *puppies*?" I asked.

"I don't know!" he said defensively. "I thought girls liked puppies. I guess, just, dream about something awesome?"

"It's a deal," I promised.

Lane called me every night after that.

MARINA LOOKED TERRIBLE at breakfast on Wednesday morning. She was the last of us to arrive at the table, and she didn't say anything as she slid into her seat. She just glared into her oatmeal like it was the source of all problems in the universe, and she'd already taken a bite before anyone had told her.

"What's going on?" I asked, hoping it wasn't what I thought. Marina usually went to see Dr. Barons on Tuesday afternoons, but she'd seemed fine at dinner.

"Yeah, what's up with the doom and gloom?" Nick asked through a mouthful of pancakes.

I kicked him under the table, and he kicked back at me, making a face. I swear, sometimes Nick had no tact. Particularly if it was, well, bad news of the Latham kind.

"Amit called me last night," Marina mumbled, which was just about the last thing I was expecting her to say.

"Wait, what?" I said, scandalized. "And you picked up?"

"Oh, sorry, I forgot to check my caller ID." Marina rolled her eyes over the ancientness of our room phones.

"Who's Amit?" Lane asked, confused.

"My ex-boyfriend," Marina explained. "He went home from Latham and decided to dump me via the silent treatment. Anyway. He called, finally. He kept saying he had no one else to talk to and he was really sorry to bother me."

"Please tell me you hung up on him," I said.

Marina sighed.

"No, because that would have been somewhat self-actualized of me. I asked him to tell me all about it."

"You didn't!" I moaned.

"He sounded horrible," Marina said. "Really depressed. I think he was crying, or having a mental breakdown or something."

"Over what, getting well enough to go home?" Nick asked, not very nicely.

Marina shook her head. And then she told us what Amit had said it was like for him after going home. How his parents babied him like he was an invalid, and wouldn't let him leave the house. How, when he'd finally gone back to school, everyone had been terrified that he'd relapse and infect them.

"He said they called him plague boy," Marina said. "And defaced his locker. When he sat down at a lunch table, everyone would leave. Apparently a lot of the parents at school got really upset that they let him back in, and then last night some guys jumped him and threatened that he better not come back to school or else."

"Or else?" Nick said skeptically.

"That's what he said." Marina shrugged. "Maybe it's just his school, or whatever, maybe a lot of kids were getting sick there."

I listened to all of this in shock. Nick looked as horrified as I felt, and Lane was shaking his head like he couldn't believe things like this happened. But I believed it easily. I knew all too well how cruel kids could be, how relentlessly they could taunt you and make you feel like no one would ever be your friend again.

"Maybe," Charlie said. "It can't really be that bad, can it? Getting better, I mean?"

"It wasn't like that at all where I'm from," Lane said. "I never knew anyone who got sick."

"Yeah, but all it takes is one person who wants to stir up trouble, and suddenly everyone's panicked," Nick said. "Look at history if you don't believe me."

"*Game of Thrones* isn't real," I told him, and Marina snorted.

"The weird part was that Amit said he wished he'd never left Latham," Marina went on. "He kept saying that he didn't have any friends out there, that he was all alone. At least here he felt like he belonged. At least here he had a life."

"Some life," Nick deadpanned.

"Girlfriend, friends, your own room, no homework, and no chores?" Marina laughed. "Yeah, I'd say that's a pretty good life."

"Well, not all of us have that," Nick said, with a look in my direction that was almost accusative.

CHAPTER THIRTEEN

LANE

I FELL ASLEEP dreaming of Sadie every night that week.

Sometimes we were in the woods, and she was taking photos of a monster I couldn't see. "No one will believe this," she'd say, getting closer and closer while I shouted for her to run away with me to safety, even though she promised the monster wouldn't hurt us.

And sometimes we were lying in a field surrounded by flowers, and she was holding my hand, which was covered with numbers. "Come on, Lane, let's jump," she'd beg, and suddenly we were at the edge of a steep cliff. I'd watch in horror as Sadie jumped off the cliff, giggling. But she'd float gently to the bottom, as though held aloft by an invisible parachute. And then I'd jump, trying to follow, and there wouldn't be a parachute after all.

Each time, I woke up drenched in sweat, my body curled around the telephone. And each time, I looked around my dorm room with relief, convinced I was waking from a nightmare.

ON THURSDAY AFTERNOON, we were all in the library, using the router trick to get internet. Marina was at the computer, while Nick and Charlie were at the back tables.

Sadie and I had gone off together into the stacks and were sitting on the floor with our backs against the encyclopedias. Her hair was wet from the shower and knotted up in a bun. It smelled amazing, like mint and oranges and old books, although I guessed the last part was the library.

We both had our laptops out, the same MacBook everyone used. Hers was battered and dinged, like it had survived a war. I kept mine in a shell, with a silicone keyboard cover so it wouldn't get scratched. When I'd taken it out, Sadie had laughed at me and asked why my computer was wearing a condom. Just hearing her use the word "condom" had sent my brain spiraling down all sorts of dirty alleyways, and I was having a hard time concentrating.

She was so close to me that occasionally, when she typed, her elbow brushed mine. I wanted to lean over and kiss her. I'd wanted to do that for a few days now, or maybe even longer, but I didn't want to ruin things, and I didn't know how to begin.

I glanced over at her screen, in case she'd found something interesting, but she was just scrolling through pictures of random pretty people posing in random pretty places with balloons and cupcakes and stuff. I was on the Stanford website, clicking around.

Dr. Barons said my vitals looked better and that my new X-ray had shown some improvement, so it turned out that not doing homework and participating in naptime and getting nine hours of sleep a night was actually a solid game plan. But he still didn't have an answer on when, or if, I'd be able to go home. All he'd say was "as soon as you're better," with that bullshitty grin, like he had no idea what I was so eager to get back to, and my AP assignments weren't still locked away in some secret drawer in his office.

Stanford listed their admissions deadlines on the website. Early action was almost up, and I knew I'd miss that, but regular decision wasn't due until January. I'd wanted to see if it was possible, and it looked like it might be. If I got out of Latham within three months, my application would just make it. Getting in, with my name and social security number registered in the national database of active TB cases, was a completely different story. I was pretty sure Stanford wouldn't want to risk assigning me a roommate even if Dr. Barons certified that my TB was inactive, because there was always the chance that I'd relapse. I'd tried to ask Dr. Barons what most kids did about college once they left Latham, but he'd given me a stern look and told me to "focus on the now," which made me want to strangle him with his stethoscope.

I *was* focusing on the now. But that didn't mean I

couldn't still wonder about what came after.

Sadie leaned over and asked what I was looking at, and I tilted the screen so she could see a picture of the campus.

"That's pretty," she said.

"Yeah," I said wistfully, and then I clicked over to Facebook to make myself stop obsessing, which in retrospect might not have been the best idea.

The barrage of "get well soon" messages had stopped. Zero notifications. My account felt dead and forgotten, and I wondered how I'd missed the funeral. My high school's homecoming dance had taken place over the weekend, and my feed was filled with pictures of it. Group photos in limos, everyone in suits and dresses, girls pointing their toes together to show off their brightly colored Converses.

I'd always skipped homecoming. It took place the weekend before the first big exams, and even if it hadn't, I wouldn't have had the nerve to ask anyone. Not when the first question they'd have would be whether my dad was one of the chaperones. I wouldn't have known if they were turning me down, or turning down the idea of going with Mr. Rosen's kid. It had seemed like a miracle when Hannah had been interested in me, Hannah who had transferred to our school in tenth grade, and had missed the memo that my dad sucked. Hannah who said yes to being my date that year, which was my last chance to participate in something along with everyone else.

But there weren't any more homecoming dances. I'd

missed all of them. I hadn't thought I'd care, but now that the opportunity was gone, I sort of did. Everyone looked so happy in the pictures, and if I could have done it over last year, I would have just asked someone to go with me. I scrolled a little farther, through pictures of everyone lined up in each other's driveways and in the backseats of limos, and then I stopped cold.

It was a photo of Hannah and this guy Parker. Her hair was in fancy curls, and Parker was wearing sunglasses with his suit, even though it was clearly dark out. They were at the dance, with a butcher-paper banner and bleachers in the background.

But that wasn't what I was staring at. It was the Facebook announcement above the picture: Hannah Chung is in a relationship with Parker Nguyen. It had so many likes. So many comments from kids I'd sat with at lunch or competed with in Model UN, proclaiming, "Finally!" and "You guys are everything!"

If they were everything, I guessed that made me nothing.

I closed my eyes and took a deep breath, trying not to let it get to me. What did I care if Hannah was dating Parker? I knew him a little from Model UN, and he was a bit douchey, but mostly okay. He always wore a black button-up shirt with a red tie to our conferences, because red was a power color. He was forever saying crap like that, about how using pen on a test makes you seem more sure of yourself, and traveling to colleges to interview on their campuses looked more serious than taking a local interview.

"Hey," Sadie said. "What's up? You look like you've just seen a ghost."

More like I've just become one, I thought. We were all ghosts at Latham House, because we were all haunted by lives that were no longer ours. Only I didn't say that. I just shrugged and tilted the screen so she could see the smiling photograph of the happy, perfect couple in the middle of their happy, perfect senior year.

"Wait," she said, realizing. "Is that *Hannah* Hannah? Your ex?"

"The very same."

I tried to tell myself that it didn't matter. That high school had never mattered to me like that, that Hannah didn't matter, that none of it was a part of me anymore. It was October, and I was at Latham, and the rest of my life didn't have anything to do with my former classmates' Facebook accounts.

I had more important things to worry about. Things you weren't supposed to worry about at seventeen, like blood tests, and X-rays, and my parents' health insurance premiums, and the DNR forms we'd signed in Dr. Barons's office before I was given my med sensor and removed from everything that remotely resembled my past life. And now it was too late to do anything more than march grimly forward and hope.

"It's fine," I said, mostly to convince myself. "Hannah

can do what she wants. It's just that I didn't expect to be so easily deleted from my old life."

I sighed, and Sadie put her hand on my shoulder.

"It wasn't even that good of a life," I went on. "I did nothing but study, and even when I had a girlfriend, we just went to Barnes and Noble to do our homework and hung out at Model UN conferences. I knew everyone else was going to these parties and dances and beach trips or whatever, but I thought it was stupid, because the moment we all got to college, high school would be erased. Except now it's me. I'm the one erased. Or I guess I'm not even that, because the thing about being erased is that first you have to leave a mark."

I stared miserably at the screen, and Sadie scooted up even closer and leaned her head on my shoulder.

"You're not erased," she said. "Erased means you disappear. It's more like you've just been . . . forcibly evicted from your old life. You're still leaving your mark, you're just doing it somewhere else."

"Forcibly evicted," I echoed, testing it out.

"Exactly," Sadie said. "And now you're here, in the library, with me. That part's pretty nice."

It really was, and I tried to summon the nerve to tell her that.

While I was still summoning, Charlie wandered over to see what we were up to.

"Internet just cut out," he said. "What's with the cuddling?"

"We're allowed to cuddle," Sadie retorted.

"Yeah, but why do you look so unhappy about it?" he asked.

"Lane's depressed about Facebook," Sadie said.

"About my ex-girlfriend," I clarified. "Not, like, the website in general."

Charlie shook his head.

"Delete," he said. "I keep telling you."

But I couldn't. Even though I wasn't sure what the point was anymore. No one kept in touch, they just kept up. And then, when they couldn't keep up anymore, they forgot.

I wished I could take all of it back. The afternoons I'd sat home wondering what everyone was doing but not having the courage to ask. The countless nights I'd fallen asleep at my desk. The subdivision pool I'd walked past for years without ever stopping for a swim. The way I'd always driven straight home after taking classes at the community college, because it had never occurred to me to just drive around for a while and see where the night took me.

Maybe Sadie had it right, scrolling through fantasies of impossibly pretty people having picnics beneath the Eiffel Tower, instead of looking at a chronicle of everyone she used to know having fun without her. Or maybe I was just upset that my life back home had been so small and so pathetic. I wished I could take all of it back.

I realized then that I hadn't had a life, I'd just had a life plan. And it wasn't that I didn't still want all those things—Stanford, summer internships, graduate school—I just wasn't sure I'd gone about achieving them the right way. If everyone at college shut themselves in their rooms and studied every night, what would any of us really get out of being there? It was like Latham: sometimes the point wasn't being the best, because it didn't mean you had the best life, or the best friends, or the best time.

I didn't want to spend the next six years falling asleep at my desk with headphones on to block out the noise of everyone else having fun. I didn't want to rush through all the moments that I wouldn't know I wanted until they were gone. I could see my future narrowing, with options like football games and school dances being squeezed out, until trying not to die had become my main extracurricular activity. And if the road did stop narrowing, it would never be as wide as it had once been. I wasn't going to get my life back, and even if I could, I wasn't sure I wanted to. I didn't know what I wanted anymore, except to fall asleep every night to the sound of Sadie's voice over the phone, at Latham house, and after we'd both gone home.

"I HAVE AN idea," Sadie announced, putting down her sandwich. It was lunch on Friday, and we were all eating grilled cheese sandwiches, except for Nick, who had sawed his into strips and was arranging them into shapes on his plate.

"Someone already invented sarcasm, sorry," Nick said,

- 171 -

smirking into his sandwich strips.

Sadie rolled her eyes at him, which was something I'd noticed between the two of them more and more these days. How Nick seemed upset all the time, at the two of us in particular.

"Whatever," Sadie said. "I think we should go to movie night."

Charlie was doodling in his notebook, and his head snapped up at this.

"We never go to movie night," he said, sounding suspicious.

"I'm aware," Sadie said.

"*Why* would we go to movie night?" Marina asked.

"Aha!" Sadie said. "See, *that* is the type of question the rest of you should be asking. Why would we go to a lame, chaperoned pajama party in the gym with healthy snacks and just about everyone we can't stand?"

"You're really selling this, by the way," I said, stirring my soup. It was tomato, and awful, even with half a grilled cheese sandwich stuffed in. I had a suspicion that it was actually watered-down spaghetti sauce.

"It's such an excellent plan that it sells itself," Sadie promised. "Wait for it . . . instead of wearing our pajamas like everyone else, we'll dress up fancy. I'm talking ties, boys."

Sadie leaned back in her chair, a look of triumph on her face.

"Fancy?" Nick said, considering it. "Could there be booze?"

"If you have booze, there can be booze," Sadie said.

"So it's like Dapper Day," I said, and everyone stared at me blankly.

"Seriously?" I said. "Am I the only one from SoCal? Once a year, there's a day where people get dressed up and go to Disneyland. It's a thing."

Although I only knew it was a thing because I'd seen pictures of my classmates who had gone without me.

"That's awesome," Sadie said. "So, tonight is Dapper Day."

"It can't be day if it's night," Nick pointed out.

Sadie stuck out her tongue at him.

"A day is twenty-four hours, so yes it can," she said. "Now shut up. We're doing it."

AFTER LUNCH, CHARLIE insisted on holing up in his room, and when Nick and I tried to make him come out and do something, he said he was working on his music.

"He gets like that sometimes," Nick told me. "He'll snap out of it in a day or two and won't stop bothering us to listen to whatever new song he's written."

So Nick and I went up to his room and played this vampire-killing game that I, uh, sucked at. I suggested we play something else, but Nick insisted I just had to get the hang of it.

- 173 -

"Are you really getting dressed up for the thing tonight?" he asked as his avatar loaded a crossbow.

"If we're all doing it," I said with a shrug.

"You just go along with everything Sadie wants, don't you?" Nick challenged.

"What's that supposed to mean?"

On the screen, his guy killed three vamps at once. I had a theory there was some extra button he pressed to do that, but I didn't want to ask.

"You could have your pick of girls at Latham, you know," Nick said angrily.

"Whatever," I said, because he couldn't be serious. But apparently he was.

"Come on. Any one of those girls in our French class would let you butter their croissant."

"'Butter their croissant'?" I repeated.

"Whatever you want to call it," Nick said. "Any of them would be interested. Except you're only interested in Sadie. It's fucking unfair."

I was about to say, *Unfair to whom?* and then I got it. Maybe *Sadie* was just friends with Nick, but the feeling wasn't mutual.

"I thought you two were just friends," I said.

Nick killed another vampire before answering.

"For now. That's how it always starts out with me. It's a long con."

Except we both knew it wasn't.

"Do what you want," Nick said. "I'm just saying, there are other options, and probably more likely ones, if you want to get laid."

"But none of them are Sadie," I said.

"No, none of them are Sadie," Nick said.

And then one of the vampires got to me, and my avatar fell to the ground, twitching, as Nick smirked.

I DIDN'T KNOW why my mom had packed a tie and dress shirt, but she had, and thankfully, it wasn't too wrinkled. Despite his complaining, Nick put on a tweed vest with a watch chain, and I found him in the hall bathroom frantically combing pomade into his hair and muttering. Even Charlie got into it, wearing a blazer and a scarf and eyeliner, which Nick called "a sad tribute to David Bowie."

"You can David Blow Me," Charlie retorted. "At least I'm not cosplaying as Professor Slughorn."

I tried not to laugh. We were on the porch with pillows under our arms and blankets shoved into our backpacks, waiting for the girls.

"Who's cosplaying?" Marina asked, waving.

"Well, if it isn't Audrey Hepburn," Charlie said, and Marina struck a pose.

She was wearing this black dress and long white gloves, and she looked fantastic. But then I spotted Sadie, and I almost forgot how to breathe.

She had on this green dress that was like something from an old photo, and her hair was curled, and she was wearing heels. She looked like one of the models from those pictures she scrolled through on the internet, girls too perfect to be real.

Except she was real. And she was walking toward me. She stared at me, this wonderful smile rising to her lips, and I don't know that I'd ever seen someone so beautiful.

"Wow," I said.

And then she whacked me with the pillow she was holding. I went to hit her back with mine, but she squealed and ducked away, begging me not to ruin her hair. While we walked over to the gym, I kept jokingly raising my pillow, and she kept saying, "Don't do it!" And I kept teasing, "I'm gonna do it!" and I'm sure we annoyed the hell out of everyone.

I'd never been in the gym before. It was your average high school gymnasium. The bleachers had been pushed back, and everyone was in their pajamas and sweats, with blankets and pillows spread on the floor.

A bunch of people gave us odd looks about our clothes, but Sadie just laughed.

"They wish they thought of it," she whispered to me.

And I wished I was wearing a T-shirt instead of a tie, but I didn't say that.

We spread our things in the very back, making a patchwork out of our blankets and pillows. A nurse I didn't recognize came by and smiled at us.

"Don't you all look darling," she said, and then she gave us packs of organic fruit snacks and chocolate milk cartons, like we were five.

I stared down at the fruit snacks in dismay.

"No popcorn?" I asked.

"You wouldn't be able to hear the movie over all the coughing," Marina said. "Although check out the water bottles."

She was right. There were a lot of suspicious-looking Nalgene bottles being passed around.

"Speaking of," Nick said, unzipping his backpack and pulling out a bunch of apple juice boxes. It was one of the annoyingly healthy snacks that they sold in the commissary, and I'd never understood why anyone would want them.

The juice box Nick passed me had been tampered with; there was a piece of tape over the hole. I stared at him questioningly, and he rolled his eyes like it was obvious.

"I modified them," he said.

I poked my straw in and cautiously took a sip of what turned out to be vodka apple juice. Very strong vodka apple juice. I coughed, not expecting it.

"You'll get used to it," Charlie told me, laughing.

I took another sip, and now that I was prepared, it wasn't half-bad.

"Stop moving, you're ruining it." Sadie pouted at Nick.

She'd brought her camera, and she kept taking pictures

of us, then giggling and showing them to Marina. She told me to come over to where she was sitting, so I did.

"Smile," she said, putting her face next to mine. And then she held the camera at arm's length, snapping a selfie. She turned the camera around so I could see.

It was a perfect close-up of the two of us, Sadie smiling wide in her fancy dress, and me in a shirt and tie, my hair on point for once. In the background, you could just make out the wall of the old gym, with its faded pennant from when Whitley Prep had qualified for some basketball league. It was exactly like the photos everyone from my high school had put up. Exactly like Hannah's picture, come to think of it. We looked like we were having a great time, and we could have been anywhere. Even at a homecoming dance.

"This is great," I said.

"I thought you could put it on Facebook. To document your new life after being evicted from your old one."

"It's perfect," I said. And it was. The joke of putting it online was too good, of it looking like something it wasn't. Of us looking like something I wanted us to be. Or, I guess, a lot of things I wanted us to be.

"That's why I had everyone dress up," she said, except she grinned like she was kidding, so I couldn't quite tell. "The whole thing was just an excuse for a photo I wanted you to have."

A nurse I didn't recognize finished setting up the projector, and the lights dimmed and the movie started. *Ferris*

Bueller's Day Off. It was a good movie, and I'd seen it before, so I didn't have to pay attention too closely.

We all snuck sips from our juice boxes. I'd had a few beers at some of the Model UN overnights, but never hard alcohol. I hadn't exactly pictured my first time drinking vodka to be at a pajama party, out of a juice box, while wearing a shirt and tie, but I guessed it was a good story. I didn't have a lot of stories, but ever since I'd arrived at Latham, it seemed I was collecting them.

I wasn't used to drinking, and the vodka kept making me cough. If we'd been anywhere besides Latham, we probably would have been busted. But that night, whenever one of us would cough, we all grinned like it was a private joke.

I was lying on my stomach with my elbows in my pillow. On the screen, Ferris Bueller claimed he was Abe Froman, the sausage king of Chicago, and everyone laughed. The room was spinning gently, I supposed from the alcohol, and even though it was a dumb chaperoned event full of sick kids in their pajamas, it was one of the best nights I'd had in a long time.

I was there with the right group of friends, and we were up to a small, ridiculous act of mischief, and I never once worried that I should have been at home studying instead of out watching a movie.

About halfway through the film, Sadie scooted her blanket closer to mine.

"Hi," she whispered.

"Hi," I whispered back.

"Mind if I watch from here?" she asked, and then she put her pillow right next to mine and settled in.

It was dark in the gym, and it was just the five of us, sitting apart from everyone else. Something about Sadie lying there felt more intimate than any of the other times we'd watched a movie. I was mesmerized by the curve of her bare back in that dress, and she was so pretty that I didn't know where to begin.

I propped myself on one elbow, facing her instead of the screen, and she copied me.

"Sorry it's not a real dance," she whispered.

"That's okay, it's a real gym."

"And you didn't stand me up."

"I'd never do that."

Sadie smiled at me, and it felt like she was holding the universe together.

"I know," she said.

After the movie ended, we walked back to the dorm. Nick was sulking and had polished off at least three juice boxes. I could feel Marina silently cheering as Sadie and I walked together and I carried both of our pillows. Charlie kept moaning about how he'd had to pee for, like, half the movie, and how it wasn't funny, and could we please not make him laugh unless we wanted to be personally responsible for the consequences, which would be pee.

There were twenty minutes before lights-out, hardly

enough time for anything, but I'd consumed a juice box full of alcohol while wearing a shirt and tie, so the weirdness of that night was already out of my hands.

Charlie beelined for Cottage 6, and Nick followed.

"Um, I'll see you later," Marina said with a yawn, heading back toward the girls' dorm.

And then it was just Sadie and me standing on the grass, with me awkwardly clutching our pillows.

"Why don't we put these down?" Sadie suggested, so I dropped them on the porch swing, and then we stood there wondering what came next.

Everyone streamed around us in their pajamas, talking and laughing in this excited but exhausted way, and it felt so strongly like we were at summer camp. Like we'd never left but had grown old there separately, and had only now found each other again.

"Wanna take a walk?" I asked.

"A promenade," Sadie said, giggling. "Come, fair gentleman, let us take a turn about the garden."

She rested her hand on my arm, and we walked toward the gazebo.

"Nope," I said, steering her away. "That's a sad place. We don't go there."

"That's okay, I have a better idea."

"You always have a better idea," I teased.

"I can't tell if that's a compliment," she said, and then she grabbed my hand and pulled me into the woods.

The moon wasn't quite full, but it was still bright enough to see by. It had been a long time since I'd been in the woods at night, and they seemed to twist around me, to chirp and hum and vibrate from every direction.

"Where are we going?" I asked.

"Shhhh, we're time traveling."

Sadie bent down to take off her heels, and then she stepped ahead of me, in that green dress with the achingly low back, her spine pale in the moonlight as she pulled me deeper into the woods.

"We're here," she said, stopping suddenly.

"Where?"

"Camp Griffith, four summers ago. The night of the dance."

Behind her was an enormous rock, like the legendary one from camp. I laughed at the reference.

"You brought the rock all the way here?" I joked.

"Yes, I did," she said seriously. "Because I've considered it and have concluded that the make-out rock is the most romantic place in the world to have a first kiss."

"Well," I said. "Who am I to argue with the world's most romantic time-traveling rock?"

I was awestruck by my good fortune, and by this profoundly gorgeous girl who was staring at me in the moonlight. And then she stepped forward, and her lips parted mine, and nothing else mattered. Not that we were sick and might never get better, not that we'd missed so much and would miss more still, and not that the band around her wrist wasn't a corsage but a med sensor.

The world melted, and it was just us, in the woods, our mouths pressed together as we found the kiss that had been waiting for us since we were thirteen.

"Well," she said.

"Well," I said.

"I guess now I have your TB," she joked.

"I guess now I have your first kiss."

"Took you long enough," Sadie said, biting her lip and staring up at me. "There's a second kiss with your name on it, too, but it'll have to wait or we'll be late for lights-out."

And even though I could have stayed there forever, her hand grabbed mine, and we hurried back through the woods toward the soft, warm glow of the cottages.

CHAPTER FOURTEEN

SADIE

I COULDN'T SLEEP after we got back from the woods. I lay awake under the too-warm covers, my whole body thrumming in the aftermath of that kiss. I felt the ghost of where his lips had been, and remembered the pressure of his hand on my back, the smell of his soap, the way his mouth had tasted faintly of apples.

I didn't care that I'd promised myself I'd stay away from Latham boys, that I'd rolled my eyes whenever I saw other couples sneak off toward the woods or duck behind buildings to engage in Latham's favorite pastime. I didn't care about any of that. I just wanted to tiptoe over to Cottage 6 in my pajamas, and push open the door to Lane's room, and crawl under the covers with him so the feeling of our lips touching never had to end.

Kissing Lane was like the first time you hear a song that you'll listen to on repeat a hundred times. It was like the first spoonful of ice cream of the whole cup. But mostly, it was the strange and lovely experience of something being even better than I'd imagined.

What were the odds that out of the 150 of us at Latham, there'd be a boy whose smile did flippy things to my stomach, and who liked me back, and who made jokes about Harry Potter? And what were the odds that it would be a boy I'd known, and had wrongly despised, for years?

I'd been at Latham long enough that I no longer quite believed in second chances, but in the moments before I drifted off to sleep that night, I wondered if maybe Lane was the miracle Latham had promised, and if that miracle would be big enough.

Lane was waiting on the porch the next morning. He bounded out of the glider when he saw me, this big, goofy grin on his face. His hair was wet from the shower, and he was wearing these horrible athletic shorts with a giant Aeropostale logo on the leg.

"Really?" I said, making a face at the shorts.

"Hey, you already kissed me. No take-backs," he joked, and then he leaped down the porch steps two at a time.

It was just a small thing, but it struck me how much healthier he looked than when he'd arrived. How the nurse never seemed to stay in his room very long when we hid our phones during lights-out, and how he rolled his eyes after a coughing fit, instead of struggling to catch his breath.

I wondered what I'd do if he left, *when* he left, without me. Maybe it hadn't occurred to him, since I never seemed that sick. And I wasn't. Month after month, my X-rays and blood tests came back the same. And I didn't know which change would be more terrifying, the death sentence I'd been dreading since sophomore year, or the ticket home to a life I'd missed far too much of to ever fully recover, and a world that would always treat me as an outsider if they knew.

All I knew was that Lane was smiling at me, and even if it wasn't too late to back away, I wouldn't have been able to.

"So, can I walk you to breakfast?" Lane asked.

He looked so earnest, and so excited about walking with me to the dining hall that I had to laugh.

"This plan of yours will never work, you know," I told him.

"What plan?"

"This plan to fatten me up and feed me to the circus elephants."

"I'll keep that in mind," he said. "In the meantime, pancakes?"

"In the meantime, pancakes."

And then I took the porch steps two at a time, copying him, and pretending it didn't make my chest ache.

I HADN'T THOUGHT that breakfast would be weird or different that morning, but I could feel people staring as Lane and I waited in line. Staring at *us*. At first, I thought something horrible must have happened, but Nick and Charlie were at the front of the line, and I'd seen Marina in the bathroom ten minutes ago, trying to even out her gel liner.

"What's going on?" Lane whispered, confused.

"Your shorts are just that terrible," I said, reaching for the muffin tray.

"I've got it." He held it out to me with a flourish. *"Mademoiselle, quelque chose du sucre?"*

I melted into a puddle, and when I was done melting, he was still there, and still smiling at me from behind the platter of lopsided cafeteria muffins.

"I can't ever tell if the droopy ones taste better or worse," I said.

"So much better," Lane said. "Droopy muffins for the win."

"That would be an awesome insult," I said. "'Don't go out with her, she has a droopy muffin.'"

We laughed, and behind us, someone huffed impatiently. It was Angela. She narrowed her eyes at me.

"Can I help you?" I asked.

"Take your time," Angela said, smiling sweetly. "I just wanted to remind you both that it's impossible to walk with the Lord when you're lying down."

For a second, I had no idea what she was talking about, and then I burst out laughing.

"Oh, wow," I said. "Thank you for calling me a slut in New Testament. That's super nice of you."

I glanced over at Lane, who was still holding the muffin

tray and trying so hard not to laugh that he was red in the face.

Angela spluttered but didn't say anything else. I made sure to take extra long in the line just to annoy her. I caught some of the other girls from French class staring at us as well, and then I realized.

Everyone had been at the movies last night. They'd all seen Lane and me flirting and holding hands and lying next to each other in our blanket nest, and they'd watched as we'd disappeared into the woods together. I hadn't considered what it looked like—like we'd done much more than we actually had, and like we were being obvious about it, wanting everyone to know what we were up to. And I hadn't realized quite how many girls had been set on Lane until they were glaring at us from behind their yogurt bowls, eyes narrowed in resentment.

When Lane and I got to our table, he hesitated, then switched to the empty seat next to mine. He kept bumping my leg under the table with his, which was the cutest thing ever.

I expected Nick to sulk about it, like he'd been doing ever since the Starbucks trip, but thankfully, he was too hungover to do anything besides groan and attempt the world's tiniest forkfuls of eggs.

"You need to drink some water," Charlie told him.

Nick, who appeared not to have heard, swallowed thickly and lifted a forkful of eggs toward his mouth like someone had dared him to eat a snail.

And then Marina rolled her eyes and imitated him, sending us all into hysterics.

IT WAS GORGEOUS outside that morning. Indian summer. The sky was a cloudless blue, and it felt like the school year was almost over, instead of just beginning. It would have been a shame to go inside and waste one of the last warm days, so we stood around on the grass, trying to figure out what to do.

"We should go to the hill," Marina finally suggested, so we did.

The hill was this slope on the far side of the lake with a view of the grounds. It wasn't quite a hill, but that didn't matter. Charlie brought his portable record player, and Marina brought a deck of cards, and we all had books in our bags, although Lane and I were the only ones who actually tried to read them.

We sat there all morning in the soft, warm grass, listening to Charlie's collection of psychedelic pop records and teaching Lane how to play Egyptian Ratscrew.

Nick, who was apparently in agony, put his cardigan over his face and went to sleep. Charlie and Marina took turns dropping handfuls of grass onto his stomach and laughing when he finally woke up and noticed.

It was so wonderful, the five of us sitting there, and I wanted every day to be like this. To be us, in the sunshine, in no hurry to be anywhere else.

After a while, Lane and I took a walk down to the lake. There was a single paddleboat at the water's edge. It was chained there, half-sunken and rotting away.

"That is one sad metaphor of a boat," Lane said, pointing at it.

"You're right. It's a metaphor, which is like a simile," I joked, and he playfully shoved me.

"You're going in the lake," he warned.

"You're coming with me," I promised, even though he was so much taller he could probably pick me up and toss, like I was a Frisbee.

"I'll take my chances," he said, menacing toward me, and I shrieked and ran up the little slope to the nearest bench, trying not to cough.

He sat down next to me, looking contrite.

"Sorry," he said. "I wouldn't really throw you in the lake."

"Except as a metaphor." I couldn't resist.

"Oh, you're really gonna get it."

And then Lane was kissing me again, his hand cupping the side of my face. They say your skin is the largest organ in your body, but I'd never really appreciated that before, the way his fingertips slowly tracing the curve of my jaw could travel down the entire length of my body, covering me in goose bumps. The way he could make me feel flushed with something that wasn't a fever.

"Listen," Lane said. "I want to ask you something."

He cleared his throat nervously, and I was so afraid of what he might say that all sorts of terrible questions flashed through my brain.

"Would you go on a date with me?"

He looked so nervous about it, like he thought there was a chance I'd refuse.

"I think that would be okay," I said.

He grinned triumphantly and scooped me onto his lap, and he was so tall and messy-haired and perfect, and he really was asking me out this time, it wasn't some mean prank by the girls in my cabin.

"So, where are we going on this illustrious date?" I asked. "The dining hall? The library?"

"I was thinking Fall Fest," he said. "Next Friday night?"

I had no idea what he was talking about. Latham didn't have a Fall Fest. We had, like, decorative gourd painting and a screening of *Hocus Pocus*. And then I realized.

"You mean in Whitley?" I asked.

Lane nodded, holding back a grin.

"I remembered the flyers from when we were there last time."

"What happened to Mr. There Are a Hundred Reasons Why We Shouldn't Go to Town and I Will Stubbornly Stand Here Listing Them All?" I asked.

"Well," Lane said, "I realized that was no way to impress a girl."

THE REST OF the week was the way summer camp should have been. The way my life should have gone four years ago, if only either of us had been brave enough or bold enough to say hello back then. It was a week of board games on the porch, and frozen fruit bars from the commissary, and trading flash drives full of music. We read paperbacks on our stomachs in the grass after dinner, and watched the sun set over the lake, and ducked into the woods to kiss.

Every night on the phone, we'd read each other the funny parts from our books, or talk about the TV shows we'd watched as kids, or what we would do if we were really there in each other's beds, except mostly joking. We said absurd things, like how I'd suck the back of his knee, or he'd run his toes through my hair, and pretended they sounded amazing.

The warm weather was gone by Friday, and that evening was foggy and cold. I had to abandon the cute dress I was going to wear in favor of jeans and my green parka. When Lane picked me up, he was wearing this black fleece jacket zipped up to his chin, and I joked that he looked like a Dracula.

"A Dracula?" he asked. "Like, one of the many Draculas?"

"Shut up."

"I vont to suck your . . . type A blood. The other Dracula, over there, he is interested in type B," Lane went on, in this ridiculous Count Chocula voice.

"Oh my God, I'm gonna kill you!" I said, laughing.

We set off into the woods. I was in charge of navigating us down to Whitley, and at one point Lane looked around, confused.

"I remembered it being that way," he said, pointing.

We'd veered a little farther west than I'd thought and were almost at the place where I usually met Michael. He was pointing even more west, which wasn't right.

"It's this way," I said, and explained where we were.

"So, you just picked a random point in the woods to meet some strange dude?"

"*I* didn't pick it," I said, and I explained about how Phillip had run the black market before Nick. I inherited it, and anyway, he and Michael were like half cousins or something.

We were almost there, and I took out my bag of cough drops and passed one to Lane.

"Do these actually work?" he asked.

"Yes, and you're cured now," I teased. "You're welcome."

"How can I ever thank you?"

Lane got this mischievous grin on his face and pulled me toward him for a kiss that tasted like cherry medicine. And then his hands were in my hair, and his tongue was against mine, and I accidentally swallowed my cough drop.

It wasn't much farther into town, and when we got there, the main street looked so festive with lights in the trees and all the shop windows decorated for fall. The street was blocked off to traffic, and crowded with booths, and a jazz band of old dudes was playing in the old gazebo.

There were rides, too, a miniature Ferris wheel, and a giant slide, and a chair swing. It reminded me of the county fair, and how I used to go with my mom and sister, enviously watching as other girls my age roamed around in friend groups.

"Reminds me of my school carnival," Lane said with a lopsided grin.

"Fancy school," I teased.

He shrugged.

"I never went to the thing, anyway. They always had teachers in the dunking booth."

I didn't know what he meant at first, but then I remembered how he'd said his dad taught at his school.

"Then we have to make up for all the carnivals you missed," I said, dragging him toward the line for ride tickets.

Everything was pretty expensive, so we just got tickets for the swing ride.

"You have to try and grab my hand while we're in the air," I said. "That's the rule."

"What do I win if I do?" Lane asked.

"A wish," I promised.

It was exhilarating going on the ride and lifting into the

air, my feet dangling beneath me. You could see a lot from up there, the road that led to Latham, the bell tower through the trees, and the neat yards of the houses in town. It was strange seeing both worlds at once: mine, and the real one.

The swings were pretty far apart, but Lane still tried, twisting around in his seat and looking back at me with his hand outstretched. I leaned forward, too, as far as I could. But we could never quite reach.

"Guess I didn't get my wish," Lane teased as we staggered off the ride.

"Don't worry, it wasn't a very big wish," I assured him. "It was like a medium soda of a wish."

"Well, now you've ruined it, and I know I'm missing out on a medium soda."

"Or possibly half a plain funnel cake," I said.

"Or possibly half a plain funnel cake," he repeated in mock despair.

Lane held my hand as we wandered through the booths, and then he bought us apple ciders. They were too hot to drink, so we sat on the hay bales outside the pumpkin patch, waiting for them to cool off.

It felt strange being in town, but it always did. I hadn't lived in this world for so long that it was weird to see that people were still drinking green juice and taking out their phones whenever they had to stand in line.

"This is so nice," I said, and then I sipped the cider and made a face. "Ow. Hot."

"Still?"

"Why don't you try it and find out?"

"I'm not falling for that one," Lane said, laughing.

Nearby, little kids ran through the pumpkin patch, hyper from sugar and covered in face paint. I leaned my head against Lane's shoulder, thinking about my sister, who was twelve. Too old to be enthusiastic about this stuff, but still young enough to dress up and get free candy.

"What was your worst Halloween costume?" Lane asked me.

"I was Hermione Granger, like, five years in a row," I said. "By the time that was over, I'd gone through my embarrassing years."

"I was a gorilla once," he told me.

"You were not!" I laughed.

"I was," he insisted. "I think I was five. I saw the costume in one of those Halloween Castles, you know, those stores that pop up for a few months and then disappear?"

I nodded.

"Anyway. That was it. Gorilla. So my mom took me trick-or-treating, and she made me go really early, just to the houses on our block. And that year it was, like, eighty degrees out." He glanced over at me with this lopsided grin. "Which means it was at least a hundred degrees in that thick, hairy gorilla suit. The mask was off by the third house, and then the feet, and then the gloves. And after ten minutes I was standing there covered in sweat and crying in this hairy black jumpsuit, wanting to go home."

We both laughed. I tried to picture five-year-old Lane in a hairy gorilla suit, and it was surprisingly easy. I'd known him when we were thirteen, after all.

"I want to see a picture," I insisted.

"Fine, then I want to see you in that Hogwarts uniform." He raised his eyebrows.

"Oh my God, I was ten!"

"Hey, you were pretty cute at thirteen," he teased.

It wasn't true, though. I'd been skinny and frizzy-haired at thirteen, with weird-shaped boobs, like cones. But it was still nice of him to say.

Our ciders had cooled down enough, so we sipped them, watching the sunset and listening to the terrible music that drifted from the bandstand.

"I bet they sell kettle corn," I said.

"I bet you're right," Lane said.

"I'll go get us some."

Lane asked if I wanted him to come with me, but I shook my head. I didn't want it to seem like I was forcing him to buy me kettle corn, too.

"I'll be right back," I promised.

And then I did something I hadn't had the pleasure of doing in a long time. I disappeared into the crowd. I felt so free, even with the med sensor around my wrist, like I wasn't making the best of Latham, but was actually doing something seventeen-year-olds did, for real.

I was on a date with a cute boy, and he'd bought me apple cider and told me an embarrassing story about when he was five, and afterward, maybe we'd make a detour in the woods so I could show off my seriously uncomfortable blue lace bra, and then we'd smooth down our hair and he'd walk me to my front porch and kiss me good night.

I found the kettle-corn lady and bought a bag. I couldn't resist eating some on the way back. The kernels scratched at my throat, and I ducked into a little alleyway between two shops, trying not to cough on anyone.

I was just catching my breath when a side door opened and these three preppy-looking bros in ball caps and boat shoes staggered outside. It was the back door to a bar, I guessed, since it was dark inside, and I could hear a sports game playing on some television.

The guys were college aged, and they stared at me in this uncomfortable way that I thought was only reserved for girls in tight dresses, and not girls in jeans and striped shirts.

I was still coughing, and the blond one walked over, laughing.

"Hey, you okay?" he asked.

"Kettle corn," I said, trying to catch my breath.

"You wanna come back inside? I'll buy you a drink," he said.

I realized he thought I'd been in the bar, which made sense, because I was standing right outside.

I shook my head.

"I have to meet someone," I said.

"We'll walk you," the guy said, suddenly pushy. "Won't we?"

His friends nodded and said that yeah, it was no trouble, they'd walk me.

"That's okay."

I started to edge away, and he sort of blocked me.

"What's wrong?" the guy asked. "You don't wanna talk to us anymore?"

I glanced toward the passage that led back onto the street.

"I told you, I'm meeting someone," I said firmly, and then I walked away.

"Come on, beautiful, where are you going?" one of them shouted.

Without looking back, I knew they were following me. I could hear their footsteps behind me in the alley but forced myself not to turn around.

I could feel the panic rising in my throat as they followed me through the edge of the Fall Fest. I didn't know how to make them leave me alone, and I didn't want to get anyone else's attention, because they might ask questions about me.

"C'mon, we're really nice, just stop a second," one of them said.

I whirled around.

"I told you no," I said sharply. "Go away."

They laughed. They were so close, and so much bigger than me, and they didn't seem to comprehend how terrible they were acting.

"But we said we'd walk you," the tallest one said. "And a gentleman never breaks his word."

"Then be a gentleman and stop following me!" I insisted.

And then I started coughing. It was pretty bad, and I hadn't been expecting it. The stupid kettle corn had been my worst idea ever.

When I caught my breath, the tallest one had taken a step back.

"Whoa, that sounds pretty serious," he said.

"I have asthma," I said defensively.

"Didn't sound like asthma," the blond one said, smiling like he enjoyed taunting me. "Sounded contagious. You're not gonna give us the plague, are you, blondie?"

"Not if you leave me alone," I said, whirling around.

But his hand shot out, and he grabbed my wrist. I twisted away, and my parka pulled back, revealing my med sensor and its blinking green light.

They all stared at it, and at me.

"Oh shit," the blond one said. "She's from that creepy hospital."

"We could have fucking TB now," his bearded friend said. "What the fuck?!"

"Wait, she said she was meeting someone. There's more of them here," the tall guy said.

My heart was hammering. I didn't know what to do. If I went back to Lane, they'd follow me. And if I tried to get someone's help, I'd be in an even bigger mess. I was Frankenstein's monster. Typhoid Mary. The guy who kept sneezing really loudly on an airplane.

I stared at them in horror, and then I heard a boy's voice.

"What the hell are you doing?"

It was Michael, with his work boots and tattoos, walking toward us. I'd never seen him look so angry, or so intimidating, as he frowned at the three drunken bros.

"I asked you a question," he demanded.

"She's one of those contagious kids from the TB place on the hill!" the blond guy said. "And there's more of them here!"

I stared at Michael, pleading silently for him to vouch for me.

"That's ridiculous," he said. "This is my cousin."

"Your cousin?" one of the guys asked, frowning.

"I'm Phillip's little sister," I lied.

They looked unsure.

"I'm *fifteen*," I said, making my eyes wide and scared. That at least got through to them.

"Shit," the bearded one muttered, believing me.

"Then what were you doing in a bar?" the tall one said.

Michael glared at me.

"I wasn't *in* a bar, I was standing outside eating kettle corn, and they started harassing me," I said.

"You're drunk," Michael told them, "and bothering underage girls. So you can stop lying about how and why that happened. Go home, sober up, and read *Jezebel*."

Michael stalked off, and I followed him, gratefully.

"Thank you," I said.

He whirled around, still upset.

"I didn't do it for you, I did it for business," he said.

"Yeah, okay."

"You can't keep doing this," he said. "Those guys were about to turn this place upside down until they found your friends. You have to stop coming down here. You're going to infect everyone!"

"We are not, we're just sitting by the pumpkin patch," I said.

The color drained from his face.

"My kid's over there!" he said.

"You have a kid?" I asked.

"Yes, I have a kid," Michael said angrily. "He's two and a half, and if anything happens to him, I swear to God. If I see you in town again, I'll turn you in myself. Now get your friends, and get the hell out of here."

"Fine," I said, stalking off. It wasn't fair. Those beer-sloshing bros were the ones putting everyone in danger, not me. I wasn't even doing anything. I wasn't even near anyone. But I believed it then, what Amit had said about leaving Latham. There were people out there who panicked, and all it took was one to start a witch hunt.

Lane looked worried when I got back to the hay bales.

"That took a while," he said. "Everything okay?"

I didn't want Lane to freak out. He looked so hopeful, and so happy, that I couldn't say anything and ruin our date. So I rolled my eyes and held up the kettle corn.

"The line took forever," I said. "Everyone had the same idea. We should probably head back, though, since it's getting late."

"Yeah, of course."

And then he followed me back toward the old hiking path. I dug into my purse for my flashlight and compass and handed him the kettle corn.

We ate it as we walked back, not caring that it made us cough. And when we came to the rock in the woods, which almost looked like the one from camp, I was much calmer.

Nothing bad had really happened. It was just some drunk guys deciding that my walking around and being female was an invitation for creepery. That sort of thing went on all the time. And to be fair, it wasn't like they were still afraid of me after the doctors said my TB was inactive. I was a pale, sick-looking stranger with a bad cough—of course they were on their guard. But it was over now, nothing to worry about. And I wasn't going to let it ruin my first real date with a boy. A cute boy, who'd bought me cider and held my hand and been a complete gentleman.

- 203 -

Lane stared at the rock, and so did I.

"I bet you'll never guess what color my bra is," I said.

"Probably not," he said. "But I know one way to find out."

CHAPTER FIFTEEN
LANE

MY FIRST MONTH at Latham House came to a close, although it seemed wrong to measure time like that, to consider the start of my days at Latham to be something that didn't have to do with Sadie Bennett.

I talked to my parents on the phone every few nights, and when they asked me how was I sleeping, and how was I feeling, and what had I been up to, I actually answered them. I figured I owed them some assurance that I wasn't lying on my deathbed four hundred miles away, trying to keep up with my AP Euro packet. And the weird thing was, they were enthusiastic when I said I'd made friends in my French class and that we played cards and traded books, and they didn't seem to mind when I said I'd put aside my schoolwork to focus on getting better.

The longer I was away, the more my specific annoyances with them faded. Sure, they'd always been strict, but I'd never given any indication that I wasn't happy with the way things were. I'd wanted to be the best as much as they'd wanted it for me.

I'd been the one who had decided to give up drama class to take AP Art History my freshman year. It wasn't like I'd discussed it with them, or pleaded to keep taking drama; I'd been convinced it was a necessary sacrifice, and they'd praised me for "making a mature decision."

Before I even knew what high school was, I'd already let my fear of not being the best at it make me miserable. And I was starting to think that if I hadn't gotten sick, I would have done the same thing with college, rushing toward internships and grad school and a job. Somehow, without realizing, I'd made high school into a race toward the best college, as opposed to its own destination. It was only now that I hadn't done the same thing at Latham that I could see it, and that I realized how unhappy it made me.

The last SAT date for early admission passed. I don't know what I was doing that day. Lying in a field of overgrown grass, reading a Douglas Adams novel on my stomach. Pulling Sadie behind a building to kiss her on the way back from Wellness. Lounging in bed in the middle of the afternoon, listening to Charlie's records through the open windows while the shadows of tree branches played across my wall.

Whatever I was doing that day, I wasn't hunched over a too-small desk in a high school gym with a plastic bag of sharpened pencils, trying to raise my score another thirty points, even though it was already in the ninety-ninth percentile. I wasn't terrified that if I screwed up a single question, my entire future might disappear. Probably, I was wondering if Sadie and I could slip off somewhere after dinner, and what else we'd slip off.

WE WERE IN French class when it happened.

Sadie was sitting under the window reading a John Green novel, and I'd slid her worksheet onto my desk and was busy filling it in with the most hilariously wrong answers I could think of, since I'd already finished mine.

It was almost lunch, and I was starving. I kept hoping my stomach wouldn't growl and give me away.

Mr. Finnegan was at his desk for once when this kid Carlos pushed open the door. Carlos wasn't in our class, and Finnegan looked up from his iPad with a frown.

"Everyone's supposed to go to the gym immediately," Carlos said.

The whole class looked around, confused. It was Tuesday morning, and as far as I could tell, it was a pretty unusual request.

"The gym?" Mr. Finnegan repeated.

"Immediately," Carlos said.

Our teacher thanked the kid, who disappeared out into the hallway. And then Finnegan shrugged and told us to stop working.

"Are we coming back?" Nick asked, but Finnegan didn't

know, so some of us took our bags, and most of us left our books open on our desks.

Everyone was in the gym, spread thinly across the rows of bleachers, which were meant for far more than 150 of us. I remember Sadie making some joke about it being a terrible time for a pep rally, and Nick chiming in about how come nobody told him we had a basketball team.

I was too nervous, and too confused, to say anything. I didn't know what was going on, and I hated that. There were adults I'd never seen standing around the edges of the gym, teachers and nurses, which felt ominous, like whatever was going to happen was so bad that they thought we might try to escape.

Dr. Barons and this administrative lady Mrs. Kleefeld, who'd given my parents my admission forms, were discussing something behind an ancient wheeled lectern.

"What's going on?" Sadie whispered, and I shrugged.

Some young tech-looking guy was helping to set up, and the microphone came to life with a squeal and then static. Everyone clapped their hands over their ears, making a much bigger deal of it than it actually was. Latham had never felt so much like a high school as it did then. Except for the small fact that most high schools have a survival rate higher than 80 percent.

Mrs. Kleefeld angled the microphone down and smiled tensely at us. Her pearl necklace was so tight that it almost looked like it was choking her.

"Good afternoon, children," she said, which seemed like the wrong word to use, although I didn't know what might have been the right one. She paused, as though waiting for us all to chant "Good afternoon, Mrs. Kleefeld!" back at her, but we didn't. I glanced at the clock on the wall, which read 11:23. Not afternoon, but still morning.

"As you know," Mrs. Kleefeld continued, "being at Latham House is a special privilege. The data that your medical sensors collect has helped scientists to understand so much about your illness. And these scientists have been working day and night to make advances in the treatment of total-drug-resistant tuberculosis. We thought it best to gather everyone here as quickly as possible to avoid the spread of rumors and false information. I suppose I should let Dr. Barons explain."

Everyone else looked as confused as I felt. And then Dr. Barons stepped behind the podium. He wasn't wearing his white coat, just a fleece jacket a lot like mine, and it was strange seeing him in a high school gym and not a medical building. The only thing we'd done so far in here was to watch movies, and I was pretty sure he wasn't announcing a surprise screening of *The Goonies*.

"Thank you, Mrs. Kleefeld," he began, and then cleared his throat nervously. "There has been news this morning that the FDA has classified a serum called protocillin as a first-line treatment for total-drug-resistant tuberculosis. The protocillin has been approved for clinical testing and is moving forward into production."

The gymnasium was silent, hanging on his every word. He couldn't be saying what I thought he was saying.

"And as of thirty minutes ago, it has been confirmed that the first doses of protocillin will be ready in six weeks, and that Latham House will be participating in the initial trial." He paused and beamed at us. "What this means is that in six weeks' time, the TDR strain of tuberculosis will be curable."

There was a moment of stunned silence, and then the gym erupted in whoops and cheers. All around me, people were laughing and hugging and crying. Genevieve and her crowd were on their knees, thanking God for inventing science, I guessed.

I couldn't believe I'd been so wrong about why they'd gathered us in the gym. It wasn't something bad at all. It was something incredible.

"Sadie," I said, turning toward her.

"Oh my God," she said, fighting back tears.

We hugged each other close, and she sniffled into my shoulder as I struggled to wrap my head around the idea that we were going to be cured. All of us. Not temporarily stable but having to take it easy to avoid a relapse. Cured. Forever. In no time at all I'd be transported back to my former life, and Latham would melt away like a bad dream.

Except it wasn't a bad dream. It was card games in the

grass, and stolen internet, and Sadie in that green dress, and Charlie's records, and subtitled Japanese movies, and Marina doing an impression of Nick eating scrambled eggs. It wasn't the life I'd wanted, but it was the life I had, and I was finally starting to accept that.

"If I can have everyone's attention," Dr. Barons said, and the gym gradually quieted. "I'm sure you have a lot of questions, and I'm going to attempt to answer some of them now. Your parents will be notified over the next few hours by our medical staff. Protocillin will be administered by daily injection over the course of eight weeks. For the first four weeks, you will stay here so that any side effects and symptoms can be monitored and recorded. After that time, arrangements will be made with hospitals in your area so you can continue receiving daily, observed treatment at home for the rest of the course. Your hall nurses will be distributing more information to you and to your parents as soon as it becomes available. And we'll be temporarily suspending phone and internet access until everyone's parents have been contacted by our staff."

Dr. Barons went on, thanking us all for listening and saying what an honor it was to share this news with us.

"Look at Finnegan," Sadie whispered.

I glanced over. Finnegan and his wife, who was wearing scrubs, were holding each other so tightly that it looked painful. I'd never seen him so happy.

Actually, I'd never seen Latham House so happy. I hadn't noticed before quite how grim everyone was, even if it was a cheerful, morbid sort of grimness. We were all trapped on the same hellish island together, except now, in the distance, someone had sighted a lifeboat.

CHAPTER SIXTEEN
SADIE

I HATED THAT there was a voice in the back of my head telling me it wasn't true, but for whatever reason, I couldn't quite believe that protocillin was real. All I could think about were the last two times scientists had claimed they'd created a serum that cured tuberculosis:

The first time, one of the guys on Nick's hall had found it on the internet and printed out the *Daily Mail* article, and it was all over Latham by dinner. Except it turned out to be a hoax. A researcher in Korea had faked the data, and the next morning there were at least a dozen articles accusing him of fraud. That was during my sixth month at Latham House. And then, a few months later, rumors had spread about a new super drug. I'd let myself hope, only to be disappointed again when it failed miserably in lab testing.

So I didn't want to get my hopes up for protocillin. Even if it did seem real this time. Even if it was all over the news that afternoon.

I stood around the common room with everyone else, glued to the television as reports trickled in that a group of scientists at the Hospital of the University of Pennsylvania had developed a first-line treatment for the previously total-drug-resistant strain of tuberculosis. That this was the first new tuberculosis treatment in fifty years, and the first major medical breakthrough to treat an infectious disease in what doctors were now definitively calling the post-antibiotic era.

Someone would switch the channel, and it would be another report, about how patients and carers at long-term treatment facilities would receive the initial course of protocillin, and how vaccinations were being developed for the general public.

They were the first news reports about tuberculosis that I could remember where the correspondents didn't look worried as they explained that the contagious illness known as TDR-TB had been declared an epidemic by the CDC two years ago, with more than 280,000 active cases reported across the United States alone this year. If anything, they looked hopeful, like the disaster was behind us, and the scare was almost over.

October was coming to a close, and I'd been at Latham House for seventeen months. I'd missed the end of my sophomore year of high school. I'd celebrated my sixteenth birthday in the hospital playing Uno with my mom and sister while they wore surgical masks, and I'd been at Latham for almost a year and a half, longer than nearly everyone.

I wasn't sure I knew how to leave Latham. I'd never let myself think for certain that I would, or when that might be. Except now everyone was saying we'd be home by January. I didn't know how to feel about any of it, or even what I was feeling, just that I was overwhelmed.

No one said much of anything at dinner. We were all too busy thinking about what had just happened, and what it meant to have our futures slip back into place while we were sitting quietly at our desks, trying not to cough all over our notebooks. We were no longer incurably ill, and for so many of us that had been our defining thing for so long.

It had hurt to accept what was wrong with me, but it hurt even more to have hope.

I didn't want protocillin to be real because I didn't want to go home to the dreary, unappealing life I'd left behind. I wanted Latham to stay Latham forever, for us to have a million more days of playing cards in the sunshine, and a million more nights of whispering into the phone and knowing that when I woke up, Lane would be waiting on my porch, his hair still wet from the shower.

Latham was my Hogwarts, and protocillin was the cure for my magic. It would turn me into a Muggle again, one who had to worry about standardized testing and mean girls and tardy slips.

After we bused our trays, Lane and I walked down to the lake. He kept glancing at me shyly, like he thought I wouldn't notice, and then he reached out and grabbed my hand. We walked like that down to the far edge of the lake, with the sunken boat, and lay on our stomachs in the grass.

I looked over at Lane, at the nearly invisible white hairs that dusted his earlobes, at the freckle on the center of his neck, at how absolutely thrilled he seemed, and I told myself to quelch this weird darkness that was twisting inside of me. So when he smiled and nudged me with his sneaker, I nudged back, forcing away my traitorous despair.

We had the perfect view of Latham across the water. The half-moon of the cottages, the collegiate-looking classrooms, the dining hall with its stained-glass windows, the bell tower atop the gymnasium, and just a white corner of the medical building.

"Do you think Latham's going to shut down?" I asked.

"Probably," Lane said. "Maybe it'll become a boarding school again and the students will tell ghost stories about the kids who died here."

"Maybe it'll become some terrible artists' colony with a bunch of nude ladies painting fruit," I suggested, not entirely kidding.

Lane shook his head, smiling.

"We'll have to visit and check," he said. "We can get butterbeer lattes and everything."

I tried not to let my smile falter as I told him that sounded great.

"You live where again? Calabasas?" he asked, and I nodded. "That's, like, eighty-five miles. It's nothing. I'll be at your doorstep with bagels every Saturday morning."

"I didn't know you had a car."

"Oh, yeah. My dad's old Honda. It's covered in a million political bumper stickers, but it has spirit."

I smiled at the thought of him pulling up outside our condo, and us driving to the beach or one of the canyons to have a breakfast picnic. It sounded so wonderful, like something I'd dreamed up. But part of me was afraid it wouldn't work. That he'd make the trip once or twice, to be polite, and then he'd make excuses.

"I can't believe we're talking about this," I said. "About being home two months from now, and you showing up at my door."

"Well, I'd text first," he said.

The absurdity of having phones again, and being able to text each other, made me giggle.

"It's so weird to think about any of it. About going back to high school," I said.

"Well it's even weirder to think about college," Lane said. "I hadn't really wanted to get my hopes up, you know, before."

He went on to explain how he'd been afraid that Stanford wouldn't grant him housing, and that Dr. Barons might say he wasn't fit for full-time study, and that he'd get sick again and have to drop out. But protocillin would change all that. Our lungs would suck, so we'd never be marathon runners or anything, but we'd live.

I wished I was more excited about it, but all I could think was that I was going home for what should have been my last semester of senior year, to a school I'd left as a sophomore. I was pretty sure I'd be held back, since I doubted I could keep up with kids who'd taken precalc and chemistry. I'd be remedial, when I used to make the honor roll. I didn't have my driver's license, or even a permit. I hadn't taken the SATs, or even started to study for them.

None of those things had been a part of my world for so long that it was terrifying to find them rushing back toward me.

My mom's new boyfriend, whom I'd never met but who my sister said was nice, apparently stayed over all the time. It weirded me out to think that there was some guy around who wasn't Dad. That the world hadn't been put on hold, and things had changed, and an accountant named Drew had filled our fridge with protein shakes.

Lane and I had only a few more weeks together before everything changed. A few more weeks to be the Latham versions of ourselves. And I was determined to make them count, to enjoy the last scraps of happiness while I could still pick them out of the rubble.

I was certain that I wouldn't be cool and offbeat the way I was at Latham. The girl with the red lipstick and tough boots, who talked back to the French teacher and made a joke out of the cafeteria rules. The girl with the camera and contraband, always sneaking away with her friends like they were up to no good, always laughing the loudest and giving the impression that even alone in my room I was doing something interesting. All of that would be gone, whoosh, and I'd be the weird new girl who'd been out sick for so long that everyone had forgotten about her, even her family.

MY MOM CRIED, although I could hear her smiling through the tears. She told me that my room was waiting for me, and that she'd wash the sheets before I got home, like my sheets had gotten up to all sorts of nefarious business while I was away. She said we'd go for tacos, and she couldn't wait for me to meet Drew, and Erica had a gymnastics meet right before Christmas, and I just *had* to see her floor routine. She sounded so happy that I went along with it, because from the way she was rambling, I had the impression that she'd prepared herself a long time ago never to need to wash those sheets.

I HAD AN appointment with Dr. Barons on Thursday, so he could change the battery in my med sensor. It needed to be swapped out every couple of months, and the whole process made me feel like a robot. I'd had the sensor for so long that for the few moments when it was off my wrist, I felt untethered, like something was missing.

When I was younger I'd had this star necklace I used to wear, which I never took off, not even to shower. My dad had given it to me. I'd unclasped it the night my parents told me they were getting a divorce, and I overheard them whispering about the truth; that my dad loved some woman from his office, apparently more than he loved us, because he'd rather be with her than his family. For the next week, I'd reach up to grab my star necklace, forgetting not just that I'd taken it off, but that I was no longer my father's North Star, and he no longer wanted to find his way home.

Apparently, I'd been lost in thought, because Dr. Barons was like, "I'm going to need to put that back on you, sweetheart."

"Oh, sorry."

I held out my wrist, watching as he took out a tiny wrench and screwed on the plate that kept it shut. He smiled at me reassuringly, fiddling with the clasp. He screwed the back panel into place, but the green light didn't turn on, and he made a face.

"Hmmm. Let me reset it," he said, taking a paper clip out of his pocket and inserting the end of it into one of the tiny holes on the side of my med sensor. He held it there until something clicked, and then the green light flicked on.

"These things shut off sometimes," he explained. "Just need a reset to get them going again."

"Yep, Gatsby should be able to spot me now," I said, and Dr. Barons smiled at me distractedly.

"All set." Dr. Barons took out his tablet, making sure I was back online. But then he furrowed his brow at the data.

"Everything okay?" I asked, hopping off the exam table.

"Your temperature's a little high," he said, scrolling down his tablet screen. "Heart rate, too."

He swiveled toward the computer and typed something in, pulling up a series of X-rays and tabbing between them.

"Are those mine?" I asked.

Dr. Barons nodded, then pivoted toward me on the stool.

"Is anything wrong?" I asked.

Dr. Barons smiled at me.

"No, no . . . nothing that a dose of protocillin won't fix."

CHAPTER SEVENTEEN

LANE

LATHAM HAD NEVER felt more like a summer camp than it did in those first few days after news of the cure. Suddenly everyone was talking about the future and making jokes about adding each other on Facebook. Camp Latham was almost over, and everyone was getting overly nostalgic about even the smallest things.

Halloween was that Friday, and although Sadie had been joking about decorative gourd painting, I hadn't quite believed her. But it turned out she hadn't been kidding. The nurses set up tables outside the cottages and taped down about a million trash bags so we wouldn't make a mess.

Charlie's was a masterpiece, and Marina's was a Dalek, which Nick flipped over and tried to copy while she glared at him. Of course mine, a lopsided ghost-thing, came out so badly that Sadie joked it was lucky I'd never taken an art class.

"Take that back!" I insisted, brandishing my paintbrush.

"Nope. The grade still stands. D-minus. Good-bye Stanford."

I swiped my paintbrush at her, landing a dot on her cheek. She squealed and tried to wipe it off, but only smeared it bigger.

"You're gonna get it now," Sadie said, leaning over and painting an orange stripe down my nose.

And suddenly the five of us were in the middle of a paint fight, or, I guess, the four of us, while Charlie hovered protectively over his gourd, begging us not to wreck it.

His gourd, like many civilians in war, was a casualty.

"Exterminate?" Marina said innocently, holding her still-dripping paintbrush.

"Oh, I am going to *kill* you!" Charlie said, staring at his mauled gourd. And then he picked up his paintbrush and joined the fray.

When it finally ended, everyone was staring at us like we were crazy. And maybe we were. We were covered in paint and surrounded by smashed and sabotaged gourds. One of the nurses came over and got really angry about it, and I could still feel flakes of paint in my ear that night while we watched *Hocus Pocus* in the gym.

"This movie is so lame," Sadie whispered, shaking her head.

"I loved it when I was little, though," Marina said, and we all agreed that yeah, we'd loved it when we were kids.

Nick had booze for us again, but he said that was the last

of it until they restocked on Friday.

"We need some serious boozage for my birthday next Saturday," Marina said, and Nick promised he had it covered.

Charlie had fallen asleep, and maybe it was the way he was curled around his pillow with his head thrown back, but his breathing sounded pretty ragged.

Is he okay?" I asked, nodding toward Charlie.

Nick peered over at him. "He's fine. He always falls asleep during movies."

"I think he stays up all night writing in that notebook," Sadie said.

Nick nudged Charlie with his foot, and Charlie shifted, coughing a little in his sleep.

"Don't eat the walrus, it's poisoned," he muttered, his left foot twitching.

"Yeah, he's good," Nick said.

We went back to watching the movie, which was pretty cheesy. It gave me flashbacks to the Year of the Gorilla Suit, which I couldn't believe I'd told Sadie about. Way to seem cool, Lane. Way to make a girl fall in love with you.

Up ahead of us, these three girls in pajamas and drawn-on cat's whiskers giggled at the screen, actually enjoying the movie. A group of boys eyed them. The boys were from Charlie's floor, and they passed around a Nalgene bottle, coughing like they were swilling straight alcohol.

Next to me, Sadie sipped her juice box, our bare feet

tangled together. Her toenails were painted blue, and her hair was down and wet from the shower, and she was so beautiful that I didn't know what I'd do when I couldn't see her every day, when I had to fall asleep catching up on my AP coursework instead of catching up with her.

Sadie caught me staring and grinned.

"Hey, trick or treat?" she asked.

"Trick?" I said hopefully.

"Too bad, I only have a treat."

She pressed the last fun-size Twix into my hand. I tore it open, and the chocolate oozed out, getting everywhere.

"It's all melty," I complained, and Sadie smiled sadly.

"Not even chocolate lasts forever," she said.

CHARLIE REFUSED TO hang out with us on Sunday night. He didn't have the bridge right on his new song, he said. It wasn't working, and no, he couldn't just leave it, he'd lose the momentum.

So it was just Nick and me. Nick still wasn't happy about my dating Sadie, but he was getting better about it. I guess it didn't bother him as much now that we'd get out of here so soon. He talked constantly about how the girls back home would think he was so deep, and his biggest problem was going to be keeping up with all his ladies. I didn't want to ruin his fantasy, so I nodded and said, yeah, totally.

That night, in a fit of nostalgia, Nick insisted that we play Mario Kart. Except he'd loaned his disc to Carlos from the second floor, so we went down to try and get it back.

But Carlos couldn't find it. We stood there in the door-way while he sifted through the endless crap in his drawers, looking for the thing.

"I swear I had it, like, this week," he said. "Hold on. There's only five places it would be."

Carlos opened his wardrobe and started tossing stuff onto his bed, like he thought maybe he'd hung up Nick's disc by accident.

Nick rolled his eyes over it.

"We could play something else," I said. "You could show me the crossbow trick on that Blood Stakes game."

And then we heard a shrill electronic beeping from another room. It sounded like an alarm clock, or a timer. Except louder, and somehow more foreboding.

Beep-beep-beep beeeeep! Beep-beep-beep beeeeep!

Nick and Carlos stiffened immediately.

"Shit," Carlos said, letting the sweatshirt he was holding fall to the floor.

The beeping continued, and I wondered why no one turned it off, and why everyone was reacting so strangely.

"What's going on?" I asked.

"Med sensor," Nick said grimly.

My eyes met Nick's. He looked afraid.

"Come on," he said, yanking me into the hall.

The beeping continued. Other doors started to open, the residents of the second floor looking around. Some guys from the third floor had come down the stairs and were poking their heads over the banister.

"Who is it?" someone asked.

An Asian kid in a towel pushed open the door to the bathroom, shampoo still in his hair.

"Chandler?" he called.

"Not me, dude," a heavyset kid said.

"Shit," Nick whispered. "The nurse is coming!"

Most of us were in the hallway at that point, rubbernecking, and Nurse Monica had to wade through it.

Med sensors went off only if your vitals spiked pretty badly, if you needed immediate medical attention. Most of the time anyone that sick was already staying in the medical building.

"Move!" she snapped. "You know better!"

"Where's Charlie?" I said.

"Oh God," Nick said, going pale.

The beeping was coming from Charlie's room.

Nick and I started pushing to the front, and I couldn't remember being more terrified. My heart was hammering, and I felt like I was going to throw up. It couldn't be Charlie. It couldn't be.

Nurse Monica banged open the door.

And there was Charlie, hunched over his desk, while two naked dudes went at it on his giant cinema display. From the huge bottle of lotion and his lack of pants, it was obvious what he was up to.

The entire hallway was in hysterics.

"Oh-oh," Nurse Monica said. Clearly she'd been expecting a different kind of disaster.

"Fuck!" Charlie gasped. "Shut the door!"

"Yo, that's dude on dude," this guy Preston called out, thinking he was very astute.

"Gross! Turn it off!" someone yelled.

"More like turn it *on*!" someone else said.

"That's enough!" Nurse Monica scolded. "Go away! Back to your rooms!"

And then she barged into Charlie's room and shut the door.

I could hear her in there, trying to calm him down while he yelped, "Get away, oh my God, I'm fine!"

"That," Nick said, "is probably my greatest fear."

"Is he going to be okay?" I asked.

"Oh, he'll never live it down," Nick said gleefully, and then he saw the look on my face. "Yeah, dude's fine. He just jerked off so hard he triggered his med sensor."

"I thought that was an urban legend."

I mean, I'd never had that problem? And I'd assumed from the, uh, general activity on my hallway that it wasn't a usual thing. I'd heard some guys joking about it, but I'd figured it was just one of those freak-out-the-new-kid things.

"Nah, it happens sometimes, if you're, like, really going at it. The thing is not to rush. You've gotta get your heart rate down *just* enough—"

"Shut up," I said.

"You've gotta do, like, *yoga* breathing," he continued.

"Seriously, shut up."

"Hey, I'm just giving you some free advice here," he said. "So you don't wind up being the next victim of the med sensor."

"No offense, but I don't want to think about you when I've got my dick in my hand."

"Aha!" Nick accused. "Aha! So you and Sadie *haven't* yet made the tiny little love muffins!"

I didn't even know what to say in response. Or why Nick thought our love muffins were so tiny. Maybe we had massive love muffins. How did he know?

"This really *is* the darkest timeline," I said, shaking my head as we walked back upstairs.

"Of course it is. We're all sick virgins. Except for Charlie, who's a sick gay virgin dumb enough to tilt his computer screen right at the freaking door," Nick said, shaking his head. "I wouldn't want to be him tomorrow."

FROM THE WAY Charlie slunk into the dining hall the next morning, it was obvious he wanted to disappear. And I didn't blame him. The guys in our dorm were still laughing over his misfortune, and I was pretty sure the story was about to make the rounds, if it hadn't already.

"What's going on?" Marina asked suspiciously, narrowing her eyes at us.

"Nothing," I said, shrugging. But Nick must have smirked, because Marina stared us down until he told her.

"Um, Charlie's sensor went off last night," Nick said, and then quickly took a huge bite of toast so he didn't have to say anything else.

Marina gasped.

"Charlie, are you okay?" Sadie asked, looking concerned.

Charlie sank even lower in his seat, until his chin was level with the table. He looked awful, like he'd been up all night.

"Dontwannatalkboutit," he mumbled.

That guy Preston sailed past our table.

"Hey, homo, hands where we can see 'em," he called, laughing.

"Hey, Preston, you're an asshole," Nick called back.

Charlie put his head down on the table and sighed.

"Nick," Sadie said, sounding stern. "Tell us right now."

And so, laughing the entire time, Nick told them.

When he was finished, Marina was grinning, and Sadie was having a hard time keeping it together.

"Just one of the many reasons why it's better to be a girl," Sadie said, which just about killed me, thinking of her doing that.

"The entire floor saw?" Marina said. "Like, *all* of them?"

"Seventy-five percent. Plus Lane and me," Nick said.

"It isn't funny!" Charlie wailed. "And it wasn't even

Nurse Jim, it was Nurse Monica! She's like a mom!"

"She *is* a mom," Nick said. "Her kids are adorable. I've seen pictures."

"Oh, shut up," Charlie said. "I hate this stupid sensor. I wish I could just disable it."

"Actually . . . ," Sadie said, and we all stared at her.

"You know how to turn it off?" Charlie asked eagerly.

Sadie shrugged, exactly the way she did when she tossed a bag of contraband candy onto the bed, or got held after class by Finnegan. Like it wasn't a big deal, and she was trying to play it cool. But the hint of a smile gave her away.

"Of course I do," she said. "Dr. Barons was changing the battery, and mine glitched, so he reset it."

"Can you show me?" Charlie sat up, his eyes wide with excitement.

"It's easy. You just poke a paper clip into the middle hole until it clicks," she said.

"That's amazing." Charlie grinned.

"Great." Nick rolled his eyes. "You've created a monster."

"Hey, I just want to make the most of having my own room," Charlie said. "I share with my kid brother at home, and he's *nine*."

"You think *your* life sucks? I have to go to an all-girls' Catholic school," Marina complained. "With uniforms and nuns. And I'm the only black girl."

Another guy from Charlie's hall walked by the table,

snickering. Charlie sighed, then burst out coughing. It sounded terrible, and at the end of it, he was gasping for breath. He shoved his handkerchief back into his pocket without bothering to look at it, even though it sounded like he'd coughed up blood.

"I'm going back to my room to channel this crap into my music," he said, standing up to bus his tray.

"We have class in ten minutes," I pointed out.

Charlie let out a ridiculously fake high-pitched cough.

"I'm too sick to go," he said, smirking.

ON TUESDAY, MR. Finnegan was waiting for us in French class with a paper bag on his desk and a bowl of mini Halloween candy. He grinned at us when we filed in.

"*Bonjour, classe,*" he called, still smiling. "*Ça va bien? Vous avez passé un bon Halloween?*"

I shot Sadie a questioning look, and she shrugged as if to say she didn't know, either. I'd never seen Finnegan so chipper. And the bowl of candy on his desk was totally bizarre. It was like something in him had woken up, a part of him that remembered that he was a teacher, and we were a French class. Or maybe it was the promise of the protocillin, which, if Sadie's theory was correct, would cure his employment problem.

"We're going to do something different today," Finnegan said. "A game. And the winning team gets this leftover, half-priced Halloween candy. I have a bag of French tongue twisters. Each of you will pick one and read it aloud. If you get it right, your team gets a point. If you get it wrong, your team loses a point."

"What are the teams?" Nick called.

"Does boys against girls seem fair?" Finnegan asked.

We said it did. And then we spent the rest of class trying to pronounce *les virelangues* like *"Ces cerises sont si sûres qu'on ne sait pas si c'en sont"* without messing up.

The girls won, and they triumphantly descended on the candy bowl.

"Homework," Finnegan said while we were packing up.

Everyone paused, and Nick actually snorted, thinking it was a joke.

"Your homework," Finnegan continued, "is to come up with your own *virelangue*. If you want to borrow a French-to-English dictionary, they're on the bookshelf in the back."

We all stared at him, confused.

"Well," he said, shrugging. "If you're going back to high school next semester, you should get used to doing homework. Class dismissed."

CHARLIE HADN'T BEEN in class, and he didn't come to lunch, either, so the four of us ate quickly, then drifted over toward the cottages to check on him.

I didn't blame him for sulking, since a lot of the guys in our dorm still hadn't let it go. Nick said that if the video clip had been girl on girl, Charlie would have been a hero, and I hated that he was probably right.

A frantic ukulele solo spilled through Charlie's window, and we took turns throwing stones through it until the music stopped.

Charlie came to the window. His hair was a mess, and his face was flushed, his eyes glittering feverishly. He stared down at us like he couldn't figure out what we were doing, or even what day it was.

"You alive in there?" Sadie called.

"I'm working," he said, peering down at us. "I need to get this song out before the emotion is gone completely."

He walked away from the window, and we could hear him coughing. A moment later, the music started again.

"Perfect," Marina muttered.

She and Nick went to see if a library computer was free, and I was going to follow them, but Sadie grabbed my hand.

"Everything okay?" I asked.

She'd seemed worried lately, like there was something on her mind that she didn't want to tell me. And I hoped it was just the enormity of going home with tuberculosis-free futures.

"Of course," Sadie said, and I wondered if I was imagining it. "I have a proposition for you."

"I'm listening."

"Wanna sneak a girl into your room?" she asked, grinning.

"Do I ever."

Sadie and I crept up the stairs and onto the third-floor hallway. When I opened the door to my room, you could still hear Charlie's music, the sad, high croon of his voice, and the wild strumming of his ukulele. I couldn't tell if it was any good, but it was certainly heartfelt.

"Sorry," I said. "His room's almost directly below mine."

"It's fine. Just put something on and we'll drown it out," Sadie said, so I started a Belle and Sebastian playlist on my computer.

Sadie surveyed my room with a smirk.

"Were you planning on moving in?" she teased.

"I unpacked!" I said, although it did look pretty temporary.

My room wasn't like Nick's, with all his electronics and action figures, or Charlie's, with his records and weird assortment of musical instruments. I had clothes in the closet and notebooks on my desk, and the picture Sadie had taken of us in the gym printed out and propped against my desk lamp.

She picked it up, smiling.

"Our fake-dance photo," she said.

"That was a pretty good night."

"I almost didn't make it back in time for lights-out," Sadie said.

"Me neither. I had to climb into bed still wearing my tie."

My room was so narrow, and she was standing so close

to me in those tight, dark jeans of hers that I could barely concentrate on anything else.

"Well, if we'd had more time . . . ," I said, and then I kissed her.

Her lips were soft and warm and tasted like coconut, and her leg wrapped around the back of mine, and it was so sexy that I couldn't take it, I just wanted to press her against me until there wasn't any space between where I began and where she ended.

"You're going to set off my med sensor," I teased.

"Well, lying down lowers your heart rate," Sadie suggested innocently.

She smiled up at me, all mischief through her eyelashes. God, I wanted to throw her on the bed. I wanted to do everything I thought about when I was alone in my room with my evil little med sensor, going slow.

"So?" she said. "What do you think?"

What did I think?

"Yeah, that would be cool," I said, and Sadie laughed at me for pretending I wasn't completely freaking out.

She sat down on the edge of my bed, and I was like, "It's bigger at home."

I don't know why I said it, because it made Sadie almost die laughing.

"Um, I don't think that's how anatomy works?"

"I meant my *bed*," I said, humiliated. "And my room,

which actually has posters up, and a view of—"

And then I didn't say anything else because she was kissing me, and it was all I could do to take terrified yoga breaths through the whole amazing thing.

CHAPTER EIGHTEEN

SADIE

AS THE DAYS went on, I began to accept that Latham wouldn't last forever. And I wondered if maybe I could be something of my Latham self after I went home. I didn't have to go back to my old high school. I could always transfer to another one, or to an arts high school, or get my GED and be done with it.

Part of it was Lane, with his unflagging optimism about the future, and his determination not to miss out on anything. And part of it was having an answer to the question of how much sand was left in my hourglass, and how many plans I could realistically make.

I tried to picture all of us in a few years, sitting in some late-night diner over winter break and catching up on each other's lives. Charlie with his music, and Marina with her fashion, Nick already building his business empire, and Lane, all collegiate, and still looking at me like I was the person he wanted to see most in the world. Maybe it was possible, and I'd study photography at some art school in San Francisco, near Stanford. Maybe Lane and I would drive to the diner together.

There was another collection on Friday, and Nick came with me, I suppose because he knew I'd "accidentally" forget his alcohol if he didn't. It was cold that night, and dark, with almost no moon. The woods didn't feel dark so much as thick, and finding a path through them was a challenge.

Nick didn't say anything until we were halfway there, and then he sighed, loudly.

"What?" I asked.

"So you and Lane," he said.

"That's not a sentence, an opinion, or a question," I told him.

He snorted, clearly not amused.

"Well, good luck with that," he said.

"What are you talking about?"

"You're not actually thinking you'll stay together after Latham, are you?" He said it with this wide-eyed concern, but I could see right through him to his trembling, jealous little soul.

"Maybe. What's it to you?"

"I just don't want to see you get hurt."

"Wow, thanks for the concern," I said. "You're such a good friend."

I hadn't meant it to come out as sarcastically as it did, but it was too late now. Nick scowled at me in the moonlight.

"I never wanted to be friends," Nick muttered.

"Well, haven't you heard?" I said. "Life is full of disappointments. I'm sorry you didn't get the chance to check my name off your fuck-it list."

"Is that what you think I wanted?" Nick asked, shocked. "I thought you knew."

Knew what? I wondered as his expression softened. And then he pulled me toward him, going for a kiss.

"Get off!" I said, pushing him away. "I can't believe you!"

"Sorry," Nick said, embarrassed. "I'm really sorry."

"Nick Patel, you can be a real buttpocket," I told him.

"Just forget it happened," he said. "Please."

"Fine," I said. "Whatever."

We'd reached the place where we usually met Michael, but he hadn't arrived yet. So I stood around seething at Nick and wishing he'd get over himself. Or, I guessed, over me.

After a minute, I heard leaves crunching in the distance, and then the beam of a flashlight passed across a nearby tree trunk. It was Michael, carrying our stuff.

"Sorry," he said, doing this combination cough and sniffle thing. "Not feeling that great. You have the money?"

Nick handed over the envelope, and Michael counted it out. He charged us triple, and while paying thirty dollars for a ten-dollar bottle of vodka wasn't a bargain, it was the only option. I guess Nick and I were supposed to mark things up even more and take a commission, but we never did. Well, except for the people we couldn't stand. Genevieve's Milk Duds had cost her five bucks a box.

"Looks good," Michael said, stashing the envelope in his jacket. "I'll see you in two weeks."

"Yep," I said.

"You kids stay out of trouble now." He stared straight at me while he said that last part, like it was a warning.

MARINA'S BIRTHDAY WAS on Saturday. She was turning seventeen, the youngest of our group, and we'd always joked with her about it when we watched R-rated movies or smuggled Nick's booze, even though none of us were old enough for that.

I always hated having my birthdays at Latham House, because I wondered if anyone actually cared that it was my birthday, or if they were just so relieved that I'd made it another year. This was Marina's first birthday at Latham House, and she'd missed the awkwardness of what it had been like for Nick and Charlie and me. But we gave her our tradition anyway.

We stuck an unlit candle in a plate of pancakes and sang to her at breakfast.

"Happy birthday, dear Marina, happy birthday to you!" we finished.

"And many morrrre, since there's a cureeeee," Charlie added, before coughing into his handkerchief. His notebook was out, and his eyes were glittering like he'd been up all night slamming contraband energy drinks.

"How's the music?" I asked.

"It's good," Charlie said. "Yeah, I'll let you guys hear it soon."

"We can already hear it," Lane reminded him. "Open windows, remember?"

"That's just the bare bones," Charlie said. "I'm doing the whole thing on the computer, adding in different layers with virtual instruments and stuff. You'll see."

"Oh really, *that's* what you're doing on the computer?" Nick said, and we all laughed.

"Shut up," Charlie muttered. "I'm trying to create a legacy here. There's a specific energy to different moments, and once you lose it, it can't be recaptured. You've got to record it, or you've got nothing."

He stood up to bus his tray.

"Where are you going?" Nick asked.

"To keep working," Charlie said.

And then he stalked off.

MARINA INSISTED ON having a birthday party that night, and the plan was to sneak out of the dorms and rendezvous in the woods for some late-night revelry. We'd meet at the dried-up creek bed a little bit west of the rock. It was far enough from Latham that flashlights wouldn't be visible, but not too deep in. The theme was a toga party, and the plan was to bring our bedsheets. We could just stick them in the contaminated laundry chute, for bloodstained sheets, so it didn't matter if we ruined them.

Marina and I spent the afternoon with craft glue and leaves, attempting to make laurel crowns for the party. Mostly, we just wound up ruining our manicures, since the craft glue got everywhere and refused to dry. In the end, we had to staple the leaves together, which took about thirty seconds and made us feel like idiots for not thinking of it in the first place.

That night, Marina and I went through the routine of putting on our pajamas, just to make it feel even more illicit, and then we went back to our rooms and waited for the hall nurse to come check.

Lane called, which he usually did.

"So, what are you wearing?" he asked.

"Lane!"

"I mean under your toga."

"Mm-hmm, sure," I teased.

"Although, come to think of it, what are you wearing?"

I giggled, and then I heard footsteps in the hall.

"It's the nurse," I said. "Wear jeans and a hoodie. I'll see you later."

And then I hung up and tried to look innocent.

"You're running a bit of a fever, hon," Nurse Heather said. "I'm gonna give you this."

She handed me an aspirin, and I rolled my eyes and gulped it down.

"You're a champ," she said, reaching for the light switch. "Sleep well now."

Which, obviously, I didn't.

Marina knocked on my door an hour later, wearing her backpack.

"Ready to go?" she whispered.

I grabbed mine and flipped up my hood, and we snuck down the dark hallway together. The dorm echoed with coughing, and I wondered if I coughed in my sleep, too, and if it sounded that bad.

It wasn't hard to get out of the dorms after lights-out, just a little inconvenient. The doors locked, but the windows didn't. So all you had to do was slip out the window that led onto the back porch, and then jump down onto the grass. I couldn't remember the last time we'd properly snuck out. The real thing, not just snuck into the boys' dorm before lights-out.

Marina and I wiggled out the window and jumped off the porch, and then, in the thin light of the moon, we crept across the grass and into the woods.

I switched on my flashlight as soon as I dared, illuminating the tree trunks and the thick, moldering leaves that covered the ground. I loved the woods best in the summer. They felt warm and welcoming, with golden shafts of light filtering through the trees. But the woods were changing now that it was November. They felt cold and bleak, almost like they were dying.

It was farther than I'd remembered to the clearing, and somehow the woods were darker that night, wet and thick with the scent of decay.

Marina and I were the first ones to arrive. We took our sheets out of our backpacks and tried to fasten them into togas, which we probably should have practiced. Lane arrived just after we finished pinning them. Relief washed over him when he saw us.

"I thought I was lost," he said.

"First star to the right, and then straight on till morning," I said.

"Not a lost boy, lost in the woods." Lane shook his head, grinning. "Happy birthday, Marina."

"Thank you," she said, giving her toga a twirl. "Welcome to Toga Night. We're going to party like Jay Gatsby."

Lane snorted.

"What?" I asked.

"Well, no one wants to party like Jay Gatsby," he explained. "Because he doesn't even attend his own parties. When he does, he just stands there, sober and unhappy and waiting for a girl who never arrives."

Marina made a face.

"He's right," I said apologetically.

"Fine," Marina said. "We're going to party like guests at one of Jay Gatsby's parties, but not like Jay Gatsby himself."

"Yes, we'll party like nameless minor characters in a novel about someone else," I agreed.

"Perfect," Marina said. "The theme for my party is both togas and forgettable literary characters from misunderstood classics."

Lane shook his head over the two of us.

"Mind helping me get this thing on?" he asked, holding up his bedsheet with a pleading look.

I'd never realized how intimate it was to wrap a sheet around a boy, how my hands would hover in all the wrong places, and how he'd smile at me the whole time, like we were both enjoying a private joke too dirty to say out loud.

"Toga! Toga!" Nick chanted.

I was still pinning Lane's, and Nick was like, "Look at you two, between the sheets."

"Hilarious," I said. "Want Marina to help with yours?"

"I can do it myself," Nick said, and then draped the sheet around his neck like a cape.

"You look ridiculous," Marina told him.

"Who has a toga party in the woods? *That's* ridiculous," Nick shot back.

"Well, next year, you can have one at your lame engineering frat," Marina teased.

Small, casual comments about the future weren't usual at Latham, and it still felt weird to hear people making them. To hear my friends joking not just about going home but also about growing up.

"I will," Nick said. "And it'll be awesome!"

He opened his backpack and took out a bottle of rum, presenting it to Marina with a flourish.

"Happy birthday," he said.

"Thank you, Captain Boozypants."

It was actually sweet of him. Although we only had lemonade as a mixer, so the drinks were going to taste interesting.

"Should we wait for Charlie?" Marina asked, twisting the top off the Captain Morgan like she really didn't want to.

"Hell no, he oversleeps, it's his loss," Nick said.

We put on the laurel crowns, which actually came out pretty great. The boys fetched rocks and sticks, and we had Nick build up a campfire, since he'd been a wilderness scout.

Marina had brought a bongo drum she'd borrowed off one of the hippie boys, and we swilled the rum, and took turns drumming the bongo, and danced around the fire in our togas. At first it felt stupid, but after more rum, and more drumming, the woods seemed to spin like we were about to rocket off the planet and launch our tiny, contained world straight into outer space.

"Hey, come here," Lane said, pulling me away from the fire.

We ducked behind a tree, and the not-too-distant firelight made the woods seem to flicker. Lane looked so handsome in his toga that I wished I'd brought my camera to capture it. Then he cupped my face in his hands, and instead of taking a picture, I settled for stealing a kiss.

Our lips were sweet and sticky from the rum, and I could taste a faint hint of his toothpaste, and something about that melted me. I kissed him like there was no tomorrow, like all we had was this moment in the woods, even though that wasn't true. We were seventeen, and we'd graduate high school and go off to college and grow old and boring and tell stories about when we were young and sick and falling in love. Being at Latham didn't mean what it used to. The rules, the treatment system, all of it was just a ceremony now, just a way to waste time until the first batch of protocillin was ready. And maybe we could be *Pride and Prejudice*, with a happy ending, with neither of us burying, or forgetting, the other.

"You know how much I adore you, right?" Lane said.

"I'm crazy about you, too," I said, leaning my forehead against his chest.

I wished that we were brave enough to use the real word, instead of deliberately choosing the wrong one. But we had time to gather our nerves. We had so much time.

We went back to the group and joined the dancing again. The four of us spun and twirled in our togas, and the fire crackled, and we laughed, getting more than a little drunk. And even though the woods were dark, we were this tiny, perfect circle of light.

"I'm going to miss you guys," Marina said, stopping to catch her breath.

"Don't say that," I told her. "You're not allowed to mourn the future."

Lane, who was drumming on the bongo, stopped.

"Isn't that all we do, though?" he asked.

"Keep bongo!" I insisted, a bit tipsy.

Lane started drumming again, a soft patter.

"I mean it," he said. "We mourn the future because it's easier than admitting that we're miserable in the present."

The combination of his pattering on the drum, and the intensity with which he said that, made it sound like a spoken-word poem, and I thought about it for a moment, probably more seriously than I should have.

"Then maybe we're not mourning the future," I said. "Maybe we're mourning ourselves."

"Okay, no more rum for you," Nick said, taking the bottle away from me and sloshing it. "Crap, it's almost out."

The woods were still spinning, even though we weren't anymore, and we were all pretty drunk. And I wasn't sure if it was the rum or the late hour, but I was suddenly so cold, and so exhausted, and so ready to be in bed, as opposed to just bedsheet.

"Is Charlie really not coming?" Marina asked.

"He probably fell asleep," Lane said, yawning.

But yawns, like tuberculosis, are contagious. And soon everyone had caught his.

"Lane!" I accused.

"Sorry," he said. "It's the rum. Clearly I'd be a terrible pirate."

We packed up our things, and Nick kicked dirt over our fire.

"Should we take these off?" Lane asked, motioning toward his toga.

"Leave them on," Marina said, so we did.

"No one takes off their togas until we're back at the dorms," I warned. "Or you are a suckbeast. Nick is already a suckbeast because his is a cape."

"You never said toga, you just said to wear your bed-sheet," Nick complained.

"Yeah, to a *toga party*," Marina said.

We set off in the direction of the cottages, exhausted and still wearing our togas.

Lane slipped his hand into mine.

"Hi," he said.

"Hi back," I said, smiling at him.

He looked so amazing in his toga, with his floppy hair and the crown of leaves, like he'd walked out of the Greek Acropolis, or whatever it was called. Like there was a statue of him somewhere, in marble, missing its private parts.

"You're cute," I said.

"You're drunk," Lane said.

"Which is the only time you're cute, otherwise you're a potato."

I giggled. God, I really was drunk.

To my left, a twig snapped loudly. My heart sped up, and I swung my flashlight beam around, but it was just one of those silver rabbits the woods were full of, its eyes luminous in the dark.

"Nothing," I said.

"I wish Charlie had come," Lane said.

"I do, too." I squeezed his hand, and we squelched through a particularly muddy pile of leaves. Our sheets were going to be ruined.

Marina and Nick had veered a little off course, and I called out to them.

"Hey, is it muddy over where you are?"

But they didn't answer. They were stopped, still as stone, and in the beam of my flashlight, they were the ones who looked like statues.

"Hello?" I called, shining my flashlight at Marina.

The look on her face was devastating.

"Sadie—" she choked out.

Something was wrong. I knew it as Lane and I ran toward them, our togas dragging and ripping on rocks and branches. We coughed as we ran, but we didn't stop running. I guess that's what people mean about racing toward disaster, how in the last moments before everything comes crashing down, you never walk.

And then I saw what they were staring at.

Not what, who.

It was Charlie, his body unnaturally splayed in the leaves.

CHAPTER NINETEEN
LANE

IT WAS AS though we'd stepped into a nightmare. We shone our flashlights down on Charlie's body, barely registering that it was real. The white fabric of his bedsheet was tangled around him, splattered with bright-red arterial blood. There was blood smeared around his mouth, and he was so still, lying on the carpet of rotting leaves.

I didn't say anything. I couldn't say anything. I stood there in horror, not fully processing the enormity of what had happened.

"Charlie—" Sadie wailed. She got to her knees, shaking him. "Come on, Charlie! You're okay, come on. Please!"

He wasn't okay, though. Any of us could see that.

"Is he . . . ?" Marina asked, but she already knew. We all did.

Nick went pale and staggered away, and we could hear him vomiting.

We were drunk, and cold, and covered in mud, with

bedsheets pinned over our clothes. And until that moment, it had all seemed so silly. The sneaking out, the woods, our trips into town, the nurse barging in on Charlie with his pants down. We'd been playing a game where we hadn't quite believed the stakes. But I believed them then, staring down at the first corpse I'd ever seen, the first person I'd known who had died.

"He can't be dead; his sensor would have gone off!" Sadie insisted. She reached for his wrist, and at first I thought she was taking his pulse, but then she pushed up his sleeve.

The light on his sensor wasn't green, or flashing yellow in warning. There was no light on his sensor at all. It was just a black silicone band.

"That's why no one came," Sadie said. "Because Charlie had his sensor off!"

The enormity of what that meant washed over me, and I felt my stomach sour and twist, like I might be sick as well. We'd joked about Charlie's sensor in the dining hall, laughing at him when it had gone off, instead of being concerned. And now it was too late to be concerned. Now it was too late to be anything except sorry.

While we'd danced around the fire in our togas, and beat our drum, and thrown back our booze, Charlie had lain there dying. Alone. In the woods.

I didn't realize I was crying until I tried to put a hand on Sadie's shoulder to steady her, and found that I was trembling as well. I swallowed thickly and glanced over at Marina, who looked as distraught as I felt.

Nick staggered back, pale and sweating.

"Fuck, Charlie, you don't turn off your sensor! You don't ever do that, you hear me?" Nick said.

But of course Charlie didn't hear him. The dead never listen when you want to tell them anything.

Charlie wasn't supposed to be dead. None of us were. Not now that they'd announced a vaccine, and what we had was curable. We were supposed to be cured, all of us, with medication that would be ready in four short weeks.

It hadn't occurred to me that some of us might not have four weeks left.

"This is my fault," Sadie said, blinking back tears. "I showed him how to shut off his sensor. I didn't think anything would happen."

"None of us did," I said, wondering how Sadie could think that.

"Charlie was really sick," Nick said. "We all knew he was doing the worst of any of us."

"Having the worst symptoms doesn't mean anything," Marina said. "We never saw his charts or his X-rays. Sometimes people seem really healthy, and then they die. And sometimes they seem sick, and then they just *go home*."

I'd had too much to drink. We all had. The woods were spinning in this uncomfortable, dizzying way, and I tried to steady myself by putting my hand against a tree, but it was slick with sap. The woods no longer felt like our sanctuary. They were dark, and twisted, and full of phantoms. Now I knew why everyone else stayed within the narrow confines of Latham, only venturing up the well-marked path on afternoon nature walks.

The whole night had taken on this strange, nightmarish tone, and I struggled to believe any of it. Any moment, I expected to wake up back in my dorm room, my heart pounding and my T-shirt clammy, wondering what the hell was wrong with my subconscious.

"If we're the only ones who know, we have to tell someone," I said. "A nurse. Someone who'll know what to do."

Everyone stared at me like I'd suggested calling the police.

"We *can't*," Nick said, his voice cracking.

"Nick's right," Sadie said. "No one can know we found him here."

There was a terrible silence where we were all thinking the same thing.

"So we just go back inside?" Marina asked.

"Yes," Sadie said. "We go back inside, and climb into bed, and in the morning, when Charlie isn't at breakfast, they'll look for him."

"We can't just leave him here," I said.

"Yes, we can." Nick's expression dared me to argue. "Unless you can think of a better option?"

"Maybe a nurse would understand," Marina said.

"Understand *what?*" Nick said angrily. "Do *you* want to tell Dr. Barons that we all decided to sneak out and get super drunk in the woods, and oh yeah, Charlie turned off his med sensor and died, but we weren't with him or anything, which we can't prove, but we found his body and can take you to it, and please don't punish us for breaking, like, every rule at Latham House that actually matters."

When he said it like that, it sounded terrible. Like we'd been up to something awful. Like it was our fault.

"But they can't really punish us, can they?" I asked.

They all stared at me like they couldn't believe they had to spell it out.

"Are you *kidding?*" Nick said. "We get kicked out of here, we're out of the drug trial."

The drug trial. It was one of the reasons my parents had sent me to Latham, after all, instead of one of the cheaper, public places. Instead of the holistic hot springs, or the homeopathic place where everyone slept in yurts and farmed their own kale. Latham gave us med sensors, and sent that data to researchers, and it put us at the top of the treatment list for any experimental drug trials. Like the one for protocillin.

Nick was right, and we all knew it.

"Okay," Marina said. "So we walk away."

"We walk away," I agreed.

"Like we were never here," Sadie said hoarsely.

"Like we have no idea Charlie isn't asleep in his room,"

Nick said. "None of us gets in trouble, and in a couple of hours, it will all be over."

Except that's the thing about dying, or experiencing death. It happens, but it's never over. So we stood there one final moment together. And then, slowly, regretfully, we walked away.

I WOKE THE next morning convinced it had been a bad dream. And then I looked down at the tangle of mud-streaked sheets, and at my filthy sneakers, and was horrified to realize it had actually happened.

It was early, and Sunday, which meant breakfast began slightly later than usual. My head was pounding, and my mouth tasted terrible, but I dragged myself out of bed. I put my sheets down the contaminated laundry chute and rinsed my sneakers in the shower.

Breakfast was an ordeal. I don't know how any of us managed to act normally. We were all pale and gray from the alcohol, and just the sight of pancakes and eggs made my stomach churn unpleasantly. But I piled my tray high, because I didn't know what I'd do if Linda made me go back through. And then the four of us sat around our table, wan and silent, while the rest of the dining hall talked and laughed and hummed with energy.

Nick stood up early to bus his tray.

"We should head back," he said, staring at me. "We have to do that thing."

I followed him over to the tray return, and across the grass, and back into Cottage 6. He didn't say anything. And he didn't have to. I knew what we were doing—cleaning up before the lockout.

One night in the dorms, Nick had been talking about how, in the army, when a soldier dies, the other soldiers wipe all the porn off his computer before it's returned to his family.

"You'd do it for me, right?" Nick had said. And we'd all agreed that yeah, we'd do it for each other. It had seemed like a joke, the way everything did then, when we did what we wanted because nothing bad ever happened. But now the joke was on us.

It felt wrong going into Charlie's room without his permission, like the room was still his, instead of just filled with his things.

"You check his computer, I'll see if I can find his stick," Nick said.

I told him that sounded good, and then I went over and woke up Charlie's computer. The whole thing had been restored to the original settings, with the generic outer space background.

"Nick?" I said.

Nick was holding a shoe box, an unreadable expression on his face.

"I've got everything," he said.

"That fast?"

"It's all here. Let's go," Nick said.

We went back to his room and set the box on his bed. It had *PROPERTY OF NIKHIL PATEL* written across the top in black Sharpie, but I recognized it as Charlie's handwriting immediately.

"What's in it?" I asked.

Nick lifted the lid. Inside was a stack of Moleskine notebooks, a bag of peanut butter M&M's, an iPod, and two USB sticks. One was suspiciously titled "Math Homework," and the other was labeled "Gone to His Narrow Bed— Charlie Moreau."

Nick picked up the second USB stick and popped it into his computer.

It was an album. Charlie's album. With hand-drawn and meticulously inked cover art. He'd finished it.

Nick pressed play, and for a moment, nothing happened, and then a familiar melody drifted from Nick's speakers. I'd heard Charlie play this song so many times, but the finished version sounded different. It was darker, and richer, and full of anguish.

He sang about getting sick, and about making art, and about time, how we never had enough of it. I closed my eyes and listened, my heart breaking with each track.

"I am a grave man, children play in my graveyard/ skipping stones on headstones/It's time to rest these too young bones/If anyone asks, I've gone to my narrow bed."

The last song finished, and when I opened my eyes, I

was crying, and Nick was, too.

"Fuck," he said, sniffling. "All that time I thought he was writing love songs to One Direction."

I laughed, and then felt horrible about it. But there was something about the box that was bothering me. Charlie had spent the last few weeks working almost constantly on his music, with an intensity I hadn't understood. He'd skipped class, barely left his room, hardly eaten anything. . . .

"Do you think Charlie knew?" I asked.

"That he didn't have much time?"

I nodded.

"Yeah," Nick said finally. "I do. I just think he didn't want us to worry about him, since we'd all started talking about going home and stuff."

We were silent a moment, considering it.

"He left that box right there, on his bed," Nick said. "So we'd find it when we went into his room for our army mission. It's like he wanted to make it easy for us."

"Then why the notebooks, and the music?" I asked. "Why wipe his computer if he kept all the X-rated stuff on a stick?"

"Haven't you ever thought about it?" Nick asked. "What you want to leave behind, and what you don't?"

"Not really."

It had never occurred to me that I had anything to leave behind at all. Everything I'd done had been focused on the future, on impressing college admissions officers, but it was just empty paper. Just numbers and letters on a transcript and a list of clubs I'd belonged to.

I remembered what Charlie had said about shutting down his Facebook, as a preemptive strike against it turning into a memorial wall. About needing to finish his music. About trying to create a legacy, because if he didn't record his songs, he'd have nothing to leave behind.

"If he knew he was that sick, why didn't he just stay in bed last night?" I asked.

"Would you?" Nick said, and for a moment I didn't understand what he was saying. And then, horribly, I did.

Charlie hadn't wanted to pass away in the hospital ward, wasting his last days waiting to die instead of spending them living. And he hadn't wanted to die in his bed, beeping, while the whole dorm woke up and crowded the hallway to see what was going on.

We'd gone into the woods, and he'd known that, but he didn't have anyone else. He'd turned off his sensor so he wouldn't get caught, and he'd gone to find us. He just hadn't made it.

There was nothing we could have done. No way we could have known. Because he hadn't wanted us to know, not until right at the end, and then, it had been too late.

"You'd think if there was a god that Charlie would have had five more minutes to come find us," I said.

Nick shook his head. "It makes me so sad that I'm not even sad anymore, I'm just angry. Dr. Barons said we'd be cured. He didn't say we'd be cured *if* we all lived six more weeks, but heads-up, guys, some of you might not live that long."

Nick was sitting on the floor, his back against the wardrobe, and he pulled his knees and arms in, curling himself into a ball.

"Maybe he thought it was the right thing, giving everyone hope," I said.

"Maybe he's just an asshole," Nick muttered. "I knew it was too good to be true that we'd all go home and have fucking *Skype chats*. Four weeks till the cure, a hundred and forty-nine of us to go."

Nick got up, pulled a water bottle of vodka out of his desk drawer, and took a swig.

"Want some?" he asked, coughing.

I shook my head, and Nick lifted the bottle in salute.

"To Charlie," he toasted. "For finishing his art."

CHAPTER TWENTY

SADIE

I WATCHED FROM my window as the nurses and doctors scurried back and forth in the overcast morning, frantically searching for Charlie. I tried to pretend I was backstage at a play, watching the chaos as everyone scrambled around before curtain, but part of me knew that I wasn't. That all our games and jokes had finally twisted into something serious and terrible.

I hadn't been able to sleep. I'd just sat there watching the sky and listening to this one bird that didn't understand it was night, and wondering if I'd ever sleep again. I was terrified of what I'd dream, of whose corpses I'd conjure up when I closed my eyes.

It was all my fault. Charlie was dead because of me. I hadn't meant for it to happen, but that didn't make it any less true. I'd just wanted to show off about the med sensor, but if I'd thought about it, I would have realized it was a terrible idea.

Charlie had always been sicker than the rest of us. We'd never made a big deal about it, because that sort of thing could change in an instant. Any week, one of us could have come back from an appointment with Dr. Barons, our face ashen as we moved our things to the hospital wing for round-the-clock care, and our parents were summoned, and we were given a pain pump instead of an aspirin. Any week, one of us could have come back from the same appointment with a copy of our latest chest X-ray and a release date.

I'd been waiting for the latter to happen. For the people I cared about to leave me behind, one by one, like I was an imaginary friend they'd outgrown. I wasn't prepared for any of us to leave the other way, with the doors locking behind us, and a hearse driving quietly through the back gate.

We were the ones who got dressed in the morning, who stole internet and staged photo shoots in the woods during naptime, who hid phones in our beds after lights-out and snuck into town to get coffee. We weren't the ones who died here. We couldn't be.

Everyone in the dining hall stared at our table during lunch. They all knew, or they guessed. Charlie had missed two meals, and the nurses had been running into the woods all morning, and where Charlie Moreau had once sat, there was now a definite ripple.

I stared down at the sandwich and fruit cup and salad on my plate, because I knew I should eat them, even though I wasn't hungry. I could feel Charlie's empty chair at the edge of my vision, and I wanted so badly for him to sit there bent over his notebook, scribbling away. I wanted to hear the high strum of a ukulele coming from his window as I walked back to the cottages. I wanted him to play me a record with this huge grin on his face, delighted by the antiquated technology. I wanted him to dress up in eyeliner and velvet again, and to do his spot-on impression of Dr. Barons, asking us to rate our pain on a scale from one to ten.

Except right now I didn't want to rate my pain. I wanted to rate my grief. And there wasn't a number high enough.

I left lunch early and went back to my room, collapsing onto my bed in tears. I cried until it made me cough, and when I took my handkerchief away from my mouth, it was stained with blood. I was surprised, but I wasn't. I hadn't been taking care of myself. None of us had. We'd rolled our eyes and skipped rest periods and stayed up late and drunk Nick's booze.

It was no wonder Charlie had gotten so sick. Oh God, Charlie.

The memory of last night seared through me, and I curled up in a ball, clutching that horrible handkerchief, and cried some more. I knew Natalie Zhang would be able to hear it through the wall, but I didn't care. I cried for the way Charlie had died, and I cried that I hadn't gotten a chance to say good-bye, and I cried that the last thing I'd said to him was, "You better not oversleep." I cried because, while Charlie was dying alone in the woods, I was so close, pressed up against a tree with Lane, kissing him like nothing else in the world mattered except how the two of us felt about each other, and naively thinking how wonderful it was that all of us had so much time.

DR. BARONS CAME into the dining hall that night to make an announcement: med sensors were not to be turned off or tampered with. To make sure that our sensors were working properly, nurses would periodically access our data throughout the day and night. Furthermore, all ground-floor windows in the dormitories would be fitted with bug screens.

There was a collective groan as Dr. Barons exited the dining hall. It felt like everything had fallen apart, like I'd blinked, just for a moment, and when I'd opened my eyes I was surrounded by ruins.

I stalked off to bus my tray, and Lane followed me.

"Sadie, wait," he called.

He looked terrible. We all did, I guessed, except now it worried me in a way it hadn't for weeks. I couldn't tell if the dark circles under his eyes were serious, or if his cough sounded worse. And I hated that I wasn't looking at Lane with a melty feeling in my stomach, that instead I was scanning him for symptoms.

I slotted my tray into the return.

"What?"

"I haven't seen you all day," he said.

"I haven't wanted to see anyone all day."

"Not even me?" he asked, biting his lip and staring at me adorably.

I wished he wasn't so cute when he did that. I wished he'd already gone home and left me behind without calling. I wished I didn't have a fever, and he didn't look so tired, and we hadn't just eaten dinner while brooding over a friend's death.

I hated that I was in love and grieving, because I didn't know how to be both. It was just too much. Too many things that could go wrong. And there was too much potential pain for us to keep going.

I don't know what made me do it, except some combination of sorrow and anger and the stupid fever I couldn't get rid of, and the feeling of everyone at Latham staring at our table in that awful hushed way, but I sighed and shook my head.

"Sorry," I said. And then I fled the dining hall.

FINNEGAN HAD GIVEN us homework, but I'd completely forgotten about it. We were supposed to write a poem or something, and I felt so embarrassed when everyone else took out theirs. I'd been out of school so long that it felt strange having homework. I wondered if bereavement was an excuse, although at Latham, probably not.

And then Finnegan came in, looking as miserable as I felt. Wordlessly, he set down his coffee, picked up a whiteboard marker, and scribbled an assignment. *Chapter 15, exercises 8 and 9.*

"You can leave when you finish, no need to hand it in," he said.

With a sip from his mug, he was out the door.

"What the heck?" Nick muttered. "I thought we were doing poems."

"I did, too," Marina said. "Whatever happened to 'you need to be prepared for high school'?"

"What do you think?" I said bitterly. "Homework adds unnecessary stress. Finnegan wouldn't want any of us accidentally getting sick from his French assignments."

Lane sighed. He was staring at me again in this pleading, can-we-talk way, but I pretended I didn't see.

I didn't know what to say. Now that there was news of a cure, everything at Latham felt different. It wasn't the same "we can treat the symptoms but not the disease, so if you're feeling tired, how about a rest" bullshit that Dr. Barons had always pushed. No doctors would ever say that again. Now there was this frantic new undercurrent of "let's just keep everyone alive until the protocillin arrives," as though any of us could keel over at any moment, and it would somehow be fifty times more tragic than if we'd done it a month ago.

GRIEF IS A strange thing. I'd thought, for the longest time, that being at Latham was a constant grieving for an answer.

Live or die. Return home or succumb. But it wasn't grief at all. It was fear.

I knew at least that much after Charlie died. Because I could hardly breathe through the pain of thinking about what had happened, but underneath that, I was so, so scared that there were more casualties to come. That I'd gotten too attached to the idea of us, of Nick and Lane and Marina and Charlie and me as being untouchable, while the invisible hand of tuberculosis hovered there, drumming its fingers impatiently.

I remembered the look on Dr. Barons's face when he'd pulled up my X-rays, and the way Lane's cheeks had seemed flushed at dinner, and how Marina sometimes walked away when she had a coughing fit, so we couldn't hear how bad it was, and how I knew Nick skipped the contraband collections because he often went to the nurse's station for narcotics.

The saying at Latham was "Welcome to the rotation," but the unspoken second half of that phrase was "you can exit through either of two doors." I'd always had a theory which door would be mine, but I'd been careful not to make predictions for anyone else.

Lane called me every night, and every night I ignored him, turning away from the ringing phone and turning up the volume on my music. I knew it was a bad plan, but I didn't know what else to do. The idea of giggling and flirting after what had happened struck me as horrible. It was like something in me had snapped. I could feel my emotions floating there, just beneath the surface, but I couldn't access them. All I could get was numb, and horrified, and occasionally angry.

But I couldn't avoid Lane's calls forever. You can't end a relationship by ignoring it, you can only hurt the other person's feelings and make the inevitable breakup even worse. It was like Lane had said that night so long ago in the gazebo: being someone's ex isn't an existing condition you find out about later, it's something you know about the moment it happens to you.

And so, on Thursday, I called him.

"Hello?" he said after the third ring, his voice uncertain.

"It's me," I said.

"I'm so glad." I could hear his smile, and I wished he didn't do that. I wished he could just talk to me without sounding like I was the one person he wanted to talk to more than anyone. Without making me feel so guilty.

I took a deep breath, trying to summon my courage. I didn't want to do this. I hated myself for doing this. But I had to.

"Lane," I said softly, "I can't do this anymore."

Lane waited, unsure.

"Do what?" he said.

"We can't be together," I explained.

It was very, very quiet on his end.

"We can't, or you don't want to?" Lane finally asked.

"Both," I said.

"I'm sorry."

"You're sorry?" I asked, confused.

"I'm sorry, but I don't accept your breakup. Meet me in the gazebo of sadness and breakups."

"It's almost—"

"We have twenty minutes, so you better hurry," he said, hanging up.

I put on a coat over my pajamas and smoothed my ponytail, and when I got to the gazebo, he was already there, slouched on the stairs.

"What's going on?" he asked.

I sat down next to him, and we stared out at the woods, and I felt sick over them, like they were full of corpses. I glanced over at Lane, and he looked so beautiful, his cheeks pink in the cold, his hair in need of a trim, the way he sat with his fingers curled, like he was clutching something tiny and secret in his palm.

Latham felt like a shipwreck, and I didn't know how many places there were in the lifeboats. I wanted both of us to be okay if we turned around and found we had the last seat. So I was shutting us down preemptively, before the pain became too much to bear.

"We can't be together," I said, trying not to cry. "We hooked up, and it was great, but it's like summer camp. These things never work in the real world."

Lane was quiet a moment, and still.

"I thought I was going to drive to your house with bagels when we got out. And we'd text. And we'd make it work," he said.

"But it *won't* work," I said angrily. "You'll go home and want to catch up on your schoolwork so you can graduate on time, and it won't be worth driving for hours to see me when you're going away to college in the fall."

"Of course it will be worth it," Lane said.

"You're just saying that because you're nice."

"I'm saying that because it's true," Lane insisted.

"What, so we can have breakfast? So I can tell you about how fun it is being the oldest person in my classes and the only one who doesn't know how to drive?" I asked.

"It wouldn't be like that."

"It might be. You get your life back, but I don't."

"But I don't *want* my life back," Lane said. "I wasn't even using it. I was just . . . waiting for everything to be different. Except I was the same me when I got to Latham that I'd always been. I didn't want to change, but I did. And now I want to figure it out as I go. But I know that I want you to be in it."

He looked so earnest in the moonlight. Like he really believed the world was this place where good things happened to good people, and anything to the contrary was an accident.

I wished I'd never let it get this far. I'd always been fine on my own. And I'd be fine on my own again. Now, if we broke up, it would just be that. A breakup. You don't mourn a breakup. At least, I didn't think you did, having never personally experienced one.

"Well, I don't want you in my life anymore," I said, feeling myself crumble. I was crying because it wasn't true, and because it was. And because I'd been right to be skeptical of happy endings and love stories where no one got hurt. Someone always gets hurt. But what no one ever tells you is that you can get hurt more than once.

So I stood up and walked back inside, away from the one boy who made me feel like I wasn't alone, because he was the one person I couldn't stand to lose, or disappoint, or watch fall out of love with me when I stepped out of Latham and transformed back into a potato.

CHAPTER TWENTY-ONE
LANE

SADIE IGNORED ME the next day. We sat at the same table in the dining hall and everything, but with just the four of us, there was lots of room to space out, so it was me and Nick, and Marina and Sadie, with the empty chairs between us. We'd been a group once, but Sadie's and my breakup had thoroughly wrecked that. The awkward, thick silence that had settled over our table since Charlie's death seemed to close up, sealing us inside in permanent misery.

I spent that weekend alone in my room, reading old books from the library. I was on this Vonnegut kick, which seemed to fit my mood. He had this dark, awful sense of humor that was just about perfect, and he wrote about war and death and tragedy in this irreverent way, like misery was inevitable. I'd never properly wallowed before, but I did it then, listening to the most depressing music on my iTunes with my eyes closed, and wearing two-day-old T-shirts and not shaving, even though it gave me this weird, French-looking mustache.

What was the point anymore? Charlie was dead, and Sadie had decided to shut herself off from the world, and Nick was medicating away his sorrows, and Marina sat there writing fan fiction like if she tried hard enough, she could pretend she was at Hogwarts.

So I sat and read Vonnegut, and listened to the Mountain Goats, and slept a lot, and spent too long in the shower. It was Latham House the way Latham was supposed to be, without illicit trips to town, or girls snuck into the dorm, or classroom pranks. And I couldn't stand it, any of it. The loneliness, or the fear, or the grief.

I wondered what Sadie was doing. I wanted to call her. A couple of times I picked up the phone, but I always put it back down. Cowardice, through and through.

She didn't come to Wellness anymore, and I didn't blame her. Really, what was the point? Latham had become exactly what I'd wanted it to be before I'd known better: something to get through before we could go home.

And every time I saw Sadie walking back to the cottages after dinner, or tapping her pen against her notebook and staring out the window in French class, I ached in a way that wasn't a symptom of being sick. It's strange how we can lose things that are still right there. How a barrier can go up at any moment, trapping you on the other side, keeping you from what you want. How the things that hurt the most are things we once had.

And I wanted Sadie. I wanted our relationship back, for us to try and stay together. Even if it was a bad idea, and even if she didn't want a reminder of this place, because I did. I wanted to remember who I'd been when we were together, because I liked the Latham version of me so much better than the Lane I'd been before. I wanted to be the Lane who kissed a girl in a bedsheet toga and stole internet and wore a tie to a pajama movie night. I wanted to be Sadie's Lane, not the Lane who ran the Carbon Footprint Awareness Club just so I could put "club president" on my college résumé.

And I was scared that I couldn't be Sadie's Lane without Sadie, that I wouldn't be brave enough to put down my books and go on an adventure if she wasn't beckoning me toward the woods, a smile on her lips promising that everything would be okay.

I STARTED TAKING walks around the grounds at night, thinking about everything. About Sadie, and Charlie, and about what I wanted to leave behind in this world, when the time came. I was tired of being an empty box, of maintaining a checklist instead of a passion, of having skipped so many rites of passage that were lost to me now.

One night, I stayed out a little later than I'd meant to, and it was almost lights-out when I came back inside. As I walked across the deserted common room, someone called my name from the nurse's station.

I walked over to investigate. Nick was in there, alone,

lying on one of the cots. He was reading *A Storm of Swords* in his pajamas and bathrobe.

"Hey, thought that was you," he said.

"Is everything okay?" I asked, concerned.

"Fine," Nick said. "I'm almost out of vodka, so I was thinking what to do about that, and then I realized . . . oh man, my chest *really* hurts."

He rolled his eyes while he said it.

"So you wanted to come down here and lie on the cot?" I asked, not understanding.

"Codeine, dude. They don't even question it. I just have to stay here, is all." He grinned, pleased with himself. "It's awesome, I'm all floaty."

"Well, have fun," I said.

"Hold on," Nick said, pushing himself up in bed. "You okay?"

"I'll live," I muttered. I hadn't meant it ironically, but Nick snorted.

"Look, I'm sorry about you and Sadie," he said.

"Really?" It shot out of my mouth before I'd thought about it.

There was an awkward pause.

"No, I'm secretly glad, I want all my friends to be as depressed and lonely as I am," Nick said sarcastically. He leaned back and closed his eyes. "Sure you don't want some codeine? It's great. The room's spinning like a trampoline."

"Trampolines don't spin," I reminded him.

"Well, they should. And Sadie shouldn't have done that to you. Shit, why are girls so impossible?"

"I don't know," I said, sighing. "Everything was going great with us, and then Sadie preemptively dumped me because she thinks we won't last."

"You probably won't," Nick said.

"Thanks a lot."

"Nothing lasts," he said. "Even this awesome floaty feeling. We all reach for whatever we think is going to dull the pain, and sometimes we don't even want whatever it is, we just want to *not* be miserable, you know? So anyway, I'm sorry I was a dick."

"It's fine," I said.

"No, shut up, I'm atoning. We have seven more weeks at Latham, and then all this is over. It's like the end of senior year. It's the last chance to go for things. Otherwise you always wonder." He shifted on the bed, coughing a little. "I want us to be cool, so we can all keep in touch. That's all we're going to have left, you know? Each other."

He was right. Latham would close down, and TDR-TB would be curable, and it would be hard to explain to anyone who hadn't gone through it what it had been like at a sanatorium, and what it was like to have this weird past that was filled with blood tests, instead of standardized ones.

"We're cool," I said. "Don't worry about it."

"Did I already ask if you want some codeine? Because it's awesome, like a trampoline. . . ."

- 279 -

"Think I'll pass. But thanks."

I went up to my room thinking about what Nick had said, even though he was pretty out of it. I didn't want to wonder about Sadie, I wanted to be with her. But I'd never given her a reason to think I really meant it.

I'd never asked her to be my girlfriend, not officially. And I'd never said that I loved her. I'd taken the coward's path, telling her that I adored her, and that I was crazy about her, using every other phrase that I could instead of the one that I meant.

And now, even if I did muster the courage to say it, she wouldn't want to hear it. She might not even believe it.

CHAPTER TWENTY-TWO
SADIE

I HADN'T EXPECTED Latham without Lane to hurt as much as it did. I'd made a mistake, and I knew it as I lay in bed each night that week, alone and lonely, with no company except my own horrible thoughts. I had trouble falling asleep, so most nights I'd curl up on my side and stare out the window at the inescapable woods. I tried to see beyond them, past Whitley and the dust-covered avocado stands along PCH, all the way down the coast to Los Angeles, to home.

But I couldn't. All I could see was Lane's face in the gazebo, the way he'd crumpled, the way he'd stared at me like I'd torn apart the universe and handed him the shreds.

I hadn't known it would be like that. I didn't have experience with boys, or experience with much of anything, except having TB. But Latham House was closing down. It was like Nick had taken to saying, that these were the last days of the empire.

He was wrong, though. The sun had already set on our

little empire, which was the only one that really mattered. Our group was splintered, the energy that once made our table the center of the dining hall sucked dry. There was no empire anymore, just the ruins of a once-great civilization. Just the memories of a once-great relationship.

It took me three days to build up the courage to even sneak a glance at Lane again, and to stop pretending that whatever picture was in my fashion magazine wasn't the most fascinating thing in the world.

And when I glanced at him, I wanted to cry. He looked the same as always, my Lane, with his floppy hair and green-brown eyes, except he wasn't mine at all. Not any-more.

Marina knocked on my door the Thursday after I broke up with Lane. I was curled up in bed with Adele on repeat, in this little nest of electronics and books and chargers, and she snorted when she saw me.

"I see you've made a cave," she said.

"I'm regressing. Next I'll sprout gills and slither into the pond," I said.

Marina shook her head.

"What's going on?" she asked. "I thought this was what you wanted."

"I don't know what I want!" I said. "Except to sit in my mope cave."

"Well, your mope cave has company."

Marina shut the door and held up a USB stick.

"I just talked to Nick," she said. "Have you listened to this?"

"What is it?"

"It's . . . well, it's Charlie's album," she said.

I sat up.

"Charlie made an album?"

"Before he died," Marina said. "He finished it. Left it in a box on his bed."

I hated talking about Charlie. It made me feel like I was back there again, standing over Charlie's body, looking for his green light.

But this was different. This was new.

"Can we play it?" I asked.

"Nick made you a copy," she said. "So, here. All yours. I've been listening to it on repeat all day."

She tossed the stick onto my bed. I stared at it.

"Thanks," I said.

"He was coming to find us, you know," Marina said. "Charlie. He knew he wasn't doing well. He was trying to say good-bye. That's why he was in the woods. Not because we guilted him into attending a toga party."

I stared at Marina. She smiled sadly.

"Not that it's worth anything," she said. "I just thought you should know."

She shut the door behind her when she left.

I popped the stick into my laptop, and plugged in my headphones, and played it.

I'd heard Charlie's music before, in snippets. A line, a chord progression, the acoustic version on the ukulele. But this wasn't a rough draft. It was his finished verse. It was Charlie, back from the dead and sitting right there next to me, confessing everything about how it felt to be young and dying and terrified that there was something you still hadn't finished, that you wouldn't have enough time.

When the album ended, I was sobbing. Charlie had barely finished making this. And I'd been so stupid to abandon Lane. We hadn't finished becoming anything yet, because I'd been so terrified that whatever we were was only temporary.

And I'd been so, so wrong. Being temporary doesn't make something matter any less, because the point isn't for how long, the point is that it happened. Like ancient Greece. Like Latham. Like Lane and me.

I tried my best to smooth my ponytail, and I put on the last of my favorite lip gloss, which I'd been saving for a special occasion, and then I bolted down the stairs and knocked on the door of Cottage 6.

It was evening, not too late, and this kid Tim opened the door, looking puzzled.

"Thanks," I said, slipping in past him.

"You're not supposed to be in here," he said, but I didn't care.

I ran up to the third floor and down the corridor to Lane's room.

I knocked, and his voice called, "Come in."

"Hi," I said.

His room was a mess. Piles of books, clothes, misery. It was so different from the pristine dorm room I'd made fun of a few weeks earlier. So much more lived in.

He stared at me like I was the last person he'd expected to show up at his door.

"Hi," he said cautiously.

I closed the door and stood there, staring at him, wondering what he was thinking.

"I'm sorry," I blurted. "I'm so sorry, I didn't mean to break up with you."

"You didn't?" he asked, like he didn't quite believe me.

"No. It was the worst mistake I've ever made, and I brought tie-dyed shorts to summer camp, so that's saying something."

"I remember those shorts," Lane said, grinning.

And then he wrapped me in a hug. He squeezed me so tightly that I could almost feel the holes in my lungs, the missing parts that TB had pressed out of me, and how being with Lane made me feel like I was whole.

"I remember your braces," I teased.

"I remember your purple rubber bands."

"I remember your red sunglasses."

"I remember staring at you when we swam in the lake, thinking how beautiful you were."

"You did not!" I said.

"Okay," Lane said guiltily, "but I should have. And I should have told you a long time ago that I love you."

I stared up at him in shock, and he grinned down at me, all eyelashes and jawline, making me feel shivery.

"Even after I broke up with you?" I asked.

"Oh, wait, now that you mention it," he joked.

"Hey," I said, pretending to be mad. But I threw my arms around him and stood on my toes to kiss him, and right before I did, I said, "And I love you, too."

And then I kissed him like I wanted to make both of our med sensors explode.

"Whoa," Lane said after we pulled apart.

I smiled at him.

"We don't have to stop," I said.

"Um, we probably do." He motioned toward his silicone bracelet. "I'm pretty sure any more of that would set off nuclear warheads."

"Yoga breaths," I told him. "Nice and slow. In and out."

"Who knew Wellness would be good for something?" he joked.

"Shush, I'm trying to kiss you," I complained.

And then my lips met his and we didn't say anything at all.

FRIDAY WAS THE next collection, and of course Nick backed out at the last minute. Lane said he'd come with me, but I told him it was okay, I'd rather go on my own.

I hadn't been in the woods since the night of the toga party. I'd been avoiding them, the way I'd avoided everyone. But Charlie wouldn't have wanted to ruin the woods for me. So I squelched my nerves down into a tiny, manageable little ball, and set out that Friday night with my backpack and knit cap, walking the familiar path with my flashlight illuminating the trees. I was trying to make peace with the woods, and to say good-bye to them.

It was almost December, and a lot of the trees were skeletons now. It was easier to see the sky through the branches, and I could even make out some stars. I read once that we're all just dead stars looking back up at the sky, because everything we're made of, even the hemoglobin in our blood, comes from the moment before a star dies.

I don't know why I was thinking about that, but it made a lot of sense right then that stars glow so brightly in their instant of death, and that Charlie's music was him glowing, and that the stars in the sky would one day burn out and become atoms inside of people who were sick with diseases we couldn't yet imagine.

Michael was waiting for me in the clearing, hunched inside a heavy coat, even though it wasn't that cold out.

"Hey," I said, waving my flashlight beam up and down in greeting.

He turned, and there was a strange expression on his face.

"Just you?" he asked.

"Nick is the worst business partner ever," I said, rolling my eyes. "Which is particularly ironic, since he'll probably wind up *running* a business."

Michael coughed then, and it didn't sound good.

"You okay?" I asked.

"Not really," he said. "Sick."

"Cold season, huh?" I asked.

He stared at me, and I realized that he didn't have any bags with him. He hadn't brought our stuff.

"TB, actually," he said, with this unsettling half smile.

We stared at each other in the dark, and I didn't know what he wanted. I didn't know what to say. And I didn't know why I felt so nervous all of a sudden.

"I'm sorry," I offered.

"You're sorry?" Michael laughed in a way that scared me. "Sorry? What does sorry do? Can it get my *job* back? Can it pay my *rent*? Or my *child support*?"

"No, I—" I broke off, unsure what I was going to say.

"*What?*" he said, raising his voice. "No *what?*"

"No, it can't, but there's a new medication," I said.

"Oh, that's right, the so-called protocillin. If that's even real," he spat, taking a step toward me. "But it doesn't matter if the medicine is real or not. They're not giving it to people like me for *months*. I have to sit and wait. I could die before they have enough."

Michael was really frightening me. He didn't look

- 288 -

scared, he looked furious. And then he took another step toward me.

"*You* did this!" he accused. "*You* gave this to me! My life is over. I can't see my kid. I lost my job. I'm not supposed to leave my *house*. And I'm going to die from this! I'm going to die *alone*!"

I stumbled back, trying to get away. But he lunged toward me, his fist connecting with my rib cage so hard that I couldn't breathe, and everything seemed to shatter. I felt myself fly backward, and there was a sharp crack against the back of my head, and something sticky, like sap, but which probably wasn't sap.

And then pain. So much pain. Everywhere, like, I was drowning in it. Like galaxies were collapsing inside of me, the stars burning out, even though they were already dead. I was filled with twice-dead stars, and everything began to go black around the edges, and I tried to say something, anything, but all I could do was curl up on my side and cough in violent, gut-wrenching spasms. I could hear Michael saying, "Oh God, oh God, oh God," and the *beep-beep-beep beeeeeep!* of my med sensor on high alert, and then darkness.

CHAPTER TWENTY-THREE
LANE

SADIE SAID TO meet her in the gazebo after the collection, but it was getting late and she still wasn't back. I waited, wondering where she was, and wishing we had cell phones, so I could have texted.

I didn't know what would happen if she missed lights-out. She could probably figure out some excuse. I just hoped she was okay. She'd seemed more tired lately, and more pale than usual, but I was probably imagining things, because of Charlie.

I was scaring myself, because I was alone in the dark and it was late and starting to get cold. Sadie would be back any minute, with that silly red cap on her head, her backpack heavy with contraband, rolling her eyes over how that black market guy hadn't shown up on time. And then she'd tuck her chin against my jacket and grin up at me, and we'd share a quick good-night kiss before dashing inside with barely enough time before the nurse check to climb under the covers still dressed.

I was listening to this playlist I'd made for her, headphones clamped over my ears. It was the story of us in music, except it wasn't finished yet. I had this plan that I'd add a new song every month, so that the playlist would keep going as long as we did. It was sort of an electronic version of adopting a tree, which I'd done in the Carbon Footprint Awareness Club, but only because it had looked good, not because I'd actually wanted to. Keeping a playlist alive sounded much more me.

I stared across the quad, at the clock tower. Five minutes until lights-out. And as much as I didn't want to, I knew I should go inside. But I didn't budge.

Come on, Sadie, I thought, fiddling with my iPod.

Sadie will be back before this song ends, I thought.

And then: Sadie will be back before this next one ends.

But she wasn't.

The song was halfway through when the nurses came running out of the cottages. They raced toward the woods, their expressions grim. I glanced back at the dorms, at all the windows lit, with everyone watching. At the kids spilled out onto the porches in their pajamas.

And then I took off my headphones and heard that dark and terrible alarm.

Beep-beep-beep beeeeep! Beep-beep-beep beeeeep!

It was coming from the woods. And I knew, beyond a doubt, that it was coming from Sadie.

Everything stopped cold, except time somehow marched grimly forward, because my heart was hammering, and there was a pounding in my ears and my head, and I knew, I just knew, that something was deeply wrong with Sadie. Panic rolled over me, a dense fog of it, choking me, and blanketing everything.

I scrambled to my feet in the moonlight, desperate for that horrible beeping to stop, even though what I really wanted was for it never to have happened in the first place.

The nurses raced into the woods. Nurse Jim clicked on a flashlight, and I didn't even think before I plunged in after them.

I didn't have a compass, but I remembered the general direction, the clearing she'd pointing out to me. I didn't know if she'd be there, but I had to try.

"Wait!" I called.

Nurse Jim turned.

"Lane, get back inside!" he said, as a tall, brunette nurse crashed into the woods behind me.

"I can't get a read on this location," she said, shaking her head. "Signal's too weak out here."

"None of us can," Nurse Jim said. "We'll have to spread out and hurry."

He glared at me.

"Back inside, now!" he insisted.

"I know where she went!" I said desperately. "Please! I can show you."

I didn't want for them to say that I couldn't. I just started running. My lungs burned, and my chest ached, and I didn't realize how painful it would be until I'd already begun. I put my hand against a tree, catching myself, and taking a ragged breath.

"It's this way," I said, pushing forward and willing myself to keep going as I raced toward that terrible beeping.

I knew something was wrong. And I wanted to kick myself for not realizing it earlier. For not going with her. For not insisting. And God, I wanted to kill Nick.

"Sadie!" I called. "Sadie!"

But part of me knew she wouldn't answer.

It was so dark in the woods, even with the thin, white beams of the nurses' flashlights. I could hear other nurses shouting to each other about how they couldn't get enough reception to track the signal as the nightmarish beeping continued, getting louder and louder until the woods were pulsing in alarm.

The clearing Sadie had told me about was just ahead, and I hurried toward it.

"Sadie?" I called again.

And then I saw her. She was curled on the ground at the base of a tree, an empty backpack next to her. At first

I thought she was sleeping, but then the beam of Nurse Jim's flashlight passed over her, and I saw that the back of her head was matted with blood. It wasn't the bright red of arterial blood. This was a different kind, darker and more urgent.

"No," I whispered, sinking to the ground next to her.

There was a deep gash on her scalp, like she'd been thrown against the tree, and she was so pale that her skin was almost translucent.

I cradled her in my arms. She was so cold, and her breathing was so shallow, but she was still alive.

"Sadie," I said. "It's me. Please. Sadie."

I was gasping for breath, and my heart had never beat so fast or so loud or so close in my ears.

Softly, Sadie moaned.

"You have to step back," one of the nurses said, but he couldn't have meant me. And then his hands were on my shoulders, and he was lifting me away from her, and I was crying and screaming, and I couldn't catch my breath, but it didn't matter, nothing mattered except Sadie being okay and not dead.

"What was she doing out here?" one of the nurses wondered.

Everything was starting to spin, and I leaned one hand against a tree and pressed the other against my hammering heart, struggling to breathe.

"Is she going to be okay?" I asked. "Please? Anyone?"

"You've got to calm down," a nurse told me. "Here, this will help."

I felt a puncture, and then the whole world melted away.

I WOKE IN a hospital room in Latham's medical building. It was just after four in the morning and eerily quiet. Something itched at my noise, and I reached up and unclipped an oxygen tube.

I was still woozy from the sedative, and it took an embarrassing amount of effort to push myself out of bed and stand without swaying. My brain was so foggy that I couldn't quite remember why I was there, or where there was. And then the fog cleared, and the events of that night hit me full force.

Sadie, lying on the ground in the woods. That gash on the back of her head. Her shallow breaths. The way the nurses had surrounded her like she wasn't a girl anymore but an emergency.

I had to find her. I had to make sure she was okay.

I shuffled into the quiet hallway. The nurse's station was at the far end, and a television played softly, flickering through the glass barrier.

I'd never been upstairs in the medical building before. It was a small ward, not a full hospital, and I found Sadie's name scribbled on the door plaque two rooms down from mine.

I tiptoed in, hoping desperately that I'd find her awake. I pictured her laughing at my terrible bedhead, then smiling sleepily and asking if I wanted to snuggle in with her until the nurses caught us.

But of course that didn't happen.

She was asleep, or unconscious, I'm not sure which. She looked so small in the hospital bed, and so delicate, with a collection of wires and tubes disappearing under the blanket. She looked nothing at all like the red-lipped girl in the knit cap who'd tramped through the woods at night with a backpack full of contraband.

"Hi," I whispered, but she didn't respond.

I reached for her hand, wanting to hold at least that much of her. I remembered writing my phone number across the back of it, and feeling her fingers flutter across my jaw as we kissed in the woods. I remembered twisting around on the swing ride at the Fall Fest, reaching toward her as she held out her hand, daring me to grab it and get a medium-soda-sized wish.

I could have used that wish now. But something told me it wouldn't have been big enough.

I don't know how long I sat there before Sadie moaned softly and opened her eyes.

"Hey, you're awake," I said, squeezing her hand.

She winced, her face pale and drawn.

"Where am I?" she whispered.

"Medical building."

- 296 -

She closed her eyes again.

"Everything hurts," she whispered. "I think I'm actually made of pain."

I looked around for something that would help, and then I spotted it.

"Morphine pump," I said, guiding her hand over the button. "Nick would be so jealous."

I waited for her to say something else, but a nurse came in. She was young and brunette and pretty, and she smiled when she saw that Sadie was awake.

"Good morning, sweetheart," she said, and then she spotted me and frowned at my hospital gown.

"Out," she insisted, daring me to argue. I staggered to my feet, still a bit unsteady from the sedative.

"I'll be back," I promised Sadie, glancing over my shoulder, but her eyes were closed again, and I couldn't tell if she'd heard me.

CHAPTER TWENTY-FOUR

SADIE

I WOKE TO beeping and pain and the smell of hospital. Lane was there, or maybe I just imagined him, telling me that I was in the medical building, that I was still at Latham. But it was the wrong part of Latham, the place you never wanted to wind up.

There was the pinch of an IV, and liquid flowing through it. It was all so hazy, so out of focus, a bad photograph of a blurry moment, and then darkness.

It felt like there were knives inside of me, straining to get out. My head throbbed as though something had punched a hole in it, and I imagined myself escaping through that hole, flying outside of the pain, and my body, and being done.

But I wasn't done. I had so much left here. I had . . . something in my hand. A button. And the nurse was talking to me, saying . . . saying to push the button for morphine.

She explained as she helped me use it that it would take

away the pain. But it wouldn't, because I'd been at Latham long enough to know that pain can't be taken away. It has to leave on its own. And I wasn't sure mine was the type of pain that wanted to go away.

WHEN I WOKE again, it felt much later, but I wasn't sure. I blinked up at the ceiling, trying not to cry from the horrible ache in my chest.

I groaned softly, and Lane was there again, bending over me with an anxious look in his eyes.

"Hi," he said.

"You're here," I whispered.

"They tried to kick me out, but I put up a fight," he said cheerfully, and then shrugged. "Not really. I'm two rooms down, I just snuck over."

"Breaking the rules," I murmured.

"Well, I learned from the best."

Lane showed me how to raise my bed so I could sit up without actually sitting, and I realized he was wearing a hospital gown.

"You're hurt," I mumbled.

"Nah. They gave me a sedative and brought me up here to sleep it off. I'm pretending it hasn't worn off yet, so I get to stay," he said with a lopsided grin.

I tried to smile back, but I probably just winced.

Lane held a cup of water to my lips, and I attempted to take a sip.

"Wow, hot," he joked as it spilled, wetting the front of my hospital gown.

"Keep it in your pants. I mean, gown," I said.

Lane chuckled, then suddenly went serious.

"Sadie, what happened last night?" he asked.

At first, I was confused. What *had* happened? I was in the woods—and then—and then—oh God.

"Michael," I whispered, the horror of it flooding back until I was drowning in the memory of it.

I told Lane everything that I remembered: that I'd gone alone to meet Michael, and that he'd told me he had TB, and it was my fault.

"That's bullshit," Lane said. "Who knows where he caught it?"

"I know," I said. "But it was—he wasn't himself. He was in a rage. He attacked me."

"I'm going to kill him," Lane said, shaking his head.

"Marina was right," I murmured, suddenly exhausted from so much talking. "People are afraid of us. We're their monsters. Except they're the ones who are afraid of what they don't understand. They're the ones who ruin everything."

I started to drift back to sleep.

"Sadie?" Lane said.

"Wake me when the nightmare's over," I told him, and then I floated off on a sea of morphine.

CHAPTER TWENTY-FIVE

LANE

I WANTED TO stay with Sadie, but Dr. Barons kicked me out, promising that her family would be there soon. When I'd asked him if she was going to be okay, he'd given me a patronizing smile and said that he sure hoped so.

It felt strange exiting the medical complex and walking through Latham's quad and pathways on a Saturday afternoon, while everyone was lying in the grass with music and books and board games. I was out of sync with Latham House again, I realized. No longer a part of its rhythms.

I went straight back to Cottage 6 and knocked on Nick's door. He opened it looking awful. He was wearing his ratty bathrobe, and his hair stuck out in a million directions. His face looked naked without his glasses.

"How is she?" Nick asked desperately. "They wouldn't let me up."

He looked so concerned, like Sadie was his to be concerned about, and in that moment I hated him. I hadn't come to give him news about his friend. I'd—well—I'd come because it was his goddamned fault Sadie was lying in a hospital bed, hurt with what the nurse said were two broken ribs and a concussion, and if I couldn't kill Michael, Nick was the next best thing.

"Not good," I said.

"I should have gone with her."

"Yeah," I said, an edge to my voice. "You should have."

"What's that supposed to mean?" Nick asked.

"That you should have gone with Sadie like you were supposed to instead of getting drunk alone in your room."

"Fuck you," Nick said.

"Fuck *you*."

I don't remember hauling back and hitting him, but I must have, because he staggered backward with his hands over his face, cursing, and my fist stung like hell. Instantly, I felt better. But I couldn't say the same for Nick.

"Shit! That hurts!" he whined, revealing a trickle of blood over his eyebrow.

"Might want to disinfect that cut," I said. "Good thing you keep alcohol in your room."

I WENT BACK to see Sadie that evening. The nurse didn't want to let me in at first, but I kicked up such a fuss that Dr. Barons came down to see what was going on.

"Ah, Lane," Dr. Barons said. "I'd like to speak with you in my office."

So I followed him down the corridor to his office, where he grilled me on how exactly I'd known where to find Sadie.

I told him what I knew, about how she was meeting some guy Michael from town who worked at the Starbucks, although I didn't know his last name. And then I'd filled in the part Sadie had told me, about how Michael had claimed he had TB and accused Sadie of giving it to him, and how he'd attacked her.

Dr. Barons sighed, looking grim.

"You're sure about this?" he asked.

"Positive."

He brought in the police next. Two middle-aged cops from town, who put on surgical masks before talking to me, then asked me to go over it again. The whole thing took forever, and I was anxious to get up to Sadie's room and see how she was doing.

"Is there anyone else we should talk to?" the beefier cop asked.

I didn't even hesitate before throwing Nick under the bus with that one.

DR. BARONS FINALLY took pity and let me go up to see Sadie, although not before making me put on a surgical mask and scrub the hell out of my hands.

Sadie's family was already there. Her mom, young and pretty, with Sadie's blond hair, filling out paperwork in a chair. Her sister, Erica, twelve and gangly and dark-haired, playing a game on her phone.

"You must be Lane," Sadie's mom said. Her eyes smiled at me from above her surgical mask. "I'm Naomi, Sadie's mother."

"Nice to meet you." I almost stuck out my hand, a reflex, but remembered not to just in time.

"Thank you so much for staying with her this morning," she said.

"Of course."

While Sadie's mom didn't exactly seem thrilled to have me there, she at least let me stay. I told her that Sadie and I had been at summer camp together, too, and she asked me how I'd liked it. I lied politely and kept up the small talk, because I wanted her to like me, because I was afraid she'd ask me to leave.

I must have fallen asleep in the chair next to her bed, because when I woke up, Sadie was staring at me.

"You're up," I said, stretching.

"Shhhh," she whispered. She looked slightly better, but still so pale. She tilted her head toward the hallway, eavesdropping.

Dr. Barons was out there, talking with Sadie's mom just outside the doorway. He gravely mentioned the fractured ribs and the concussion. But then his voice dropped lower as he said that Sadie had suffered a small hemorrhage in the woods, brought on by the attack. He was worried that if it happened again, she wouldn't survive it.

"Her X-rays aren't hopeful, Ms. Price," Dr. Barons said, and it took me a moment to remember that Sadie's parents were divorced. "The ribs are a problem, and every time she coughs, there's a risk one of them will shift and puncture a lung."

Sadie's eyes filled with tears as the weight of what Dr. Barons had said sank in.

"Between the rib fractures and the damage from her tuberculosis, it isn't looking good," Dr. Barons finished.

"Is there anything we can do?" her mom asked.

"What she needs is protocillin," Dr. Barons said gravely.

"But I thought that was three weeks away."

"It is. And, unfortunately, she doesn't have that kind of time. I'm so sorry, Ms. Price," Dr. Barons said.

Sadie closed her eyes, blinking away tears. I reached for her hand and gave it a squeeze, wishing we'd never eavesdropped on that conversation. There are some things you shouldn't overhear, some things that are too terrible to comprehend when other people are discussing them, even though they're happening to you.

Sadie didn't look so much overcome by sadness as defeated by it. And I don't know how I managed to hold it together. How I sat there, stroking the back of her hand, breathing raggedly but not crying, because I wasn't going to do that in front of her.

"Lane," she said after a while.

"Hmmm?"

"I'm so sorry. I always felt like there was something off about me, and now I know. I'm broken."

It wrecked me all over again to hear her say that.

"You're not broken."

"Then how come I can't be fixed?" she asked, shaking as she held back tears. "If I'm not broken, how come no one can fix me?"

WHEN SADIE'S MOM came back in, you could tell she'd been crying. Dr. Barons trailed behind her, looking grim.

Sadie squeezed my hand, and I squeezed back. And then I held her hand, like they'd told us to at camp during off-grounds trips, as though it would prevent us from being separated.

"Sadie, good to see you're awake," Dr. Barons said.

"I heard you," she told him. "Out in the hallway."

Dr. Barons blanched. Sadie's mom looked horrified.

"I'm happy to answer any questions you might have," Dr. Barons said, trying to put on a smile.

"I just have one," Sadie said. "Can you give me the medication for multi-drug-resistant TB?"

I hadn't been expecting that at all. But the moment she said it, a small flicker of hope lit itself inside of me as I remembered back to that day in French class, and our dialogue about the medication that Mr. Finnegan had called an extraordinary means of preserving life.

Sadie's mom looked to Dr. Barons, who sighed and ran a hand through his hair.

"That's a last resort, and not one we usually consider. The risks are too high," he said.

"But it could work," I pressed. "It could make her better."

Sadie's mom and I stared at Dr. Barons, and he shook his head.

"It really is an extraordinary means of treatment. The survival rate is too low, and the chance that it would work is too slim."

"But it might!" I insisted. "Please!"

"Mr. Rosen," Dr. Barons scolded. "You seem extremely agitated. Do you need to be given a hospital bed and a sedative again?"

I folded my arms and glared.

"I don't care," Sadie said. "It's my choice, isn't it?"

Sadie looked to her mom, who nodded, her lips pressed together.

"Of course, sweetie."

"Well, I want the medication," Sadie said matter-of-factly. "I know the risks. Twenty-five percent chance it'll work, twenty-five percent chance it'll kill me. And if it doesn't do anything, then we already know what to expect. Mom, don't, please . . ."

Sadie's mom had started sniffling again, and she

pressed her hands over her mask, as though to hold back her despair.

Dr. Barons handed Sadie's mom another tissue. He kept a packet of them in the pocket of his white coat, I noticed, and I wondered if he always carried tissues, or if he'd put the packet in special, before breaking the news.

"Why don't you take the rest of the day to come to a decision, and I'll check back tomorrow?" he said.

"I'm not going to change my mind," Sadie said, coughing softly. She splinted her ribs with a pillow one of the nurses had given her, going so white I thought she might faint.

Dr. Barons gave Sadie's mom a reassuring pat on the shoulder, and then paused in the doorway.

"Young man, shouldn't you be getting back?" he asked me.

"To what?" I asked.

But I could feel Sadie's mom wanting me to leave, since the nurse who'd taken Erica to get dinner would probably be back at any moment.

"I think for the rest of the night, it needs to be just family," she said.

"Yeah, okay," I conceded.

I pulled off my surgical mask and bent down to give Sadie a kiss on the cheek. I rested there a minute, my temple pressed against hers, feeling the shallow rise and fall of her chest, and the warmth of her skin, and the reassurance that she was there, and alive, and that it was possible we'd get past this.

"I'm going to be okay," Sadie promised as I left.

"I know you are," I said, except they were just empty hospital words, the kind that you wish were true because the alternative is too painful to bear.

CHAPTER TWENTY-SIX
SADIE

THE MEDICATION WAS going to work. I was sure of it. Of course my mom was skeptical and kept telling me about some miracle herb she wanted me to try. I told her it sounded great, just so she'd stop talking about it, because she was making me depressed.

When Dr. Barons came back the next day, I told him my mind hadn't changed. I still wanted the treatment. He seemed surprised, and not altogether pleased, that I wanted to take the risk. But for me it wasn't a choice. It was the only chance I had, and one of the things I'd learned at Latham was that you don't pass on second chances.

And a secret part of me liked the idea that my fate would still be uncertain. That I was back to where I'd been for the past eighteen months, unsure whether Latham was it for me, or if I'd go back to my former life after all. Except now I knew—if I did get better, if I did get to pack my things and take my protocillin and go back to high school, I'd call

Lane every night before bed, and somehow, together, we'd get through it. Maybe we'd even get bagels on the weekend, or drive up to see one of Marina's plays, or check out just how ridiculous Nick's house was, since he'd let it slip there was a tennis court in the backyard. Maybe we'd even buy some albums at the thrift store and drag a record player out to Modesto, where Charlie was buried. Maybe we'd even come back to Latham and sit on one of the porches of the boarded-up cottages and reminisce.

DR. BARONS LET my friends come visit that afternoon, and they showed up dressed like that night at the movies, when everyone else had worn pajamas, and we'd looked like we were stopping by on our way to a dance.

Nick smelled like he'd swigged a little too much liquid courage, and from the look on Lane's face, they'd had a conversation about it earlier.

"Wow, booze o'clock," Marina told him. "Have a piece of gum."

She tossed him a package of gum, and he took a piece, muttering his thanks.

Marina smoothed her dress nervously. Out of everyone, she was the most uncomfortable in the medical building. She was still perched on the edge of her seat, like she might need to run away at any moment.

"Loving the outfits," I said. "Whose funeral?"

They all stared at me in horror.

"I'm kidding," I said, leaning back and closing my eyes for just a moment. I got tired so easily now, and the pain meds made me feel like I wasn't all the way awake.

Lane adjusted his tie self-consciously. He looked gorgeous, his hair a little too long, and just the right amount of messy. I remembered the last time he'd worn that tie, for our fake-dance photo.

My mom wasn't in the room, thank God. She'd taken Erica to town for lunch, so it was just the four of us, me in my pajamas, and everyone else in their fancy clothes and surgical masks. I knew they'd meant the outfits to be amusing, but the idea that they were something I wasn't stung. I hated that I was too sick to participate, like I was no longer one of them.

"Round of Bullshit?" Marina asked, taking out a deck of cards. Everyone pulled chairs around the bed, and Marina shuffled the deck. I was the first one out, and after I lost, I lay back, listening to them play and pretending we were lying on the grass in the sunshine, instead of in a hospital room.

My mom and Erica came back while Nick and Lane were dueling it out to win the game, and they watched, smiling, at Nick's energy, and Lane's psych-out tactics. And I was glad my mom got to see my friends, and a little of my life here, because I knew she worried I was making it all up, like I had when I'd written letters home from camp about how the girls were all my best friends, and then when she'd come to pick me up, no one had hugged me good-bye.

❖

I GOT THE medication on Monday. Dr. Barons came in and hung the bag off my IV drip, choosing the lowest setting. My mom pulled over a chair and held my hand, even though it didn't hurt. For a moment, it reminded me of what Marina had said, about how Amit's parents had hovered and treated him like an invalid after he went home. But I pushed away the thought, and other, troubling thoughts, like men following me through a carnival, and Michael lunging toward me in the woods, and the way my mom had already gone through two large bottles of hand sanitizer.

I closed my eyes and pretended it was next summer, and Lane and I were camp counselors together, making sure the kids in our cabins didn't get bullied. I pictured him in a pair of cutoffs and his loafers, with one of those lanyard key chains around his neck, both of us in matching staff T-shirts. I pictured us eating s'mores at a campfire, the chocolate all over our hands. I pictured us sneaking into the same shower stall after I bet him that he didn't have the nerve. And I pictured the antibiotics dripping into my body, and binding tight to the infection, and making me better.

Except they didn't.

My fever spiked that afternoon, and one of the nurses gave me something so I'd stop shivering, but the pain in my chest was so bad by that point that I knew. It wouldn't work. I wasn't extraordinary enough.

If living and dying were really the same thing, then I'd been dying for seventeen years, and I didn't have much longer now to go. But I knew that might happen. I accepted it a long time ago. My miracle wasn't a cure. It was a second chance. But second chances aren't forever. And even miracles have an expiration date.

Mom's eyes crinkled as she smiled down at me, her hand in mine, her voice murmuring.

"Hi, sweetie," she said. "It's okay. Everything's okay."

I closed my eyes, wishing I believed it.

It's so strange how the moment of your birth is this fixed point in time, but the hour of your death is always changing based on what you eat for dinner, or where you cross the street, or who you trust when you're alone in the dark woods. But I like to think of all those little moments that add up to the final one, because it meant that my death would be my own, the result of my life, and not just something that happened to me.

Thinking about it like that made it more bearable, that we go back to God when we've had our turn, that some of us roll the dice less than we'd like, but that we're the ones who are rolling them.

When I first came to Latham, I thought this place existed to protect the outside world from us, but now I know it's the other way around. Latham protects us from them.

And the thing about trying to cheat death is that, in the end, you still lose.

CHAPTER TWENTY-SEVEN

LANE

I COULDN'T HELP but hope that Sadie would make it. That, miraculously, she'd live until the first batch of protocillin arrived. That what she had, like the rest of us at Latham House, was curable. But deep down I knew the truth.

The treatment she'd asked for didn't work, and she started to get sicker.

There were days where Sadie slept most of the time, where I bargained my way into the room and sat reading in a chair by her bed.

Sadie's mom sat there, too, filling in Sudoku squares with a pencil and the occasional tear. A boyfriend, or fiancé, came and went, bald and sagging, bringing bags of health food and looking like he didn't know what else to do. Marina sat with Sadie's little sister, playing board games and bringing her a stack of fantasy novels. And Nick came by, with drooping flowers he'd picked down by the lake, although

I couldn't tell you whether it was Nick or the flowers that looked more wilted.

On Wednesday, Sadie and I were alone in the room, and she was propped up in bed, making me paint her nails a bright purple.

"B-minus," she said, inspecting my work. "You missed, like, half my thumbnail."

"It's hard!" I complained.

"Well, you better fix it, since I'll probably wear this for the rest of my life," she joked.

My jaw tightened.

"Sorry," she said with a sigh. "Not funny. Please unremember every not-funny joke I've ever made."

"So basically everything?" I said.

"Basically everything," Sadie echoed, leaning back and closing her eyes.

For a moment, I thought she'd fallen asleep, and then she asked, very softly, "What do you think happens to us when we die?"

I wasn't expecting that, and I wasn't sure I had an answer.

"I don't know," I said finally. "Maybe it's different for different people."

"I have a theory," Sadie said. "That life is gathering the raw materials, and when we die, we get to make patterns out of our lives and relive them in whatever order we want. That way I can spend forever repeating the days when I was really happy, and never have to experience any of the sad days.

So that's how you live a really great life. You make sure you have enough good days that you want to go back to."

Sadie swallowed thickly, and I could see that she was crying.

"Do you think I could go there, too?" I asked her. "And meet you in our good days?"

"I think you could," Sadie murmured, her voice slowing. "I'll meet you there. I'll wait for you there. And I hope I'm waiting a very long time."

SHE DIED ON Friday, less than two weeks before the first protocillin injections were given at Latham House.

I wasn't there.

Her mother held her hand as Sadie died, not of tuberculosis, but of the thing she'd been convinced would cure her.

She would have made it if Michael hadn't attacked her. If she hadn't gone into the woods that night. If I had gone with her. If people were less afraid of diseases they didn't understand, and less horrified to find that, somehow, the invisible hand of contagion had come for them, too.

In AP Bio, I learned that the cells in our body are replaced every seven years, which means that one day, I'll have a body full of cells that were never sick. But it also means that the parts of me that knew and loved Sadie will disappear. I'll still remember loving her, but it'll be a different me who loved her. And maybe this is how we move on. We grow new cells to replace the grieving ones, diluting our pain until it loses potency.

The percentage of my skin that touched hers will lessen until one day my lips won't be the same lips that kissed hers, and all I'll have are the memories. Memories of cottages in the woods, arranged in a half-moon. Of the tall metal tray return in the dining hall. Of the study tables in the library. The rock where we kissed. The sunken boat in Latham's lake. Sadie, snapping a photograph, laughing in the lunch line, lying next to me at the movie night in her green dress, her voice on the phone, her apple-flavored lips on mine. And it's so unfair.

All of it.

After Dr. Barons refused to let me up to see her and told me the news, I walked back to the cottages, through the early dusk that had come with the end of daylight savings, and banged on the door of Cottage 7 until Genevieve came down and opened it.

I pushed past her, not caring, and then I realized I didn't know which room was Sadie's.

"You're not allowed in here," Genevieve called after me.

"I'm looking for Sadie's room?" I asked, and she must have seen it in my eyes that I wasn't budging, because she took me to it.

I opened the door, and suddenly, I was surrounded by Sadie. The twinkle lights wrapped around her bed, the color-coded towers of books, the old trunk in the corner, which she'd covered with Harry Potter stickers. The mint plant she was growing on the windowsill, which explained why I'd always thought she smelled of fresh mint. The mug shaped like a British telephone booth, filled with different-colored Sharpies. The world map over her bed with a cluster of pins in Southern California, and one in Hawaii.

I wanted to curl up in that room forever, along with all of Sadie's hopes and dreams. Along with her unfinished travel map and orphaned mint plant. Instead, I took the memory card out of her camera. And then I went back to Cottage 6 and tried very hard to dissolve.

THAT NIGHT WAS unbearable. I didn't want to go to dinner, to sit at our table just the three of us, as though the empty chairs were tombstones. I wanted to remember the table the way I'd seen it on my first day, when it had seemed the most vibrant of all, its occupants practically glowing as they sat there laughing. Now, it was the gloomiest table at Latham House, and I didn't think I could stand that. So I stayed behind.

Nurse Jim found me sitting on the floor of my room, in the dark, scrolling through her photos on my laptop. It was the closest thing to seeing her again, to having her there with me. But it wasn't enough. God, it wasn't enough.

"Dinner," he reminded me.

"Strike," I said.

He hesitated a moment.

"I'll put you down as sick," he said.

WHEN I FINALLY did leave my room the next day, it was to bang on Nick's door.

He opened it, looking as heartbroken as I felt. I'd gone over there to yell at him, but yelling wouldn't do anything.

"Gonna hit me again?" he asked.

"What would that solve?"

"Well, if you're not going to hit me, come on in," he said, and I went inside, noting a trash can overflowing with apple juice boxes.

"God, I miss her," Nick said, sinking onto his bed and burying his head in his hands. "I know she was your girl-friend, but she was my best friend, and I fucking miss her."

"I do, too," I said.

"I keep going over it," Nick plunged on. "And I really think it's my fault. If I'd been there, things might have gone differently."

"They might not," I said.

"I could have taken that guy," Nick insisted, coughing.

"You couldn't even take it when I hit you," I said.

He shrugged, knowing it was true.

"I really want to be mad at you," I told him.

"Because we're in love with the same dead girl?" he asked. And he looked so broken that I couldn't say any of the angry things I'd wanted to say. So I nodded and said yeah, because we were in love with the same dead girl.

THE WEDNESDAY THAT the protocillin arrived, we all lined up in the gym after lunch. The nurses sat behind tables, with piles of syringes, and I tried not to look for the place where Sadie would have stood in line to receive her injection.

Nurse Monica plunged the needle into my arm, and the protocillin pinched as it entered my bloodstream.

"Dose one of fifty-six," she said, typing it into her tablet. "Now can you rate your pain for me on a scale of one to ten?"

But I couldn't. It seemed so wrong to me then that there were only ten options, only ten types of pain. Because I'm pretty sure there are hundreds of types of pain in this world, maybe even thousands. And none of these are numbers on the same scale. They all hurt differently, and amounts have nothing to do with it. They all hurt too much, and not enough.

"I'm waiting, honey," Nurse Monica reminded me, and I tried to concentrate on my arm, on the serum that was flowing through it.

"Two," I lied.

I CAN BARELY remember those last few weeks at Latham. I know that we lined up each afternoon for our injections, and that after a few days, the tightness in my chest started to fade, and that after a week, I could take a deep breath without coughing.

- 321 -

It was strange to think that my insides were changing, that the version of myself who had been with Sadie was gone forever, and that as much as I wanted to live in the past, I had a long, gleaming future ahead of me. Latham House, which had once seemed to stretch endlessly into the distance, was now a relic of the past.

The sanatoriums were shut down, like they'd been before. We were removed from the world and then put back, as though nothing had changed. But we had. Without internet, without our phones, without being sure we had a future, it changed us. At least, I know it changed me.

And when my dad's SUV pulled up outside Latham, and my parents climbed out, Mom crying, and Dad stiff but smiling, I knew that I hadn't belonged to this place the way Sadie had. That my home was in the real world, and hers wasn't, and she'd made her peace with that a long time ago.

But that didn't make it any less painful that I wasn't helping her carry her things out to her mom's car. And it didn't make it any less awful how she'd slipped from my life, and from her own.

I used to think a lot about the future, but now I spend my time thinking about the past. It sneaks in, even when I don't want it to, while I'm sitting in a coffee shop doing my homework, or when I put on a shirt with my name inked into the collar from Latham's laundry, or when the teacher calls on me in French class. And I know that I'll eventually need to figure out what I want to do with my life, but right now, enjoying it seems like a pretty good option, since it's not like I can have what I really want.

What I want is for Sadie to be there outside her house, waiting for me on the curb. What I want is to spend a day at the beach that starts with us covering each other in sunscreen and laughing. What I want is to take her to my school carnival and promise her a medium-soda-sized wish if she can grab my hand on the swing ride. What I want is for her to grab my hand and lead me through the woods, back in time to that first moment I saw her, when we were thirteen.

Maybe, if I'd kissed her at summer camp, things would have gone differently. Maybe then we wouldn't have caught TB, or wound up at Latham, or fallen in love.

But we did all those things. We grew up, and we grew sick, and we slunk unprepared toward our respective futures. Or lack of futures.

There's a difference between missing someone and mourning them. And I hold out hope that one day I will no longer mourn Sadie, that I will simply remember her, and smile sadly, and then I'll keep going. Because that's all you can do in this world, no matter how strong the current beats against you, or how heavy your burden, or how tragic your love story. You keep going.

It took a lot of things to make me realize that. To make me see the path, as opposed to the destination. I'd been sitting in the coffee shop and thinking for a long time. It was getting late, and my parents were expecting me at home, since it was a school night. So I packed up my books and walked into the parking lot.

I climbed in my car and started to head home, my visor down against the glare of the sun. But at the last minute, I turned left, because I never had before, and because I had time to go down a different road.

ACKNOWLEDGMENTS

A couple of thank-you notes, which probably still won't get me out of sending Christmas gifts, but it was a nice try, wasn't it?

To Katherine Tegen, my amazing editor, for believing in this book even when I was convinced it was a pile of potato salad and not actually a book at all. To Merrilee Heifetz, my incredible agent, whose encouragement and guidance was overwhelmingly wonderful. To the University of Pennsylvania's Department of Medical Ethics and Health Policy, with particular gratitude to Professor Lance Wahlert, for giving me poems about tuberculosis and letting me write my master's thesis on young adult disease narratives. Emily Kern and Abbey Stockstill, for the hours spent researching together in the library, and the very sincere question of "This book looks perfect, how fluent is your German?" My parents, who were very lovely about the time I spent five days in their guest room frantically finishing this book while essentially holding their poodle hostage, and whom I should note are very lovely people in general. Bru Coffee House, you know what you did, and what you did was give me internet and coffee and a quiet place to write, so basically I'm in love with you. Nova Ren Suma, for a heroic rescue. To Corrie and Miguel, my coffee-shop companions. Development: Daniel Inkeles. No thank-you to Netflix; I am dis-acknowledging you, wrecker of productivity. And, on that note, Tumblr, too. Evidently I still can't write an acknowledgments without Tumblr. So it goes.

AUTHOR'S NOTE

The story contained in these pages is a work of fiction. There's no such thing as total-drug-resistant tuberculosis. No protocillin. No Latham House. I made it up, because I wanted to tell a story about what could happen, as opposed to what really is.

Tuberculosis is a disease that has affected mankind for most of human history. It's characterized by cough, fatigue, weight loss, and fever; and for thousands of years, no one knew what caused it or how to treat it. As time went on, tuberculosis became known by a variety of names: phthisis, the white plague, the dread disease, consumption, and, finally, TB.

The threat of tuberculosis reached its peak during the nineteenth century. TB became so prevalent that in 1815 it caused one in every four deaths in England. Its victims included such a who's who of philosophers, writers, and musicians that TB was believed to affect those with artistic temperaments, heightening their genius as they faced early death. The Brontë sisters, Jane Austen, Elizabeth Barrett Browning, Henry David Thoreau, Robert Louis Stevenson, Kafka, Chopin, Chekhov, Voltaire, Rousseau, and Rembrandt all died from tuberculosis.

At the height of the nineteenth century's Romantic Movement, illness was seen as a mark of distinction, and the pallor and waiflike appearance that tuberculosis lent its victims became fashionable. Women of high society copied the aesthetic, powdering their faces and feigning a lack of appetite. The art and theater of the nineteenth century is filled with wan, ethereal heroines, many of whom fall into a consumption brought on by a broken heart or an unrequited love, then die an easeful death. The idea that TB caused a "good" death was one that the Romantics seized upon, lauding TB as a pleasant way to die, even though it was far from the truth.

This widespread romanticization of tuberculosis may seem absurd now, but at the time, little was known about the disease, and most of the treatments offered were guesswork. Tuberculosis was considered a death sentence, and the sick were kept at home with the windows tightly sealed, passing the germs to their family members, who frequently fell sick as well. A few doctors advised their patients to set off for better climates, believing that fresh air and pure food would benefit them more than city living.

In 1854, a German doctor named Hermann Brehmer, himself suffering from TB, founded an institute that treated tuberculosis in the Bavarian Alps. After he reported beneficial results, others followed suit, and the sanatorium movement was born. Dr. Edward Livingston Trudeau founded the first US sanatorium in the Adirondacks in 1882, and later that year, German physician Robert Koch discovered the bacillus that caused TB, proving that the disease was contagious. The sanatoriums, which removed patients from their crowded surroundings, had unknowingly prevented the disease from spreading. Soon after Koch's discovery, the invention of the X-ray allowed doctors to track the progress and severity of a patient's disease. Over the next few decades, nearly a thousand sanatoriums opened across Europe and the United States.

The sanatoriums provided a dual function, both isolating the sick from the general population and enforcing rest, gentle exercise, fresh air, and healthy eating. No other treatment had any impact on the disease, and so patients set off for distant sanatoriums to "take the rest cure," as it was called, hoping their lungs would wall off the infection. But isolating children in sanatoriums made it difficult for them to continue their schoolwork. Open-air schools, which offered fresh air, rest, and nutritious food, sprung up across the United States and Europe, enrolling children with TB.

And still the cure for tuberculosis eluded doctors and scientists. Many patients spent years at sanatoriums, which ranged from crowded, state-run facilities with rows of cots, to private institutions that resembled fancy resorts. A stay at a sanatorium was a break from the stresses and concerns of everyday life, and some patients found it difficult to return home. *The Magic Mountain*, a German coming-of-age novel published in 1924, details a young man's seven-year stay at a luxurious Alpine sanatorium. Its author, Thomas Mann, was later awarded the Nobel Prize in Literature.

For a hundred years, the sanatoriums filled to capacity, until isoniazid, the miracle drug that cured tuberculosis, was introduced in 1952. Tuberculosis began to fade from memory, replaced with the far more pressing threats of HIV and cancer, until the hectic fever of the tortured artist was nearly forgotten.

These days, when we come across stories in which characters cough blood into a handkerchief, then die of "consumption," it seems like a made-up illness or a quaint melodrama. But TB is far from erased. In recent decades, a new form of tuberculosis has risen, evolving a resistance to the medications that treat it. This multi-drug-resistant TB, which is found primarily in the developing world, had more than four hundred and fifty thousand cases reported in 2012, with almost 10 percent of the victims suffering from the even more life-threatening form, extensively drug-resistant TB. While MDR- and XDR-TB are far from being a worldwide health crisis, the fact remains that tuberculosis has not yet been defeated.

So, what led me to this research, and to tell a story that reinvents the recent history of tuberculosis? I'm a bioethicist, and in graduate school for bioethics, I studied the history of medicine. It was 2009, the height of Twilight mania, and one late night in the library, I looked up the history of the vampire myth on a whim.

It turned out that the modern vampire legend was born in the nineteenth century from the symptoms of tuberculosis. Outbreaks of vampire hysteria frequently coincided with outbreaks of tuberculosis: as entire families died of TB, superstitions circulated that the first to die had returned from the grave to feed on surviving family members. I was fascinated. So I decided to write a novel about a sanatorium full of vampires.

But the more I researched tuberculosis, the more I began to imagine a less-fantastical story. While I was sitting in my Cinema of Contagion class, I realized TB had never been portrayed as part of the contagion genre. The disease was cured during the early days of germ theory and antibiotics, and had been so romanticized at its height that quarantine and fear of outbreak weren't a central part of its narrative.

The TB sanatorium, despite providing an ideal framework for a coming-of-age story, rarely surfaced in literature and was nowhere to be found in young adult fiction. But then, YA novels suffer from an absence of medical narrative in general. Adults have far more access to stories told through and about illness, both as fiction and nonfiction. Teenagers have only a handful of options that humanize the illness experience, and so, as a student of medicine and an avid reader of young adult novels, I set out to fix that.

I began to consider the journey into the land of illness as a metaphor, akin to Dante's *Inferno* or *Gulliver's Travels*. These days, that journey is more frequently represented by mental illness rather than physical: a patient is sent into confinement and, once away, enters a duplicate world with special rules. Only after they have been removed from their daily routine can they break free of its constraints and be cured, both metaphorically and medically, of what ails them.

I started to imagine an outbreak of a totally drug-resistant form of TB, not in the emerging world, but in the towns and cities of present-day America. I wondered what would happen if people fell ill with a long-term, contagious illness that modern medicine had no ability to treat. And then I wondered how a teenager would be transformed by the experience of moving from the institution of a school to institution of a medical facility. TB is a disease of the young, after I began to invent a sanatorium for teens, borrowing elements from th open-air schools and from the private, spa-like sanatorium depicted in Mann's *The Magic Mountain*, but adding in technology and a fear of contagion. Just like that, I had a setting for a no

What in *Extraordinary Means* is fact, a what is fiction? The name Latham House is borrowed from D hur Latham, a prominent English physician who published uals for the treatment of TB at the beginning of the twe century. The school-like atmosphere of Latham House owes a debt of gratitude to Hailsham from Kazuo Ishiguro's *Never Let Me Go*, another novel about an alternate medical timeline and the institutions it creates. TDR-TB, which I invented, is a worst-case scenario conjured from the increasingly worried headlines and new stories about swine flu, bird flu, whooping cough, and Ebola. TDR-TB's negative response to the MDR- and XDR-TB medications is borrowed from an article I came across in a medical journal that detailed the increased mortality rate in MDR-TB patients when given a new, second-line medication. Protocillin, of course, is a made-up cure for a made-up illness. But the idea of access to care, where wealthy, insured patients at private sanatoriums like Latham House are given the medicine first, is very real. And the concept of an extraordinary means of preserving life, or a risky, optional treatment that doctors don't recommend, is one I studied in graduate school, and one that fascinates me to this day. It's the idea that the patient ultimately controls their own fate, and that sometimes deciding for yourself is the greatest freedom you can have within a system that sees patients as their diagnosis rather than as people.

_____ and Sadie are both characters who struggle with the question _____ tly counts as living one's life. For each of them, _____ es a deeper issue. Lane arrives at Latham House so _____ his rigorous course of studies that he has become liter- _____. Sadie has internalized all her fears and, instead of _____ ction, ha _____ come afraid of living. The story in this book is not _____ y of what it _____ s to be sick so much as a story of how it feels to _____ an outsider. But _____ important, *Extraordinary Means* is a story of second chances, and _____ it means to have hope that you'll figure out your place in the world _____ that you'll be strong enough to get there.

Robyn Schneider, MBE